Enchanting Baby
Darlene Graham

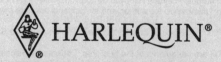

HARLEQUIN®

TORONTO • NEW YORK • LONDON
AMSTERDAM • PARIS • SYDNEY • HAMBURG
STOCKHOLM • ATHENS • TOKYO • MILAN • MADRID
PRAGUE • WARSAW • BUDAPEST • AUCKLAND

ISBN 0-373-71152-2

ENCHANTING BABY

Copyright © 2003 by Darlene Gardenhire.

"I know you *feel* like it's your baby, Greg. But the truth is—"

"No." His interruption was harsh, like a slap intended to wake her up. "The truth is, I am this baby's father, not Chad."

She swallowed and put her spoon down with a shaky hand.

"I love you, Greg, and I know what you are trying to do." She tried again in a low voice. "And that is the sweetest thing anyone has ever said to me. But you know very well where this baby comes from. And you know very well that this is not your baby. We don't have to pretend otherwise. We're both grown-ups here."

"You're not hearing me." He swiveled his chair toward her, with his legs spread wide, forming a V around the chair where she sat. He grabbed her hands, and the seriousness in his deep gray eyes scared her. "This *is* my baby."

Dear Reader,

You are holding in your hands the first book in an exciting new series set inside the Enchanted Circle north of Taos, New Mexico.

When I first visited that remote setting, I had to agree with Francis X. Aubry, an early explorer on the Santa Fe Trial in the 1850s: "There is something in the air of New Mexico that makes the blood red, the heart beat high and the eyes...look upward. Folks don't come here to die—they come here to live, and they get what they come for."

Greg Glazier and Ashleigh Logan have both fled to New Mexico for the sake of a new life—literally. As they struggle to protect the unborn baby they both cherish so dearly, they find an unexpected gift along the way: each other. True love between a man and a woman is as mysterious as the Enchanted Circle itself. And as you will see in this story, its power cannot be denied.

I joked with my editor that creating this series felt a bit like a long gestation that led to the birth of a beautiful baby. Or rather, *six* beautiful babies. Writing this series with six other wonderful authors was a blast. I thank each of them for their creativity, insights and most of all, friendship. Each of the books in THE BIRTH PLACE series stands alone, of course, but I think once you visit Enchantment, you will be drawn there again and again.

So join me now in the enchanting world of THE BIRTH PLACE.

My best to you,

Darlene Graham

I treasure your letters! Contact me at P.O. Box 720224, Norman, OK 73070. And visit my Web site at www.superauthors.com/Graham.

For Devyn, who endured so much to give us
the precious gift of Ava Rose.
And for Damon,
the most devoted and protective Daddy I have ever seen.

CHAPTER ONE

THE NAME OF THE PLACE, Enchantment, struck Greg
Glazier as slightly ironic. After all, hadn't he driven
to this remote town as if under some kind of spell,
chasing the illusion that he was going to find and
bond with the woman carrying his baby—a baby
that was nothing more, at this point, than an enchanting fantasy?

And what about the woman? What was she to
him? A cutesy television personality? A pretty face
on the screen? *Another illusion.*

On her weekly TV show, Ashleigh Logan came
across as intelligent and charming, but God only
knew what she would be like in person.

The town lay in the valley ahead like a scene from
a picture postcard. From his vantage point on the
winding highway, Greg could see a desert vista to
the south, grassy ranchland to the east, and to the
north and west, the vast aspen-rimmed pine forests
that rose to the mystical snow-capped peaks of the
Sangre de Cristo Mountains.

Greg might have attributed the breathless sensation in his chest to the stunning view if he hadn't
known it was actually altitude sickness, mixed with

a walloping dose of anxiety and fatigue. Battling a killer headache and an unslakble thirst, he took a deep pull on his water bottle, then gritted his teeth as he steered his Lincoln Navigator around another curve as the highway snaked into the valley ahead.

He should have had more sense than to travel over the mountains straight off the eastern Colorado ranching plains. He'd lived in the shadow of the Rockies all of his life, but every time he went up into the thinner air, as soon as he ascended those steep, winding roads, he got sick.

But he didn't have time to lay low now. Ashleigh Logan already had a two-day head start on him.

When Greg's efforts to contact Ashleigh at the TV station and then at her home failed, he'd tried her sister's house, but the woman had acted spooked when she answered the door.

"Ms. Miller?" he inquired while she peered at him with the privacy chain still fastened. "I'm sorry to bother you, but I'm looking for your sister. Ashleigh Logan?"

The one eye he could see grew wide with surprise...or was it fear? "Wait here" was all the sister said. Then she slammed the door.

The next thing he knew, a black-and-white patrol car came zipping up to the curb. In short order, the officer made him produce identification and vacate the premises.

That's when Greg had decided that somehow, this Ashleigh Logan woman had figured out what he was after and had bugged out on him. So he'd hired himself a detective.

In Greg's opinion the private investigator in Denver had taken too long to figure out where Ashleigh Logan had vanished to. But what did Greg know? Even in his days as a deputy sheriff, he'd never done anything this crazy. *No,* he corrected himself. Chasing down the woman carrying his baby wasn't crazy. It was vital. All-important.

But two precious days had ticked by before they traced Ashleigh Logan here, to Enchantment, New Mexico.

Enchantment. So named, Greg supposed, because it lay nestled in the heart of the Enchanted Circle north of Taos. He had to admit it was a pretty little town, with its clear mountain air, expansive blue skies, gurgling silver streams. Wide meadows flanked the curved road into town, where the highway narrowed and became the main drag of Enchantment, Paseo de Sierra. Avenue of the Mountains. The name made sense since the street pointed straight toward the Sangre de Cristo range, centering on Wheeler Peak, the highest point in New Mexico.

Centuries ago, the Spaniards had apparently thought Sangre de Cristo—blood of Christ—was an apt name for this rugged mountain range. Legend said they had come from the west and saw the range painted red by the setting sun. Coming from the east, the peaks actually looked hazy, purple, backlit by an apricot sun dipping below a bank of atomic-orange clouds. It was aspen-turning time—late September—and the thick stands of shimmering golden trees added to the feeling of rarefied light. If he hadn't been sick as a dog, he might have appreciated the stunning beauty.

In the village core he passed charming gift shops and rustic ski-rental establishments, plus a small adobe post office, a civic complex and library building, an American Legion hall, the office of the *Arroyo County Bulletin*—the town newspaper, he presumed—and an interesting-looking bed-and-breakfast. He'd come back there later, get a room and crash.

"After I find Ashleigh Logan," he muttered to himself, and took another swig of water.

Finding her might prove harder than he thought. The town looked bigger than he'd imagined. From the base in the valley, new construction sprawled far up onto the mountainsides. Southwest-style log cabins, Alpine A-frames and classic chalets shared the foothills and mountainsides with cozy hotels and weathered homesteads. Subsistence farms dotted the lower surrounding countryside, while farther up, the vast windows of the lofty retreats of the wealthy glittered in the setting sun.

The main street led straight to an old Spanish-style square where there were more shops, restaurants and art galleries. Like the name implied, it was all very…enchanting.

But the place wasn't *totally* charming. On the

southern edge of town, Greg saw evidence of poverty—dusty, dented pickups, ramshackle trailer houses.

Why had Ashleigh Logan run away to this remote place?

If it was because she already knew the truth, Ms. Logan was certainly going to a hell of a lot of trouble to evade the father of her child. But he would find her and he would demand his rights. He would not allow anything to separate him from the only child he would ever have.

As close as he could tell, Ashleigh's decision to come to this particular town was connected to a birthing center run by a bunch of midwives. The place was called—he glanced at the notes the private detective had given him—The Birth Place. It had better not be some hippie-dippy asylum where they used herbal remedies and scented oils instead of real medicine. Not if his baby was going to be born there.

He checked the map he'd printed off the Internet and turned the Navigator onto the narrow Desert Valley Road, where yellowing cottonwood trees on either side created a fluttering golden canopy overhead. He found the clinic at the end of the road.

Tucked in among sheltering pines, the place was a sleepy-looking two-story adobe building with softly rounded walls and deep-set mullioned windows, trimmed in that ubiquitous New Mexico turquoise. The little sign out front, modest enough, had the words *The Birth Place* stenciled in the same shade of turquoise against a snow-white background. A silhouette of a Madonna and babe, the clinic's logo, he supposed, completed the sign.

His tires crunched over the rock-and-sand semi-circular drive as he bumped to a halt. His was the only vehicle in sight. He chugged down the last of his water, eased out and slammed the door.

The place felt as quiet as an abandoned homestead. He hoped he hadn't arrived too late. No clinic hours were posted—he glanced at the sun disappearing over the mountain—but it had to be near closing time.

Greg stepped inside a rough-hewn cedar door, and was appalled by what he saw. His child was going to be born *here?*

The place was a cacophony of clutter, noise and activity. Behind a high reception counter, phones jangled, a copier hummed and zipped, and a teakettle whistled from somewhere beyond an open door. Muted voices came and went as doors opened and closed down a long narrow hallway. Despite the late afternoon hour, a couple of patients, grossly pregnant, still sat waiting in the small reception area. Their conversation was subdued, but their two small children were having a noisy fight over a toy in a corner play area, and lively female laughter rang out from the room behind the reception desk.

He cleared his throat and stepped up to the counter while every woman in the place, pregnant ones included, fell silent and gave him her rapt attention. Greg imagined his appearance was a little rough. He'd been traveling hell-bent all day in his worn ranching clothes. He was unshaven, unkempt, and probably looked a little gaunt and pasty to boot.

The middle-aged woman behind the desk frowned at him while she pressed her ear to a phone, holding up one finger that told him to wait.

"Sounds like her water broke," she was saying into the phone.

Greg felt like an eavesdropper and stepped back, focusing his gaze away from the desk. The place reminded him more of someone's home than an organized office. Lush potted plants rimmed the periphery of Mexican-tile floors that gleamed in the sunlight streaming through the multipaned windows. The whitewashed walls were covered with a jumble of Southwest art, photographs, homemade educational posters…even a few animal skins. A giant bulletin board held hundreds of overlapping baby pictures, as thick as leaves on a tree. In one corner, a rounded adobe fireplace still held the ashes from a recent fire. It was all very cozy, but for *his* baby, Greg had envisioned something stainless steel and sterile, a real *clinic*, for crying out loud.

"Trish!" a younger woman called as she sailed out of a back hallway. "I'm headed up to the Coleman cabin."

Was this a nurse? Greg wondered. He had been told the clinic made house calls or home visits or whatever they called them. She was tallish and slender, wearing brown overalls and clogs, with a long graying braid hanging down her back. She stepped up to the high counter and set down a box containing some kind of equipment. As she donned a jacket she continued, "Would you sign me out?"

Trish made a not-now-I'm-busy face and continued to listen intently to the phone.

"I'll sign you out, Katherine," a pleasant voice called out from the open doorway behind the reception desk. A short round Hispanic woman in a denim jumper poked her head around the doorjamb, briefly eyed Greg, and then said to the woman in overalls, "You be careful out on that Switchback Road, sweetie!"

She disappeared back into the room, and then something, the ominous-sounding name of Switchback Road, his newfound suspicious state of mind— *something*—made Greg lean back slightly so that he could see through the open door. The chubby lady was using a marker to write on a dry-erase board next to floor-to-ceiling shelves housing a rainbow of patient charts. A wildly painted cabinet—pinks, oranges, blues in an artsy design that mimicked the patterns of a Navajo blanket—snagged Greg's gaze for one instant before his eyes snapped back to the board and what the Hispanic woman was writing there, or rather, what she was writing next to…the name *Logan*.

His heart kicked against his ribs and his mouth went dry. Well, drier.

"May I help you?" The woman in the overalls stepped toward him as she studied his expression.

Greg nodded at the stethoscope around her neck. "Are you a nurse?" he asked as a stalling tactic, trying to decide if he should merely follow this woman when she left. The idea of sneaking around following people made him feel like a jackass, but on the other hand this nurse might lead him straight to Ashleigh Logan. How likely was it that the name *Logan* on that board was just a coincidence?

"No." She smiled kindly. "I'm one of the midwives. Katherine Collins."

Greg nodded and smiled, reluctant to reveal his own name. He looked around the waiting room as if searching. "I was looking for a friend who was supposed to be here, but I guess she's already gone."

"We have a couple of patients in the exam rooms." The midwife's voice was gentle and pleasant. "If you'll tell me her name—and who you are—I'll see if she's in the back."

"Uh…her name…." Involuntarily Greg's eyes darted to the big board in the room beyond.

Immediately the midwife stiffened. Her eyes cut to the dry-erase board, her cheeks pinkened, then she stammered, "Would you, uh, would you wait here, please? I'll get someone to help you." She shoved the box on the counter toward the Trish woman with a meaningful look, then shot off down the long hallway.

Greg, meanwhile, quickly glanced in the box. Sure enough, the tab on the chart inside read *Logan, Ashleigh M.* The equipment, surrounded by a nest of webbed belting, looked like some kind of fax machine. It occurred to him that the thing *could* be a uterine monitor.

With her eyes making a wary sweep of him, Trish hung up the phone and snatched the box away. The two women in the back room had sidled out to stand near the receptionist. All three cast one another covert glances. Someone, he saw, had erased the Logan name from the board in the back.

The phone jangled again and the receptionist answered it, turning her face away from Greg. She mumbled into the handset while the rest of the room grew quiet and the other women kept their gazes fixed on Greg. Greg eased away from the counter as the place grew oddly still.

The midwife reappeared, walking fast, followed by a tall, distinguished-looking woman. The midwife slipped behind the counter with the other women, but the tall older lady walked right up to Greg. She was in her seventies, perhaps, but her movements were brisk and her posture was ramrod straight.

"I'm Lydia Kane," she announced, "the director of The Birth Place." She was almost as tall as Greg, who stood at just over six feet. Her steel-gray hair was pulled back in a no-nonsense bun that accentuated her angular, rawboned features. Her outfit—a simple white linen shirt rolled up at the sleeves and a pair of well-worn khakis—would have seemed austere except for a large pendant that hung from her neck on a long silver chain. Greg collected western art and artifacts, and that thing looked like a nineteenth-century heirloom, or a convincing copy. The oval stone at the center resembled genuine rose onyx, but Greg knew it couldn't possibly be. All of the rose onyx in existence was embedded in the walls of the Colorado State Capitol Building in Denver. But the swirling patterns of cream and maroon forming the silhouette of a Madonna and infant, similar to the logo he'd seen out front, certainly resembled the rare material.

She covered the pendant with her fingertips when she noticed him frowning at it. "How, exactly, may I help you?" Her tone was wary, cool.

For a moment Greg considered making an excuse to leave, waiting down the road, then following the midwife Katherine up to this Coleman cabin. But Katherine, huddled behind the desk with the others, apparently wasn't going anywhere now. In fact, all of the women kept staring at him as if he was Jack the Ripper. Something warned him that all was not kosher at The Birth Place, and that maybe he'd better play it straight. "I hope it's not any trouble, Ms. Kane, but I'm looking for a woman who might be a patient at this clinic," he said.

"We don't give out information about our patients, Mr...." Lydia Kane waited for him to fill in the blank.

Greg didn't oblige. As a major land developer in Denver his name was fairly well known, but surely no one as far south as New Mexico would recognize it. Even so, having his identity linked to the highly visible TV personality Ashleigh Logan didn't seem wise. He wasn't ready for anyone to be privy to the reason he was in Enchantment. He hadn't even decided what he was going to do when he found Ashleigh Logan, except that he was determined to somehow be a part of his child's life. Greg was terrible at lying, and long ago he'd learned that it was better to simply be judicious with the truth. Nobody said you had to slap all your cards on the table at once.

"I understand about patient confidentiality, ma'am." Greg kept his voice low. "But I have reason to believe that the woman I'm looking for might have come to your clinic for prenatal care and I don't know how else to find her. I really need to see her. It's...it's fairly urgent."

The expression in Lydia Kane's sharp blue eyes indicated she was not inclined to divulge any information. "I'm sorry," she said slowly, making it sound vaguely like a threat instead of an apology, "I don't think I caught your name."

Greg realized, a little late, that maybe he should have sent the private investigator to Enchantment to flush out Ashleigh Logan before he came tearing down here himself. If he invented a fake name his poor lying skills would undoubtedly trip him up. But if he said anything now besides a name—*my name's not important or I'm nobody or she wouldn't recognize me*—it would sound lame, even suspicious. And if he kept up this lying now, what would they think of him when the baby came?

Again, he opted for a diversion, a partial truth. "I understand that you can't give me any information, but I have…something she needs, and I was hoping you might at least contact her for me."

Lydia Kane didn't look at all amenable to that idea, either, even though she asked, "And what is her name?"

"Ashleigh Logan."

"Ashleigh Logan…" Lydia repeated in a musing way, as if she were trying to place the name. "Ashleigh Logan." She fingered the pendant again and glanced over Greg's shoulder.

"Maybe you've heard of her?" he persisted. "She has a syndicated TV show. *All About Babies.* I mean, in your line of work—"

"I have seen that show," Lydia said slowly. "So, is this urgent business somehow related to Ms. Logan's television show?"

"Uh. No. It's personal." Again, Greg settled for a vague truth.

"I see." Lydia shot another quick glance over Greg's shoulder, toward the women clustered behind the receptionist's desk. "Is it a medical matter?"

"Well, no. Maybe I shouldn't have said it was *urgent*. It's not anything of *immediate* importance...." Greg hesitated while he did some fast thinking. His gaze flitted to the pictures of healthy babies decorating the clinic walls. If this woman ran this clinic, then the welfare of babies must be a very high priority for her. "But it might eventually impact Ms. Logan's unborn child." That was the absolute truth, so Greg had no trouble keeping his expression sincere.

"I see." Lydia Kane shot another furtive glance out the large window, then in the direction of the small waiting room, toward her patients, who appeared to be tuned in to the conversation. Even the two little children had gravitated toward their mothers and now sat still and quiet.

"I'd like to help you. But I'm afraid we're very busy right now." She smiled nervously at the women in the waiting room. "Would you mind waiting back in my office while I check on something?"

Greg decided there was definitely something fishy going on at this clinic. "Oh, that's okay," he said casually. "I'm running late, actually." He looked at his wrist as if to check his watch, and realized that in his hurry to hit the road, he hadn't put it on. The futile gesture seemed to undermine his credibility even further. "I think I'd better be on my way."

"It will only take a minute. Please. My office is

this way.'' She swept a graceful arm toward the long hallway.

The woman was clearly trying to detain him—he saw that now. It was what she'd been doing all along. And in the next instant, Greg understood why.

The whoop of a siren caused everyone to turn to the paned window. A black-and-white cruiser braked behind Greg's Navigator and a trim, muscular young cop jumped out and trotted around the trunk of the squad car. He was wearing a gray Stetson, a flawlessly pressed uniform, dusty brown cowboy boots and a sidearm in a swivel holster. He came bursting into the door of the clinic like a marine at a battle landing.

''This is the man, Miguel,'' the Lydia Kane woman said loudly. She had stepped farther away from Greg.

''Come with me, sir.'' The cop was about Greg's size, clean cut and serious-looking. His heavy dark brows formed into a sharp chevron as he indicated the door with one outstretched palm. His name tag read ''Eiden,'' but this guy didn't look German. With his hawkish nose and piercing dark eyes, he looked like he could be part Hispanic or maybe Navajo. The deep dimples etched on either side of his mouth somehow made his appearance even more threatening.

''Now, wait a minute,'' Greg said as he backed

up. Why in the hell did the cops show up every time he started asking questions about Ashleigh Logan?

"I need you to step outside, sir." The cop reached for Greg's arm, but again Greg instinctively backed away. The women and children had receded to the far edges of the room.

"Are you arresting me?" Greg demanded. He knew the law, and knew he hadn't broken it.

"I'm simply conducting an investiga—" The cop's shoulder radio squawked. He listened, then touched it off. "I just need you to come outside and answer a few questions."

"Why?"

When Greg still didn't move, the cop said, "Okay. Sir, I'll need you to turn around and put your hands behind your back."

"*What?*" Greg couldn't believe this.

But the cop had already reached behind his belt and flipped out a pair of handcuffs. His other hand was poised near his holster.

"Okay!" Greg threw up his palms like a criminal in a TV drama. What choice did he have? He wouldn't be much good to his baby if he got himself shot.

Before he could so much as blink, Eiden twisted Greg's arms behind his back and slapped the cuffs on his wrists. With one hand on the cuffs and one hand on Greg's shoulder, the cop pushed him outside.

Stunned, Greg tried to turn his face toward the man. "Officer, are you arresting me?"

The cop gave the cuffs an instructive jerk. "I could. For interference with official process. But I'll settle for taking you down to headquarters for investigative detention."

"What is this all about? I haven't done anything wrong."

The cop didn't answer. He quickly patted Greg down, making Greg grateful he'd left his firearm in the lockbox inside his Navigator.

When the cop was satisfied that Greg was clean, he said, "Please get in the vehicle, sir." He opened the back door of the squad car.

"What about *my* vehicle?" Greg jerked his head toward the Navigator.

"I'll lock it. If necessary, I can impound it later. Otherwise, I'll bring you back here to get it."

Again, Greg had no choice but to climb into the musty, plastic-lined back seat. He'd only ridden in the *front* of a squad car, never in the back. He'd never been on the bad end of an arrest, either. He felt awkward, like an animal in a cage, forced to sit sideways in the cramped space because of the cuffs. As he stared at the Plexiglas barrier to the front seat he thought, *Great. This Ashleigh Logan woman is complicating my life more by the minute.* He'd been in this backwater town less than an hour and already he was being hauled down to the local pokey.

CHAPTER TWO

AS SOON AS THE DOOR CLOSED behind the men, Lydia Kane and her staff rushed into the waiting room where the two mothers were clutching their toddlers to their pregnant bellies.

"Everything's all right." Lydia stretched her arms forth. "He's gone now. Is everyone okay?"

"We're fine," both of the patients answered at once, but their expressions remained wide-eyed and fearful.

"Was that guy dangerous?" one of them asked.

"I hope not," Lydia soothed. "But we couldn't take any chances. We have a patient here who has a restraining order against a stalker back in Denver, so we can't be too cautious." She turned to her staff. "Lenora, why don't you go ahead and move these clients back to exam rooms where they can be more comfortable?"

As soon as the patients were gone, the receptionist, Trish, covered her mouth in shame. "I shouldn't have put her real last name on the board."

Lydia patted her shoulder. "It's been a hectic day and you were just following the routine."

"Don't worry, Trish," Katherine said, adding her reassurances. "While Lydia was calling the cops, I called Ashleigh and warned her. Another officer went out to the Coleman cabin while Miguel was on his way here."

"Still, that awful man saw her name. Now he knows she's in Enchantment!" Trish wasn't going to forgive herself so easily.

"You had no idea he'd look back there," Katherine reassured her further.

"I'm so glad you were alert!" Trish's shoulders relaxed a bit.

"Yes. Good job, Katherine." Now Lydia patted the midwife's shoulder.

"And you did the right thing, Lydia." Katherine smiled at her boss. "If that is the stalker, thank God Miguel has hauled him off."

"Yes." Lydia looked out the window as the cruiser pulled away. "Miguel Eiden isn't about to let that guy hurt anybody."

THE POLICE STATION WAS BACK on the main drag, Paseo de Sierra. The sun had disappeared behind the mountains so that Greg couldn't see much through the grimy rear windows as they pulled into the gravel parking lot. But it looked like the police department was connected by a short breezeway to the civic complex that housed the library and the chamber of commerce. The building was a timber-and-adobe structure that looked as if it had been restored and added onto a couple of times.

The cop took him inside and led him down a narrow hallway to a tiny office, brightly lit and sparsely furnished. He unlocked the cuffs and said, "Take out your driver's license and have a seat."

Greg pulled his license out of his billfold, then sat down in a folding chair at a bare utilitarian table. A yellow legal pad and pen were already in place there.

The cop removed his cowboy hat and pitched it onto the table. Before he sat down he snatched up a beige wall phone.

"Ernesto? Miguel here. I've got the guy in the interrogation room. Go ahead and start the tape."

"Tape?" Greg said, "You're *taping* me? Isn't that illegal?"

The cop pulled a wry smile. "Get real." He checked Greg's driver's license, then sat in the chair facing him.

"This is unbelievable." Greg leaned forward in his chair while the cop scribbled some notes. "Are you going to tell me what this is all about?"

A pretty young woman stuck her head in the door. "Officer Eiden—" her voice was saccharine sweet "—you want this?" She waved a sheaf of papers at Miguel. Without looking up from what he was writing, the cop held out a hand and she took her time sauntering the few steps across the room to deliver the papers.

"Thanks, Crystal." Giving his full attention to the papers, the cop dismissed her.

But she lingered at Miguel's shoulder, giving Greg an avid once-over. "You think this is the guy?"

The cop cut her a sharp glance. "Crystal. You can go now."

She swished out, and the cop perused the pages, occasionally stopping to copy something he'd read onto the legal pad. He looked like he was about Greg's age—early thirties, maybe. In this part of the country there were a lot of people of Navajo descent, and this man's bronze skin and straight dark hair hinted at this heritage. When he finished reading he made a two-fingered signal at a picture-window-size mirror set into one wall, then he favored Greg with a cool, assessing squint. "I suppose you think just because this is a small town, we don't tape perps?"

"So I'm a *perp?*"

"You tell me." The cop looked at his watch and jotted something else on the yellow pad.

"What is it that you want me to tell you?"

Still writing, Miguel said, "Just answer a few simple questions…and don't forget to smile for our camera."

Greg refrained from waggling a sarcastic wave at "Ernesto," who was evidently already videotaping from beyond the dark glass.

"What's your full name?"

Through the Plexiglas in the cruiser Greg had

seen Officer Eiden writing down the tag number on his Navigator, and he assumed what the cop had in his hands was an NCIC report—and maybe some additional information from the Denver police. But Greg knew this tactic. The cop would make notes of Greg's answers to see if they jibed with the official report. "Gregory McCrae Glazier."

"Age."

"Thirty-four."

"Occupation."

"Land developer."

The cop calmly jotted down this answer without comment. A lot of people didn't know what a "land developer" did—buying and opening up new plots of land for housing and business. Greg was anxious to skip ahead. While this cop was playing twenty questions, Ashleigh Logan could be crossing another state line.

"And—" Greg leaned forward, hoping this would help move the process along "—at one time I was a deputy sheriff."

This, the cop did not calmly jot down. He fixed his gaze on Greg. "*Was?* Are you retired? Ex-cop? What?"

Greg was well aware that within the brotherhood of the badge, the difference between an ex-cop and a retired cop was vast. An ex-cop was suspect. Had he been drummed out of the force? Had he screwed something up bad? Couldn't he handle it?

"I'm an auxiliary deputy, but for all practical purposes I'm inactive."

The cop frowned. "From what agency?"

"The sheriff's department out in Last Chance, Colorado. My dad was the sheriff until he got killed in the line of duty. My grandfather was the sheriff before him. I guess you could say I inherited the job."

"Why'd you quit?"

"Technically, I didn't quit. I had to spend all of my time in Denver for a couple of years." When Kendra's kidneys had failed entirely, he'd moved her near the dialysis center. "I found a good replacement, a foreman on my ranch. Ever since, I've been inactive."

He might as well have quit. Greg was through with law enforcement. He had stopped trying to fill his father's shoes as soon as he found out how sick Kendra was. Playing deputy and keeping the ranch going in the years after his father died had siphoned off precious time that he should have spent with Kendra. Time he could never regain. But to keep from having to explain all of that to this cop, he gave the simple answer. "I still carry a commission card."

And my gun, he added mentally. He wasn't sure that fact would win points with this guy, either. "But I don't do much duty."

Eiden was a bit of a bulldog. "Why not?"

"It's pretty quiet where I'm from. The sheriff

only calls us if he needs backup on something. Not much call for crowd control out in Last Chance.''

"Okay. I get it." Eiden scribbled another note. "So, how long have you been a deputy?"

"Since I was nineteen. I was sworn in right after my father was killed."

"In the line of duty, you say?"

"Yeah. It was a long time ago." Greg was growing impatient. It was, indeed, a long time ago. And they were all gone. His dad. Kendra. Gramps. All that mattered now was the baby.

Eiden was studying him with the instinctual squint of a cop who suspected he wasn't getting the whole story, but Greg was in no mood to share. The fact that he'd made a lot of sacrifices—including his ability to father a child—in his desperate but futile battle to save Kendra's life was nobody's business.

"Why am I here?" Greg was anxious to focus the conversation back into the now.

The cop put his pen down. "Ms. Kane told me you came to the clinic looking for a woman, someone you believe is one of her clients."

Greg frowned, thinking, *So?* What a weird little burg this was. "Do you haul everyone who walks into that clinic looking for someone over to police headquarters for interrogation?" It was all so bizarre that Greg couldn't help adding, "Is that some kind of crime in Enchantment, New Mexico?"

"Would you mind giving me the woman's name?"

"Ashleigh Logan. The one with the TV show."

Greg noticed Officer Eiden didn't have to write that down. He waved the pen. "I know who she is. Why are you looking for her?"

"It's personal." That answer had seemed sufficient at the clinic. Well, no, it hadn't. The people at the clinic had called the cops.

And this cop, evidently, didn't like that answer, either. "I can detain you if you don't cooperate with me, Mr. Glazier."

"On what charges?" Greg wondered if he should call his lawyer, who was all the way back in Denver.

"I said *detain*. I didn't say *arrest*. If you're a deputy you know that I can put you in investigative detention. Now, I think you'd better tell me what business you have with Ashleigh Logan."

If Lydia Kane's furtive behavior hadn't convinced Greg that the woman he was seeking had, indeed, come to Enchantment to hide, this cop's pressure tactics sure did. Greg had the creeping sensation that he was dealing with something sinister here. That thought sent a chill through him, because if Ashleigh Logan was in some kind of danger, so was the child inside of her—his child.

The cop's eyes glittered like dark polished stones while he waited for Greg to answer. No one, Greg decided, could look more threatening.

"Look," Greg said, trying to sound reasonable. "I need to find Ms. Logan for reasons that are mine alone. It's something between the two of us. Is she in some kind of trouble or something?''

"I asked you why you're looking for her."

"I'd rather not say. I need to explain the full situation to her first. She deserves that much. Like I said, it's personal."

The cop leaned forward and braced his elbows on the table with his smooth brown hands fisted together over the legal pad. "You her boyfriend or something?"

Greg took a measure of the guy, deciding whether to trust him or not. Miguel Eiden seemed solid and clean cut. Except for a scar on his square jaw that looked as if it'd been earned in a fight. So maybe the guy had a bit of a history. Didn't everybody?

Eyeing him, Greg bet his top stud horse that the guy knew exactly where Ashleigh Logan was.

And if Ashleigh Logan was in Enchantment, the sooner he talked to her, the better. He had tried not to let himself consider this possibility, but if Ashleigh Logan had already found out about the disastrous mistake…well, she might do something rash if she was devastated enough. He had to make her see that there was more at stake than she knew. He suppressed his fears by reminding himself that she was the star of a show about having *babies,* and that her own unorthodox pregnancy had already been highly publicized. How would it look to her viewers if cute, bubbly Ashleigh Logan opted for a late-term abortion? And The Birth Place clinic didn't look like the kind of place where a woman would come for such a procedure, anyway. Still, Greg couldn't quell a certain sense of urgency. This was his child, the only child he would ever have. He had to ask.

"You know where she is, don't you?"

Miguel Eiden's mouth formed a tight line. "I asked you a question, Mr. Glazier. What is your relationship to Ashleigh Logan?"

They had clearly reached a Mexican standoff, and since the cop had the gun on his hip, Greg was bound to lose. He decided he'd have to tell the guy the truth if he was ever going to get out of here.

"I don't have a relationship with her. We've never even met."

The cop's frown deepened.

Greg could see he was going to have to tell the guy all of it. "This has to be kept confidential."

The cop leaned back and crossed his arms over his broad chest. "I'm a police officer, not a gossip columnist."

Right. As if Greg needed reminding. "Ms. Logan is pregnant."

The cop gave him a sarcastic frown that said, *duh.* Ashleigh Logan had chronicled every step of her pregnancy on her nationally syndicated cable TV show for all the world to see. "And?" Eiden pressed.

"The baby is mine."

The cop's eyebrows shot up. He dropped his threatening pose and his expression became incredulous as he leaned forward. "I thought you said you've never met her."

"I haven't."

"Then you'd better tell me what gives, Mr. Glazier." He leafed through the papers as if he'd missed something. "'Cause this deal is sounding stranger by the minute."

Greg sighed, suddenly feeling beaten down by the combined effects of his bizarre situation and the nagging altitude sickness. "*Strange* isn't the word for it. Seems like my whole life has been strange, and incredibly unlucky."

"I wouldn't call you unlucky, exactly." The cop continued to study the printout. "I guess you realize we ran an NCIC on you. They had your prints— your being a deputy and all. And Denver had more."

Greg nodded. The visit to the sister. Why were the cops so interested in him? Maybe that was the wrong question. Maybe he should be asking why they were so interested in Ashleigh Logan.

Eiden went on. "In the last two years you've made a killing off the property boom around Denver. You've been in the news a few times, doing civic stuff. On paper, you look like a real Boy Scout, unless you count a couple of speeding citations that you racked up out on Highway 63. Running back and forth to your ranch out on the Big Sandy, I'd guess." The corners of Miguel Eiden's mouth peaked downward grudgingly, as if to say Greg's profile was no big deal.

"Yeah, that about sums me up." Greg raked a hand over his face. Except for the fact that the love of his life had died a painful death at the age of twenty-nine, and his father had been shot dead by a pack of rodents, and his druggie mother had skipped off with some hippie when Greg was barely out of diapers, leaving him to be raised by his eccentric grandfather. "Could I please have some water?"

The cop went to the beige wall phone. Soon the flirtatious Crystal showed up with a plastic cup of ice water. Greg drank some, then started in. "When she decided to have a baby, Ms. Logan went to the sperm bank where she had stored her deceased husband's sperm."

The cop looked genuinely surprised at that, but he muttered, "To each his own."

"So, she got artificially inseminated and she thinks she is pregnant with her late husband's child. But I found out that's not true. They made a mistake. The child is mine. I came here to tell her that."

The cop's face showed that something had finally clicked. "And that's why you were trying to contact Ms. Logan in Denver?"

Greg nodded and the cop made a note. Greg hated to see this information go on record before he'd had a chance to explain this to Ashleigh Logan, but he supposed there was no help for it.

"You plan to tell her there was a mix-up at the sperm bank?"

"For starters."

"Is there some way for me to verify your story?"

"I could put you in touch with the sperm bank in California. They would back up my story if I told them to release the information to you."

"Okay." Eiden poised his pen. "Give me the number."

Greg pulled a card from his wallet and handed it over.

After he copied the number, Eiden said, "Okay. We're done for now. I'll take you back to your Navigator." His chair screeched on the linoleum as he stood and reached for his cowboy hat.

"Wait!" Too fast, Greg also jumped to his feet. A wave of dizziness struck as he felt himself break into a cold sweat. A sudden sense of panic mixed with altitude sickness for a moment as he clutched the table and focused on the fact that he wasn't going to leave here until he found out where Ashleigh Logan was. He had to say something to convince this cop that he needed to know where she was, *right now*. "There's something else you should know." He shook his head to clear it.

One of the cop's black eyebrows spiked up. "You okay?"

"Altitude sickness."

"Sit down."

Greg did so, gratefully. He sipped some more cold

water, then said, "This pregnancy—this baby. This is it for me. I won't get any more chances. The sperm bank...mine's all gone. They, uh, they accidentally let it...uh, defrost."

The cop looked as if he was struggling to hide a split second of involuntary disgust, then his dark eyes flitted sideways with something like sympathy. "I get it." He tugged his cowboy hat down, looking uncomfortable, embarrassed, as if he didn't like discussing another guy's sterility problems. Well, Greg didn't like talking about it, either. But there it was. He was sterile. Though he wasn't about to explain to this guy how that had come about. The salient fact was, this baby, Ashleigh Logan's baby, was Greg's one and only chance to be a father.

"Weird deal, huh?" he prompted when the cop didn't say anything.

Eiden looked up.

"So maybe you can understand why this is so urgent to me," Greg pressed. "What if she finds out the truth before I get to her? What if she's come here to do something...rash?"

Eiden put a hand up. "They don't do stuff like that at The Birth Place." He looked at Greg as if he wanted to tell him more, as if he wanted to help. "Are you staying somewhere in town?"

"I was thinking about getting a room at that bed-and-breakfast down the way."

The cop looked at his watch. "The Morning Light?"

Greg nodded.

"We'd better get you over there, then. Morning Light fills up pretty early during aspen-turning time." He tugged on the brim of the cowboy hat.

"Aren't you going to tell me where she is?"

"I'm afraid I can't do that, Mr. Glazier. For to-night, I want you to sit tight, okay? I'll give you a call as soon as I clear up a few details."

THE SUN HAD SLID BEHIND the mountains now.

After dropping Greg in the circular drive at the clinic, the cop waited, gunning the engine of his cruiser, with the alley lights blazing on Greg's back as he walked up to the door of the Navigator. Greg wondered what the guy thought he was going to do. Break into the clinic? Rifle through the file cabinets? Dig out Ashleigh Logan's records? Not a bad idea, actually. He assumed it was frustration that was making him think like this.

Greg got in his vehicle and fired it up, wondering if this whole odyssey was worth the grief. Maybe he should just head back to the family ranch and forget about this baby—if indeed there still was a baby.

The people at California Fertility Consultants had refused to give Greg the name of the man whose sperm had been confused with his, had refused to confirm that Greg's sperm had indeed been used to inseminate some unknown woman. It was only the intense publicity surrounding Ashleigh Logan's pregnancy that had finally tipped him off. When he'd seen the name of the clinic in that article in *USA TODAY,* he'd figured out the dates—her husband's sperm would have been stored at about the same time his was. The article said the sperm bank was proud of the fact that they had successfully stored specimens for that long. Well, their storage techniques weren't the problem. It was what they had done when they put the ''specimens'' into storage that had caused the damage.

Now two lives were thoroughly messed up. No, make that *three* lives. At first Greg had wanted to sic his lawyers on the idiots at that sperm bank, but after he'd calmed down, he'd realized that the threat of a lawsuit was his trump card. And he'd used it well.

Why, he asked himself again, was he doggedly pursuing this baby at all? It wasn't like he didn't have enough to occupy his time between the ranch and his business pursuits in Denver, especially now that Gramps had passed on. But the sad reality was that even though there was plenty of work to do, plenty to distract him out in Last Chance, Colorado, there was not a soul to share it with. There was no one to *love.*

In the last few years Greg Glazier's world had narrowed down to two things: horses and money. Neither one seemed like enough of an anchor to hold him for the next forty or fifty years of his life. Hell, if he was anything like Gramps—and he *was*—his

life might go on for another *sixty* years. *Family,*
Gramps had kept repeating in his final days, whis-
pering it over and over in the end, like a parting
prayer. *Family.*

Greg drove the Navigator like a little old lady as
Officer Eiden followed him back down Desert
Valley Road into the center of town. After he turned
off of Paseo de Sierra onto the short street that led
to the Morning Light, he glanced in his rearview
mirror and saw that the cop was gone, but he hoped
he hadn't seen the last of that guy. The cop knew
where Ashleigh Logan was.

Greg had no trouble relocating the bed-and-
breakfast he'd spotted earlier. He stepped through
the door and headed toward reception. A rambling
adobe villa with huge bougainvillea plants hanging
from the eaves, stuffed with antiques, Pueblo pots
and Indian trade blankets, the Morning Light was
the kind of charming place that would have made
Greg feel right at home under normal circumstances.

But tonight, the serene atmosphere did nothing to
settle Greg's churning thoughts. He followed a
friendly older woman to an upstairs room, where he
tossed his duffel bag into the closet and threw himself down to brood in a sagging horsehair chair by
the darkened window.

Right now he'd like nothing better than a good
stiff shot of his grandfather's whiskey. But he was
too nauseated to tolerate it, and what if the cop,
finally willing to give him Ashleigh Logan's loca-

tion, called? He wanted to be ready to jump back in the Navigator and go straight to her.

And then what?

He let his head fall back against the hard, scratchy back of the chair.

Then, of course, all hell would break loose.

CHAPTER THREE

ASHLEIGH LOGAN STRUGGLED to arrange her girth in a comfortable position on the plump leather couch as she waited through a series of frustrating clicks while the long-distance connection went through.

Apparently, Enchantment, New Mexico, did not have the best phone service in the West. No surprise there. This place was isolated, all right. Her cell phone had gone into remote mode shortly after they hit the road that wound up from Taos, and the signal had ceased altogether when they got up on this mountain.

She surveyed the cabin that would be her prison for the next three months—at least she hoped she could hold out for the entire three months. For the baby's sake.

The Coleman's cabin was a lodgepole pine behemoth perched high on the mountainside, at the end of a steep, winding road. The decor of the place was rustic but luxurious. The great room where Ashleigh now reclined had a high ceiling spanned by twenty-foot-long cross beams with a moose-antler chandelier at the center. A wall of glass with a deck beyond framed the three highest peaks in the Sangre de Cristo range.

The rest of the place was all dark leather, rough-hewn cedar, native stone. Thick Navajo rugs. Huge, colorful Native American paintings interspersed with tall banks of windows.

Her mother was merrily clattering around in the adjacent kitchen, which would have been rustic, too, except for the marble countertops and heated travertine floors.

Ashleigh made a wry face. She supposed she could stand this joint.

"Hello?" Finally, Megan picked up.

"Hi, Sis!" Ashleigh forced a bright, upbeat note into her voice. "We're in Enchantment. And I think we made it up here without being seen. Mom made sure the Suburban we rented had tinted windows, and I didn't even stop for a potty break after we left Taos."

Megan released a controlled sigh. "Ashleigh, let me say this again. I do *not* like this ill-conceived plan." Ashleigh's sister could cram more drama into one sentence than Ashleigh could milk out of a half hour of blather on her TV talk show.

"It's not ill-conceived. The cops okayed it. My doctor approved it. Dr. Ochoa, the obstetrician in Enchantment, is one of the best in the nation, and Lydia Kane is simply top-notch—"

"But—"

"And we've already alerted the local police—"

"Well that's *good*, because I'm trying to tell you something! After you and Mom left for Taos, a guy showed up here, looking for you."

Ashleigh sucked in a breath and sat up straighter against the couch pillows. "*What* guy?"

"The cops said his name was Greg Glazier."

"Never heard of him. Is he with the media or something?"

"No. He's some kind of land developer. Has a great big horse ranch out east of Denver."

"The cops told you that?"

"Yeah. They checked him out really well. Evidently he's very well known and respected. And he's a deputy sheriff. The cops don't think he's your stalker."

"Then what did he want with me?"

"He told the cops you two had some *holdings* in common and he needed to talk to you about it."

"Holdings in common? I never heard of this guy!"

"Exactly! Some stranger comes looking for you and the cops just let him go and now you're way off in New Mexico. I don't like any of this one bit!"

Ashleigh imagined Megan's pinched little frown as clearly as if they were standing face to face. "Now, Megan, there's no point in getting all upset. I'm doing everything reasonable to protect myself. I've practically become a hermit because of all of this." Ashleigh rushed on before Megan could argue. "But it's okay, because you should see this cabin. My gosh, it has every amenity you can imagine!''

"That cabin is also fairly remote," Megan inserted quickly, going back to her point. "What if something happens and you need emergency care? Think of all you've been through to get this baby, think of—" Megan's voice choked with threatened tears for a moment before she sputtered on with her argument against this plan—for the hundredth time.

Ashleigh listened to Megan's diatribe, thinking that she didn't need her sister undermining her resolve. Megan—a worrier, a crier, a sentimental sap—drove Ashleigh right up the wall with her roller-coaster emotions. But when it came to this baby, she supposed Megan was entitled to a little angst. From the start, this pregnancy had been incredibly emotional, for all of them. *Ill-conceived.* Ashleigh wondered if Megan realized how apropos her wording sounded.

Ashleigh had made her decision, firmly, six months ago, and in her heart, she knew Chad would support it. Ashleigh closed her eyes and bit her lip. She couldn't allow herself to go into meltdown now. Her obstetrician in Denver had warned her about that. A woman battling preterm labor had to remain calm. *Calm.* Don't think about Chad now, she warned herself. Think of the baby. His baby. At least you have his baby. Thank God they had decided to freeze Chad's sperm before he had started his chemotherapy.

"Listen, Megan," she said, finally interrupting her sister. "I'll be fine. The local cops have been alerted. And when we drove through town we even stopped to see Lydia Kane at the clinic."

"Oh. The Birth Place? How was it?" This diversion worked. Like her sister, Megan was fascinated by anything that had to do with babies.

"It's adorable! Quaint. Real adobe, nestled in pine trees."

"But do the midwives seem competent?"

"I'm sure Lydia runs a first-rate operation." It hadn't been easy, convincing her Denver obstetrician to transfer her to the care of an isolated clinic. But when Ashleigh had told Dr. Hill that the clinic was run by Lydia Kane, the impressive midwife she'd interviewed on her show a year earlier, he agreed to her plan. Ashleigh thanked her lucky stars she'd had Lydia Kane as a guest on the show and that when she needed a place to hide, Enchantment had come immediately to mind. It was geographically close enough to make a cautious road trip without stressing her system, but remote enough that the Denver media wouldn't follow her. The story of the baby guru becoming pregnant with her dead husband's sperm wasn't exactly breaking news anymore, but it was bizarre enough to attract a dogged follow-up.

She didn't blame the media. Their pursuit of her was nothing personal. Ashleigh herself had hounded sources to the ends of the earth to get something fresh, something startling.

Most important, hiding in Enchantment put distance between herself and this nutcase stalker.

"Lydia even came out to the Suburban to talk to me—" Ashleigh continued to try to sound upbeat for Megan "—so I didn't even have to walk in. Isn't that sweet?"

"I remember when you had her and those two midwives as guests on your show."

"Yeah. Remember that?" Ashleigh encouraged her sister as Megan's tone became less glum. "She's a real earth mother. She listened to the baby's heartbeat with a handheld device she called a Doppler, and she said a midwife named Katherine would come to the cabin this evening to get the home monitor set up. I'll send in a reading by phone every morning and then I'll go into the clinic tomorrow, and then once a week a midwife will check up on me here at the cabin. The cops and the staff at the clinic are the only people who will ever see me. The clinic has a private entrance in the back that leads straight to the birthing rooms. I guess it's so the moms in labor can arrive in their nighties and robes if they want to. When I've safely reached thirty-seven weeks, I can even have a home delivery with a midwife if I want. In the meantime, I'm getting plenty of rest. Right now, I'm stretched out on the biggest old leather couch you've ever seen, and that's where I'll stay until Mom fixes dinner, so stop worrying.''

Again, Megan sighed dramatically. ''I'll *try*. I just wish this were over. You know we'll do anything we can to get this baby here safely,'' Megan reiterated. ''Anything.''

Ashleigh smiled and felt a wave of pure love for her little sister. ''Right now, getting this cabin for me was the best thing you could have done. If I'm going to be on restricted activity, this is certainly the place for it. Lots of windows looking out over the mountains. Wonderful light. Very peaceful, you know?''

''I thought you'd like it. It's about as far from urban chaos as you can get.''

''Are you sure I can stay here until I have the baby? Three months is a long time to use somebody else's house.''

''The Colemans are good friends and they don't mind. They hardly ever go to that cabin now that their kids are grown. And they can be trusted to keep a secret. How does Mom like the place?''

''You know our mother. She can cheerfully adapt to anything. She's in there cramming the cabinets full of nutritious food even as we speak.''

''God, Ash.'' Megan's voice grew quiet, sad. ''Three months. I'm sure going to miss you. I wish I could come and rub your back or your feet or something.''

Ashleigh knew that Megan meant it. But they

could not risk a visit from Megan or even from Ashleigh's dad. The stalker might try to locate Ashleigh through her family.

Now that Ashleigh and her mother had made it to this remote New Mexico town, the plan was to stay put until the baby came. No one, except for Megan, their father, the local cops and people at The Birth Place, would have the slightest clue to their whereabouts.

"You just take care good of little Tyler and Justin, sweetie. When my baby is safely delivered, he'll want to play with his cousins."

"Oh…" Megan's stifled squeak at the mention of the baby sounded as if she might start to cry again. "Don't…don't let anything h-happen," she choked, "to either one of you."

"*I won't.* I'll be careful, and Mom will be careful, too, okay? I've got really good medical care. Now, don't cry. We've got to hang up now. This phone bill will probably be ridiculous."

"Okay." Megan sighed dramatically one last time. "Bye, Sis. I love you."

"I love you, too."

When they hung up, Ashleigh felt immediately bereft. She scooted down on the couch and turned onto her left side, as her doctor had instructed her. She cradled an arm under her growing abdomen and tried to imagine Chad's face, wondering if the baby would look like him. But after five years, she couldn't clearly conjure up his features without the help of a picture. With a pang, she realized she hadn't brought a picture of Chad with her. She consoled herself by thinking that soon she would see their baby's face, and that was all that mattered. All she had to do was hold on and stay safe for the next thirteen weeks. Thirteen weeks that already felt like thirteen years.

She looked at her surroundings and felt like an ingrate with her grumpy attitude.

As she'd assured her sister, the Coleman cabin was exceptionally comfortable, built to accommodate a large family on ski vacations. It wasn't as if the place was claustrophobic. A high deck wrapped around the great room and master suite, facing the mountains, and several upstairs bedrooms were connected by open walkways that looked down over the great room. At the back of the long, sunny kitchen, down a short flight of steps, there was a large, airy mudroom, with coat hooks and storage lockers for skis and winter apparel, a deep enamel sink, even a washer and dryer. She surveyed the beautiful but foreign surroundings again, then closed her eyes and steeled her emotions, ordering herself not to give in to self-pity.

She hadn't closed her eyes for long when the phone rang. *Megan,* she thought, *stop your worrying.*

But the caller wasn't Megan. It was Ashleigh's new midwife from The Birth Place, Katherine Collins.

"Ms. Logan, there's a man here at the clinic," she explained in a rush. "He's looking for you."

"Oh, my gosh," Ashleigh breathed. "You didn't tell him where I was, did you?"

"Certainly not. Lydia's on another line, calling the police right now."

"Oh, my gosh." Ashleigh sat upright, fighting to stay calm, for the baby's sake. She placed a protective hand on her belly. "Did he say what he wants?"

"No. But don't panic. He could just be somebody from the media or something." But Katherine's voice didn't sound too sure.

"What does he look like?"

"Tall, muscular, dark hair. Early thirties, maybe. Actually, he's sort of decent-looking—handsome, even. Except he's dressed kind of rough. Threadbare flannel shirt. Worn jeans. Scuffed boots. A heavy five o'clock shadow. But he's driving a new-looking champagne-colored Lincoln Navigator. I'm looking at it out the window of Lydia's office, but I can't make out the tag. Hold on."

Ashleigh heard Katherine talking to someone, then the midwife came back on the line.

"Lydia just told me that an officer is on his way up to your cabin."

"Good," Ashleigh said confidently.

But after she hung up she and her mother waited for the police to arrive like two women anticipating a jury verdict. Pensive. Intermittently clasping hands. Finally Maureen insisted on making hot tea, her cure for everything, but Ashleigh couldn't even swallow a sip.

What if Megan was right? What if this whole plan to go into hiding turned out to be…ill-conceived? What if her fanatical stalker had traced her to this remote town? Where could she go to be safe then?

It occurred to her that she should have asked Megan for a description of the strange man who had appeared at her door. What was his name? Greg Glazier? She was about to call Megan back when they heard a car engine outside.

Her mother went to look out the front window of the cabin. "It's the police," she assured Ashleigh.

The officer, an older guy with a paunch, told the women not to worry, that Officer Eiden had taken the man at the clinic into custody for questioning. He told them he'd stay parked outside until they got word.

The next time the phone rang, Maureen answered it. She said the caller was Miguel Eiden, the handsome cop who'd talked to Ashleigh and Maureen when they'd first arrived in town.

Maureen McGuinness took the phone out on the deck so Ashleigh couldn't hear. After the cop had assured her he'd keep a close eye on the Coleman cabin while Ashleigh was hiding up there, his tone had shifted, as if he had bad news. Now he was informing her that a man named Gregory McCrae

Glazier had tracked her daughter all the way to Enchantment, New Mexico.

And when Officer Eiden told Maureen *why* Greg Glazier had tracked Ashleigh here, she was glad she'd retreated to the deck. Because it was all she could do to keep from dropping the phone.

CHAPTER FOUR

MAUREEN SAT IN A BOOTH by the wide window of a small coffee shop, watching as the police cruiser rolled up at the curb. At the sight of it, her chest tightened with dread.

She reminded herself that Ashleigh trusted Officer Eiden. And for that matter, so did she. He had shown her the papers on the man from Denver and had convinced her that this man's story checked out with the sperm bank in California—the same one Ashleigh had used.

But before this man dropped his terrible news on Ashleigh, Maureen had convinced Eiden to arrange this meeting. Her daughter had endured enough stress in the last three days, the last three weeks. Truth be told, for the last five years.

Why did Ashleigh's life seem to only get more and more complicated? All Maureen McGuinness wanted out of life was for her driven daughter to settle down and be happy and for her type-A husband to finally retire and share some golden years with her.

But Marvin was working harder than ever, and her beautiful, talented daughter kept having one major crisis after another. Chad's illness had been so hard on Ashleigh, and Maureen had watched her daughter struggle to regain her balance ever since.

Maureen hadn't approved of this controversial pregnancy, not at all. She'd wanted her daughter to look to a real future, with a real relationship, instead of finding one more way to wallow in the past. She'd wanted Ashleigh to find a good man and enjoy a happy marriage, the way her sister Megan had. But Ashleigh had forged ahead, intrepid as always, making her own tough decisions, executing her own bold plans. Maureen sighed. She did admire her daughter's spunk.

But now it appeared all of the torture of Ashleigh's decision had been for naught. This baby, apparently, wasn't even Chad's. It was a stranger's baby.

Maureen's jaw tightened with resolve as a dark head and a pair of broad shoulders emerged from the passenger's side of Officer Eiden's cruiser. They would make the man prove his claims beyond a shadow of a doubt. She supposed the only logical answer was that they would perform paternity testing on the newborn. Ashleigh's baby. Her grandchild. *That* man's baby.

She rubbed her brow, having no idea how to proceed. What was the proper course of action in such a bizarre situation? After all, this was Ashleigh's child and therefore Ashleigh would have to make any decision about its welfare. Maureen was only the grandmother. Maybe Ashleigh would actually be glad to have a father for her child, if he was decent and kind.... Then a troubling thought struck Maureen. What if this man had been watching Ashleigh on TV and had some kind of thing for her? What if he was the stalker?

No. That didn't make sense. Eiden had shown her the report. Oh, it was all so confusing. She had to realize she couldn't make everyone's life perfect. And if Ashleigh found out that Maureen had secretly met with this man... Maureen felt like she was wading into very deep water here.

She hated leaving Ashleigh alone at The Birth Place, but she trusted Lydia and the midwives to watch out for her, and it was the only way to talk to this Glazier man alone. They didn't have much time. She was pretending to get milk. She would have to remember to stop at the store before she went back to the clinic. Maureen sighed. She despised subterfuge.

The little bell above the door of the café tinkled as it swung open, and there stood Officer Eiden. From behind him a handsome young man about Ashleigh's age studied Maureen as curiously as she studied him. His dark hair needed a trim, but he had compassionate gray eyes that conveyed a worried, saddened state of mind. Well, this *was* a sad situation, wasn't it? The fleeting thought that this man would probably father pretty babies crossed her mind, but she quickly banished that idea. Ashleigh did not want this man's baby. She wanted Chad's baby. What this man was claiming would throw her daughter's whole world into chaos.

The two men approached her booth, but when the young officer started to speak, she raised a hand to silence him. "Not here."

She slid from the booth, and with a jerk of her head indicated that they should follow her out onto the café's wraparound deck, which featured a panoramic view of the mountains. When she was satisfied that the picnic tables out there were unoccupied, she pulled the collar of her jacket up around her ears, folded her arms tightly under her bosom and faced the two men.

"We don't have much time. My daughter expects me to pick her up at the clinic soon. First of all, let's get one thing straight. I don't want my daughter to know we've had this conversation." With an impatience that betrayed her anger, she slapped a silvery strand of hair away from her eyes. "Is that understood?"

The man, the one claiming to be the father of Ashleigh's child, pushed a lock of his dark hair back against the mountain wind as well, then spoke quietly. "I assume you are Ashleigh Logan's mother?"

She nodded tightly, flustered that she'd charged ahead without the proper introductions. Normally, she prided herself on her self-control and impeccable manners. But this was not a Junior League tea. This was a squaring off in a strange little town, facing a man who could destroy her daughter's peace of mind, what little was left of it. A man who could simply be lying, for whatever twisted reason.

"I'm Greg Glazier." He stuck out a strong, wind-chapped hand, but he quickly withdrew it when Maureen kept hers tightly closed in the folds of her jacket.

"I am Maureen McGuinness," she said tersely.

He continued in a calm voice. "Thank you for letting Officer Eiden arrange this meeting."

Eiden had stepped away and propped a boot on the rail of the deck, keeping his back to them.

"I'm not sure I had a choice, considering your outrageous claims."

The aspen trees beside the deck made a golden flutter, and the pines whispered with a gust of wind that made Maureen shudder.

Seeming to notice her discomfort, the young man called to Eiden, "Is there somewhere where we can sit and talk privately, out of the wind?"

"I'm fine." She pressed her lips together.

"Well, to tell you the truth, I'm not."

Maureen examined Greg Glazier more closely. He did look a little wan. His eyes, she noticed again, were kind and sincere. Not the eyes of a liar.

"Greg's not well," the cop explained as he stepped up.

"Altitude sickness," Glazier elaborated. "It'll pass."

"I refuse to go anywhere where anyone could

overhear us.'' Maureen stood firm. ''My daughter has endured enough negative publicity and speculation and gossip and stress as it is. I don't want to take a chance that some hideous rumor might get back to her that might upset her again. And I don't want any media to get wind of this.''

''I understand that, ma'am,'' Greg Glazier replied mildly. ''I agree.''

''We can go sit in the squad car,'' Eiden offered, in an effort to temper Maureen's palpable antagonism.

Maureen gave a short nod of agreement, and they rounded the side of the café and descended the plank steps to the sidewalk. Officer Eiden opened the back door of the cruiser for Maureen. ''There's a Plexiglas shield. So I'm afraid you'll both have to get in the back seat if you want to have a private conversation. But I'll be right here in the front seat if you need me.''

''Thank you.'' Maureen climbed inside.

The space inside the cruiser was cramped, and with his long legs and broad shoulders, Greg Glazier made it seem even more so. As she settled herself next to him, he adjusted his muscular frame and held it stiffly canted so that his knees didn't crowd Maureen.

Maureen did not waste words on niceties. ''What is this about switching the sperm samples, Mr. Glazier?''

''It's true.'' Glazier scrubbed a hand down his

handsome face and released a tense breath. "Even though it's hard to believe. The cryo bank in California contacted me about a month ago."

"California Fertility Consultants?" Maureen bit her lip. She shouldn't have given him any additional information. She reminded herself to be careful with this stranger. He could be some kind of weird imposter, trying to get near Ashleigh. He could have made all this up, based on the storm of publicity that Ashleigh's pregnancy had created. He could even be the stalker, although that seemed unlikely. Apparently he was a former deputy sheriff.

"Yes, ma'am. California Fertility Consultants. They informed me that the mix-up actually occurred way back at the time of…the storage."

"Five years ago?" Maureen bit her lip again, rueing the slip, but she found this whole story utterly incredible.

"Yes. Your daughter's husband and I both elected to bank our sperm at the same time, in October of '98—"

"I know when it was, Mr. Glazier. It was just before my son-in-law started chemotherapy."

"I'm sorry he didn't make it." Again the man's hand scraped down his face. He was nice-looking, but right now his skin looked pale, clammy. Was that because he was lying? Maureen wondered if Marvin knew anything about this Greg Glazier. She'd have to make it a point to ask him, the next time she caught him between meetings.

"With the passage of time, our family has adjusted to Chad's death."

"I know how that is, believe me. And believe me, I don't want to cause your family any more pain, but you've got to hear me out."

"That's why I am here."

"The day the lab received your son-in-law's samples, my samples from Colorado arrived in California in the same shipment. We used the same doctor in Denver."

"I see. If I may ask, why did you elect to freeze your...sperm." Maureen felt genuinely uneasy, having this highly personal conversation with a stranger. "If I may ask."

Greg swallowed. He shot a look at the back of the cop's head that told Maureen he was as uncomfortable about having this conversation as she was. "I'd rather not say," he spoke quietly. "It's not important now. The point is my samples were somehow confused with Chad's."

"But the lab in California told my daughter that they took extra precautions. Each client was given their own separate storage unit. Each storage unit had a duplicate in another location, in another part of the state."

"Yes, the same process was explained to me."

"Then how..." Maureen's voice trailed off. It seemed pointless to argue this. No matter what he said, there would have to be paternity testing when the baby came.

"They didn't discover the error until the brown-out at their main site. When they went for retrieval of the backup samples at the alternative site, they discovered that the ones in both my storage unit and in Chad's storage unit were actually Chad's."

"Which means that both the samples at the main storage facility were yours."

"Exactly. When they went back and checked the containers that had gone bad during the brownout, they found that both storage tanks—mine and Chad's—indeed had had *my* samples in them."

Maureen covered her mouth with a shaky hand, suddenly seeing how the mishap had happened. "So," she whispered through her fingers, "they kept all of your samples at the original facility, and sent all of Chad's samples to the backup facility."

"I'm afraid so."

"And Ashleigh was impregnated with…"

"Mine."

Maureen's tears were hot and angry. "How could they make such a horrid mistake?"

"It's very rare." His voice was gentle with compassion. "Like I said, Chad and I used the same doctor in Denver. Our samples were shipped together and they got confused when they divided them up to create the duplicate containers. We would never have known any of this if the brownout hadn't occurred."

"Why not?" She dabbed at her eyes. "Weren't you planning on using your…samples someday?"

"No." His look became slightly bitter before he amended. "Not unless I remarry."

"You're single?"

"Yes, ma'am."

"May I ask why you were storing...do you have some kind of health problem? We *are* talking about my future grandchild here. It's something Ashleigh will want to know. She knows all about babies, including all the things that can go wrong."

"No, ma'am. I'm perfectly healthy, except for this altitude sickness." His disparaging smile might have been engaging, but Maureen wanted no part of it. His expression grew serious again. "My reasons for storing my sperm—it's a long story. Let's just say I wanted to be sure I could have children if that ever became possible."

"But now..." Maureen drew a sharp breath, realizing another horrible truth.

"Now," he confirmed sadly, "I have no samples left. All of my...material was destroyed in the brownout."

"But we still have Chad's."

"Yes, ma'am. That's true. And I hope that will be some comfort to your daughter in all of this. But this baby...this baby is mine."

Maureen sat as still as a stunned bird, staring at the Plexiglas shield, blinking while she absorbed the awful truth. And it was the truth, she was convinced of that now. Something else occurred to her then, and the thought made her angry. "How did you know Ashleigh was the patient who was impregnated with your last remaining sperm? The lab should never have told you that!''

''They had to tell me they…used it. But they wouldn't tell me her name, at first. I figured it out from all the publicity about her pregnancy. Seems your daughter's decision to carry her dead husband's child made quite a human interest story.''

Silently, Maureen damned the media again for what they had done to Ashleigh's life. ''The publicity, I'm afraid, has exposed my daughter to an undesirable element.''

''I don't understand.''

''Unfortunately, Ashleigh's situation with this baby has drawn a stalker. And I'm afrai—''

''Wait a minute.'' Greg thrust a palm up. ''Wait just a damn minute. A *stalker? What* stalker?''

At the anger in his voice, Maureen flinched.

''I'm sorry.'' He immediately softened his tone. ''But when somebody uses the word *stalker* in the same sentence where she's talking about *my* baby, my alarm bells go off.''

Maureen understood perfectly.

''What kind of stalker?'' He kept his voice calm now.

She supposed, if the baby really was his, he had a right to know about this threat.

''The police think it's some kind of fanatic. They only know his first name. Simon. We don't have a last name. He first called in to the Q and A segment of Ashleigh's show months ago. He seemed obsessed with the topic of babies and fertility. He started saying strange, startling things, trying to engage Ashleigh in an on-air debate. He expressed some truly bizarre attitudes about things like fertility treatments and surrogate mothers and human cloning. The producers figured out he was a nutcase and wouldn't take any more of his calls. You have to understand—'' she gave Greg Glazier a pleading look when she saw that his jaw was tightening in anger ''—almost every media personality attracts these types.''

''When did he start to bother her?''

''A couple of months ago. He's the reason Ashleigh finally took herself off the air and let someone else do the show. At least for now.''

''Why do the police think he's stalking her?''

''Well, when Ashleigh's pregnancy became public, this Simon tried to call the show for one reason or another almost every week. He seemed to think Ashleigh had no right to become a single mother. Of course, her staff never let him get through to her, except once when he used a different name.''

''Did he call himself John?''

''Yes.'' Maureen was surprised. How did he know this?

''I, uh, I taped her last show.'' He seemed embarrassed, admitting that. ''When I became suspicious about the mix-up. So this guy is the caller Ashleigh had to cut off.''

Maureen nodded. "Mr. Glazier, do you have any idea how distressing it is to be a public figure, having your privacy invaded all the time?"

"What else had this stalker done?"

"E-mails. Calls to her home phone. Notes."

"What kind of notes?"

"Messages left at the front desk at the studio, on the windshield of her car, in her mailbox at her condo. It seemed like he was trying to show her that he knew her movements and that he could get very close to her if he wanted to. And the content—very creepy stuff. Simon, or should I say whoever wrote the notes, seems to think that what Ashleigh has done is evil. He threatened Ashleigh...and her baby."

"Threatened?"

"I can't remember the exact words. But this person is deranged—some kind of pseudoscientist. He seemed to think that what Ashleigh was doing was unnatural, that she should be punished. That she doesn't deserve to be the mother of her baby. The police seemed convinced that he could do her real harm."

"So, that's why she's hiding up here in the mountains."

"Yes. We had to choose our hiding place carefully, given Ashleigh's condition, but we also hoped to get far enough away that he couldn't locate us."

"Oh, man," Greg sighed. "It must have freaked you out when I showed up in town."

"Yes. It alarmed the people at The Birth Place, too. But though the police have no real idea what this Simon person looks like, they do know his voice, and it's nothing like yours."

"I'm so sorry for the stress I've caused you." He turned his kind, sincere eyes on Maureen. "I thought she might have chosen this remote place because she was hiding from me—because she already knew about the baby."

"No. This is the first we've heard of you."

"So the people in California didn't tell her there'd been a mistake, or even about the brownout?"

"No. The lab most certainly did not contact my daughter." Maureen eyed Greg Glazier. "Why didn't they?" She had a feeling this young man knew the answer to that question.

"I, uh, managed to convince them to agree to let me be the one to tell the mother. I thought it might be easier if she met me—"

"Exactly how did you *convince* them?" Maureen interrupted, thinking he'd probably used money or influence or some such thing.

"I agreed not to sue them for the mix-up in exchange for letting me find Ashleigh in my own way and tell her the truth in my own time."

Maureen's eyes went wide, as the whole situation became suddenly clear to her. This young man had been as injured as Ashleigh had been. Ashleigh was not carrying Chad's child as she believed, but this Greg Glazier would never have *any* other children.

At least Ashleigh could still have Chad's child in the future if that's what she chose. Both Ashleigh and this man had been robbed of their dreams. Both would be completely justified in seeking legal recompense.

Greg Glazier looked up at her with an apology in his eyes, waiting for her to speak. Here was a man who valued his child, and perhaps even her daughter's feelings, more than money, more than winning, more than being justified or proved right in a court of law.

"Mr. Glazier, forgive me for being so personal, but you have to admit this is a highly personal situation here."

He swallowed and nodded.

"You are obviously a handsome, successful person." *Like my daughter,* Maureen thought, and a fleeting notion occurred to her that this man might be a good match for Ashleigh. "Someday, surely, you will marry and build a life with some equally attractive and successful young woman. Surely, under the circumstances, you don't want to complicate your future by laying claim to the baby of some other woman, a woman you don't even know."

"This is not some other woman's baby." A fierce determination undergirded his words. "This is *my* baby."

"This baby means that much to you?"

"This baby..." He swallowed again and the

sound was dry, desperate. "Mrs. McGuinness, this baby is the only person I have left in this world."

Maureen stared at the young man who threatened to turn her daughter's life inside out. "I have to think about this," she said, finding she was barely able to draw a full breath. "I have to discuss the best course of action with Ashleigh's doctor, if that's possible without her consent." She rubbed her brow.

"I understand," he said very quietly, with a slight frown forming between those dark brows. "But you have to understand that I also have to do what I think is right. I'm still going to try in every way I can to make contact with your daughter."

Maureen stared at him, hoping he wasn't remembering that she'd said Ashleigh was at the clinic. As she stared at his strong profile, it struck her again that it was a shame Ashleigh couldn't have met him under different circumstances.

"I have to go," she said.

There were no door handles on the inside, so Greg tapped on the Plexiglas barrier and Officer Eiden got out and opened the door of the cruiser. Maureen scrambled out like a fleeing prisoner.

"Goodbye" was all she said to the cop before marching down the sidewalk.

"I'll get in the front," Greg told Eiden as he scooted across the plastic-covered seat.

Maureen looked back before rounding the corner of the café. She saw Greg Glazier unfold his long frame and step out into the New Mexico sunshine with the slow, steady movements of a man who could wait forever, if necessary, to get the one thing he really wanted.

CHAPTER FIVE

THE FIRST THING SIMON FISCHER did when he got to Enchantment was locate the clinic called The Birth Place. On the way here from Denver, his car, a battered old Ford Crown Victoria, had started smoking from the tailpipe, and he wondered how far he would be able to make it once he hit the road with the baby. Mexico? That would be good.

In his trunk he had baby things he'd bought at a thrift store. He'd made up a fake e-mail address and sent one last message to Lydia Kane at The Birth Place before he had emptied his bank accounts and sold his only item of value—his computer. Then, he'd bought some photography equipment at the same pawn shop.

None of that mattered now. Simon was on a mission.

He sat in his car in front of the clinic, while the oily exhaust pumped out of the tailpipe and his tortured mind pumped out his risky, thrilling plans.

Simon felt his mind was his best weapon. When he'd discovered that Ashleigh Logan had left Denver, like a computer quick-searching files, his mind had fed him the name of this place. And then Simon remembered—oh, Simon Fischer had a great, long, ferocious memory—the *All About Babies* episode where that Lydia Kane woman and the two mid-wives had been guests. They were from this remote birthing clinic in the New Mexico mountains. A small town called Enchantment. With only a little time on the Net, Simon's search efforts were richly rewarded. He printed the maps to Enchantment, counting on two things: Ashleigh Logan would feel safe in this remote place; and these women at the clinic wouldn't mind a little publicity.

If he was wrong, he still had thirteen weeks to find Ashleigh before the baby was born. And when that baby was born...

He fantasized about getting the baby to a safe place where he'd find a job, any job, and hire a good sitter—a nice, humble, God-fearing woman, not some sharp-tongued strumpet like the child's mother. And they would live happily ever after, Simon and his baby that he had rescued from the clutches of evil, manipulative women.

Women. The very word made Simon angry. It had all started with his ex-wife—that murdering bitch.

Tears clouded his eyes as self-pity overwhelmed him, thinking of his own loss so many years ago. His wife had thought herself a brilliant reproductive researcher. He had told her and told her that the pregnancy didn't bother him. It would not interfere with her plans to finish her doctoral degree. He,

Simon, would raise their baby. Over and over, he told her. She had the abortion anyway.

A lady came out of the clinic. He shoved his thumbs under his glasses, wiped his misty eyes, then watched her closely.

She had a long gray braid and was wearing overalls and carrying a big tote bag. Her face looked nice. She pulled a sheepskin-lined jacket across her front as she crossed the gravel drive to a Jeep parked under a bare cottonwood tree.

Braving it, he turned off the engine, looped the camera over his shoulder and got out.

"Ma'am?" he said, approaching her with his most disarming smile. Simon knew that with his mild-mannered Boy Scout looks, his glasses, his thinning hair, his teddy bear build—all he had to do was add that uncertain smile and he posed no threat.

She stopped before rounding the fender of the Jeep. "Yes?"

"My name is Morris Reed." Simon had been reading Morris Reed's articles about cloning and such for some time. He'd also thoroughly searched the Internet for any pictures of Mr. Reed. There wasn't a single one. It was the perfect alias. "I was wondering who I might talk to about The Birth Place. I've been asked to do an article on midwives for *Reproduction and Sexuality*. It's a professional journal. Perhaps you've heard of it?"

"I have!" She smiled in recognition. "You e-mailed Lydia about it."

"Yes." Simon smiled, straightening his stocky frame. "Do you work at the clinic?"

The woman's smile widened. "Yes. I'm one of the midwives."

"I know it's late, but could someone possibly answer a few questions for me?"

She looked at her watch. "I can't. I'm running late for a home visit. We do have a Web site, you know."

"Oh, I know. I've seen it. But there's nothing like firsthand information…and firsthand photos." He hitched the camera up. "But I guess I'll have to try again tomorrow."

At his crestfallen expression, she said, "You could go inside and talk to the receptionist. Her name is Trish. She can give you some brochures that should help you. Someone may even have a moment to show you around."

That, Simon thought, *would be most helpful.* The more he knew about the layout of the place, the better.

"Thanks!" He smiled and waved as the midwife went on to her Jeep. As he walked toward the clinic he noticed a side drive that led around back. He'd have to check there for a rear entrance.

The first step in his plan had gone smoothly. Since he knew approximately when Ashleigh Logan was due—she'd made such a big deal out of the early stages of her pregnancy—it was just a matter of finding out when the blessed event would actually happen. That might prove harder, but he had to be there shortly after the baby's birth. But how? As he turned and watched the midwife drive away in her Jeep, Simon suddenly realized he might have a way.

He looped his camera around his neck and went inside to schmooze the women in the clinic. Would Ms. Kane give him a tour? Answer a few questions? Consent to having her photograph taken for a respected professional journal?

IT WAS EASY ENOUGH FOR GREG to find Maureen McGuinness after Eiden took him back to his vehicle. She was wearing a distinctive black wind suit stitched down the front and shoulders with a colorful Native American design. He caught up with her at the small town square as she climbed into a late model red Suburban with tinted windows. Behind those windows, Ashleigh Logan would soon be concealed.

He pulled to the curb at the opposite corner of the square and edged his Navigator into the shadow of an overhang as he watched her fasten her seat belt and start the engine.

When she left, Greg pulled into traffic and followed. The Suburban turned onto Desert Valley Road, no doubt heading to The Birth Place, and Greg slowed to a crawl while he debated about whether or not to follow. He figured his chances of being spotted along the narrow, sparsely populated road would be high. But if Maureen did see him, all she could do was avoid him or call the cops and report him. And they both knew that the cops in Enchantment already knew who he was, and why he was here.

He yanked the Navigator into a sharp turn and headed down Desert Valley Road. When Maureen's vehicle got to the clinic, she bypassed the circular rock driveway and instead took the narrow dirt lane at the side of the building that led around to the back. Greg pulled onto the gravel shoulder and parked off road, in the shelter of some low pine trees. He got out and trotted off into the trees, approaching the clinic on foot by a circumspect route, which made him feel like the very stalker he now despised. But desperation drove him. He had to have a glimpse of Ashleigh Logan, if that was remotely possible. He circled far around the back, where from a small parking lot the land sloped sharply down into a ravine. He worked his way up the slope, staying low in the sagebrush and junipers, like a cowboy sneaking up on a foe in a B movie.

He heard a car door slam, but when he raised his head to get a clear view of the parking lot, all was quiet. He found a place to hide behind some large boulders. There he waited. All he wanted was a glimpse, he told himself. One quick look at Ashleigh Logan in the flesh.

His patience was rewarded fifteen minutes later when the back door of the clinic swung open and the two women emerged. Maureen, silver-haired and

chic in the black wind suit, and a younger woman—
Ashleigh.

Unlike her stylishly dressed mother, Ashleigh was
wearing a shapeless calf-length denim maternity
dress topped with a baggy, navy-blue hooded sweat-
shirt. She hugged the jacket over her big belly as
the wind kicked up. On her feet she wore some ugly
printed knee socks and a pair of clunky Birkenstock
sandals. She slid a pair of sunglasses onto her face
as she walked toward the Suburban alongside her
mother.

She was much smaller than she appeared on TV.
And she looked more fragile, even if she was six
months pregnant. His eyes traveled to her bulging
abdomen and stayed there for a moment. Was it a
boy or a girl?

As she made her way across the gravel lot, Ashleigh's movements were gentle, feminine. When she
hitched a tiny purse up on her shoulder, her full bust
came into sharp relief. When she tossed her head,
her long, wavy blond hair caught the fire of the sun
lowering over the Sangre de Cristo mountains.

Ashleigh and her mother were walking close to
each other, talking confidentially, and when her
mother hooked her arm under her daughter's, obviously making some teasing remark, Ashleigh's face
lit up with laughter. The distant sound made Greg's
gut tighten. Her face was truly beautiful, far more
beautiful in person than her made-up TV image.

They went to their separate sides of the Suburban,

Ashleigh with the slower, slightly awkward gait of a gravid woman who hadn't had enough exercise lately. Transfixed, Greg watched her every move as she opened the door and angled herself up into the high seat, while the fabric of her dress stretched over her pregnant front. He hadn't expected his first reaction to Ashleigh Logan to be so strong. He felt as if his foundation had just been shaken and he couldn't fathom why. All he knew was that now that he'd had his little glimpse of Ashleigh Logan, it didn't feel like enough. And he had to get out of here before he did something stupid.

He turned from his hiding place, intending to go back the way he'd come, by the roundabout route down the juniper-studded slope, lest anyone from the clinic should spot him on the grounds.

But an alarmed female shout caused him to turn back around. In the parking lot, Maureen was yelling, "No pictures!" as she scurried around the Suburban toward an enormous man in a windbreaker. The guy had a camera pressed to his face.

Ashleigh, half in, half out of the Suburban, was holding her hand toward the lens while the photographer snapped away, closing in, ignoring Maureen's protests.

Greg plowed through the junipers, knocking limbs out of the way as if he were ripping the guy's arms off.

"Stop that!" he yelled, but the photographer only dodged past Maureen and swooped in closer on his prey. Ashleigh tried to pull the door of the Suburban shut to hide herself, but the guy actually blocked it with his body, leaning in to snap close-ups of her face.

The guy was bigger than Greg, but with a strategic jerk on the camera strap Greg hauled him away from the Suburban by the neck, like a trainer jerking a bear's chain.

"Hey!" the guy shouted.

"The ladies said no pictures!" Greg flung the guy to his knees.

Lydia Kane emerged from the door of the clinic, rushing forward like a tigress. "What do you think you are doing?" she demanded of the photographer.

Greg went to the door of the Suburban, where Ashleigh Logan recoiled on the seat with her hand pressed over her mouth.

"Are you all right?" he said, touching her elbow. She was trembling.

She swayed toward him and he tightened his grip. "Just lean back for a sec," he said, guiding her back in the seat.

"I'm okay." She braced a hand on his shoulder and Greg felt a surge of feelings he hadn't felt in a very long time. Was it this woman's vulnerability? Her beauty? Whatever it was, her touch felt amazingly right.

She looked at him as if reading his mind. She took her hand away. "Who are you?"

"I'm Greg Glazier."

"I'm Ashleigh Logan." She smiled, but at the same time he thought he saw a small flash of wariness in her eyes. The sister had told her about his little visit back in Denver, no doubt. Or—his heart pounded at this thought—perhaps her mother had already told her something.

"I know who you are, Ms. Logan. Lots of people do. Which is probably the reason that creep wanted your picture."

"Yes. Thank you for stopping him."

"Ashleigh!" Maureen came up to lean in beside Greg.

"Mom, he got my picture!" Ashleigh cried through shaky fingers.

"Not for long." Greg whirled around, took two bounding steps to the photographer, who'd stood up by now, and wrenched the camera off the man's neck.

He went back to the Suburban, unloaded the disk and presented it to Ashleigh. "There. No one will see these pictures now."

Behind them, Lydia was saying, "I want you off these premises!"

Greg turned back and tossed the empty camera at the guy's gut. "You heard her. Get out of here."

The heavy man stumbled around the corner of the adobe building, looking back once with a strange lopsided smile.

"Call the cops," Greg told Lydia.

"Call Miguel," Lydia relayed to Trish, who was standing in the open door of the clinic.

"I am so sorry, Ms. Logan," Lydia breathed, clutching the pendant around her neck. "In over forty years of running this clinic, I have never had anyone accost a patient like that."

"He came from inside the clinic," Greg accused.

"Yes," Lydia huffed, still breathless. "We were giving him a tour. He said he was writing an article for a professional journal. He had e-mailed me. I guess he spotted Ashleigh at some point."

"Obviously. He's another media hound," Ashleigh said. She slid off the seat, lowered her feet to the ground and straightened her shoulders. She looked defiant now as she pushed wisps of blond hair back from her brow, but Greg noted telltale stains of color on her cheeks. The incident had upset her more than she was letting on.

"Yes. Thank God you stopped him," Maureen said to Greg. "Where did you come from?"

"I followed you from the restaurant."

"I must admit I'm glad you did."

"I don't get it." Ashleigh's gaze panned from Greg to her mother and back. "You know him?"

"We met..." Greg started, but Maureen gave him a warning stare.

Greg wondered how Maureen, in this dire moment, could possibly explain to Ashleigh that she had met Greg Glazier, and that he was far from a total stranger.

But Maureen amazed him when she said, "He's the bodyguard your father hired."

"Bodyguard?" Lydia eyed Greg.

"I, uh—" Greg started.

Maureen explained further, "To provide additional protection while we're here."

"Then why haven't I met him before now?" Ashleigh turned to fully face Greg, who towered over her. She studied his face, then pulled her jacket over her bulging middle and looked away shyly.

"I was going to—" He started again.

"He's supposed to stay undercover," Maureen broke in. "Down here in the town."

Greg, unsure what Ashleigh's doctors had just told her about her condition and seeing how upset she was, felt he had no choice but to go along with Maureen's lie.

"I'll be watching out for you," he said. And that was so true.

"That's good. I guess." Ashleigh sounded unsure as she studied him again. Greg suddenly wished he'd taken the time to clean up his appearance more. "Daddy should have told me about this," she said to her mother. "Not that I'm ungrateful," she added to Greg.

"I'm just glad I could help." Standing so near her like this, looking into her beautiful eyes, Greg felt himself being assailed by a slew of surprising emotions. He backed up. "Call me if you need me, then."

"I have your number, Mr. Glazier." Maureen took control of the situation. "And we'll call you *if* we need you. I think I should get Ashleigh away from here now." She urged Ashleigh into the Suburban.

When they were gone, Lydia faced Greg. "I am very protective of my patients, Mr. Glazier. I do everything in my power to see that each of our mothers has a safe, memorable pregnancy and birth experience."

"I appreciate that. I have the highest respect for you and what you do at this clinic."

"Ms. Logan's case is special. She sought us out, hoping we could help her through a difficult pregnancy."

"Believe me, that is my goal, too. I only want to keep her safe."

"If you are Ms. Logan's bodyguard, why didn't you announce that when you first came to town?"

Greg didn't know how to answer that one. Apparently Eiden had meant what he said about not being a gossip columnist. "I needed to keep a low profile." Greg was getting really tired of walking a fine line between truth and half truth, and as with their first encounter, he felt this sharp older woman could see straight through him. "We both just need to do our jobs, Ms. Kane, and get this baby here safely."

"Agreed. I will give Officer Eiden all the information I have about that photographer as soon as he gets here,'' Lydia volunteered.

"And you tell Eiden—" Greg gave the midwife a determined look "—that if he wants to pick that dude up to call my cell. I'm tailing him right now.''

CHAPTER SIX

GREG'S NEXT FEW DAYS in Enchantment stretched into restless hours of talking to his business partner on his cell phone, cruising the roads in the area to get the lay of the land and strategizing while sipping coffee at the Silver Eagle café.

Now that he'd found Ashleigh, his main priority was clear—protecting the mother of his child. In this, Greg had found an ally in Miguel Eiden.

"The guy said his name was Morris Reed," Eiden confirmed over coffee the morning after the incident at the clinic. "And he is from the media, sort of. He really does write occasional articles for some think-tank organization called the Association for Reproductive Reform."

"There's something fishy about him," Greg said as he sipped his coffee.

"Maybe. But I didn't have any reason to hold him."

"The guy was taking pictures of Ashleigh without her consent. What if he's the stalker?"

"Lydia thought *you* were the stalker at first. And besides, you followed him. The guy's left town. Maybe he was just looking to make some easy money selling photos of a high-profile television star.''

But Greg wasn't convinced. Something nagged at him about this Morris Reed. Last night he put the videotape that he'd made of Ashleigh Logan's last live show into the VCR in his room at the Morning Light. He'd already watched it several times, trying to absorb the fact that the beautiful woman on the screen was about to become the mother of his child. Now he watched it again, this time with a different eye.

Ashleigh stood behind a table covered with an array of her favorite baby products. She was wearing a brightly striped maternity top that hugged her full bust and rounded tummy. Her blond hair was pulled up in a colorful clasp, leaving stylish wisps around her face. Flawlessly made-up, her slender fingers pointed out everything from Diaper Genies to teddy bears to pacifiers. Her guest that day was a fluffy woman named Miss Candi, who specialized in shopping for busy, affluent working mothers.

''I can usually outfit your entire nursery, top to bottom, in less than three days,'' the woman gushed.

''Wonderful!'' Ashleigh winked at the camera. ''How about coming to my house this weekend!'' The audience broke into laughter, then applause.

''Enough shopping!'' Ashleigh clapped her hands. ''Well, let's be honest, we can't ever get *enough* shopping—'' the audience laughed again ''—but we've got lots of other information you need coming up on the second half of *All About Babies,* including what to do when baby won't stop crying." A picture of a howling infant flashed on the screen. "Aw," Ashleigh said, sticking out her lower lip. "We gotta help that little guy." The audience applauded again.

"And stay tuned," Ashleigh hollered over the applause, "for a very special segment, 'Doctor Can I?' It's all about s-e-x during pregnancy. Plus," she added, pointing a manicured finger at the camera. "We'll be taking your calls right after the break. So don't go away!" Wild cheering and cut to commercial.

Greg muted the sound during the commercial he'd inadvertently taped.

On camera Ashleigh Logan smiled constantly, with dazzling white teeth and unrelenting charm. He couldn't imagine why a beautiful woman like that had chosen single motherhood over remarriage and building a family the normal way. But who was he to judge? He certainly hadn't given another woman a chance to take Kendra's place in his heart.

"Welcome back. Our first caller is John from Boulder, Colorado. Close to home, here. Hi, John! What do you think about Miss Candi's shopping service?"

At first the caller sounded pleasant, teasing Ashleigh for being a die-hard shopaholic.

Ashleigh only laughed and said, "When it comes to loving baby stuff, I plead guilty!"

But very quickly the caller's voice grew high with emotion, then vaguely hostile. "But stuff like this maternity-shopping service—that's what's wrong with our society," he said. "I think it's a sorry state of affairs when mommies don't even have time to go out and shop for their own babies."

"But, John—"

"Hey, why are you women even having babies these days if—"

Ashleigh's face clouded as she quickly interrupted him. "Well, John, some mommies must work—"

"Babies come first," the voice retorted. "A baby isn't some *toy*. It isn't some extension of yourself."

Ashleigh's on-camera smile faded and her face grew ashen as he rushed on.

"You selfish women are as bad as the scientists doing their somatic-cell nuclear transfers and par-thenogenesis—never worrying about where it will lead. Just trying to make human clones without thinking about the baby!"

"Whoa!" Ashleigh tried to rescue the situation. "Thanks for your input, John, but we're not talking about cloning today."

"It's all the same thing. It's all selfishness! The way you got pregnant is asexual reproduction, pure and simp—"

Ashleigh cut him off by hitting the line button. She forced a smile at her studio guest. "Looks like that caller thinks using a shopping service is unnatural or something. But I say a baby doesn't know if Mommy bought the goods, or if Miss Candi did.''

"Exactly." Miss Candi smiled a big, nervous smile. "What baby needs most is a happy mommy.''

"And us working mothers," Ashleigh finished cheerfully, "need all the help we can get!" She hit another line button.

"Sharon from San Diego, what have you got to say about shopping for baby?''

Greg frowned, still puzzling over the exchange with "John" as he watched the rest of the show. He played the segment a dozen times, and became convinced that this pseudoscientific fanatic—this Simon or John or whoever—was indeed Ashleigh's stalker.

Watching the tape one last time, listening carefully to "John's" voice, a snake of warning coiled in his gut. The way the guy shouted "hey" echoed with an odd familiarity. It sounded just like the "hey" Morris Reed had shouted outside the clinic. Had Morris Reed really left town?

GREG WANTED TO GET TO KNOW the area—and hopefully find the Coleman cabin. Eiden was no help in this regard. He kept his peace—respecting the wishes of Ashleigh and her mother. So Greg drove up and down every street in Enchantment, exploring the remote roads that wound up into the mountains.

Ten miles north of town he found the new ski resort, Angel's Gate, under construction. If he'd been in town on business, the potential for development on the land around the site might have interested him. As it was, the endless driving just aggravated his altitude sickness.

He stopped at the local grocery and bought some more bottled water and a quart of sports drink in an effort to replenish his depleted electrolytes. He forced himself to eat a hearty dinner at Slim Jim's, a rustic steak house on Paseo de Sierra, and thought he felt his strength returning.

The next day he had the oil changed in the Navigator, got a shave and haircut. Greg was killing time. Waiting for Maureen to call.

The quiet Hispanic in greasy coveralls at the corner gas station didn't have much to say, but some elderly locals in the barbershop proved to be more talkative. As soon as Greg walked into the old-fashioned establishment, he decided this place was probably Enchantment's Gossip Central. Two gray-haired guys were getting their hair cut and a third was lounging in a threadbare upholstered chair. All were yakking it up with the three young barbers.

Greg took the empty barber's chair, told the barber what he wanted and soon lay relaxing under a steaming towel, listening to the other customers banter about town council business, thieves in the countryside, and finally moving on to their days as World War II marines.

"The thing I remember best was those old tar-paper barracks," one of the old guys said loudly.

From listening to the conversation so far, Greg gathered that the old man speaking had, in fact, been a Navajo Code Talker. Greg glanced past the edge of the towel and studied the man with genuine admiration. He was a tall old fellow—his knees poked high and his dusty boots barely fit on the footrest of the chair. He certainly looked Navajo. Bronze skin. Roman nose. Deep, deep eyes.

"You got that right, Elkhorn," another aging voice said. "We froze to death in them old barracks." This man's speech was softer, with a touch of the ancient Moorish-tinged Hispanic accent Greg had been hearing around town. Listening to him, Greg imagined that the old man and his people had probably lived inside the Enchanted Circle for many generations.

"You froze? I thought Camp Elliot was on the ocean, near San Diego," Greg's young barber said as he unwound Greg's towel.

"It is," the Navajo gentleman named Elkhorn explained. "But there's enough elevation out there that it could get pretty frosty in the mornings. Particularly if you was lying on your belly on the ground—in the prone position, you see—" He demonstrated with a flat palm for the benefit of Greg's barber.

"Trying to hit a target at five hundred yards with an M1!" the Hispanic interjected with glee.

The Navajo gave the little Chicano a scowl. "Manny, my friend. It is rude to interrupt while a man is talking."

"Sorry, amigo," the old Hispanic said, though he continued enthusiastically, "but when you are freezing your *trasero* off, the target, it keeps moving!" He made a motion like a shivering person pointing an unsteady rifle and everybody laughed.

Even Greg had to emit a sympathetic chuckle. As a young man, he'd endured sharpshooting school in the cold Colorado wind.

The Hispanic man leaned forward, as the barber started to lather Greg's three-day-old stubble. "Don't think I seen you around here before. You new in town?"

"Just passing through. Greg Glazier." Greg gave him a nod.

"I'm Manny Cordova and this here's Daniel Elkhorn. You here for the Aspen Festival?" Manny strained the fabric of his bib as he took a closer look at Greg.

"No. Just, uh…I'm here to look up some…some relatives." This was true. The baby certainly *was* a relative. His only living relative, in fact.

"Oh, who're they?"

Greg stared up at the ceiling as his barber took his first swipe at his neck, glad that the necessity to sit still gave him time to think. He shouldn't have said that. These old men probably knew almost the entire population of Enchantment. It struck Greg then that he needed a plausible excuse if he was going to keep hanging around like this in a town of only five thousand. And there was probably no better time than now, and no better place than Gossip Central to establish that excuse.

"Well," he said while his barber wiped the blade clean, "I'm not looking for relatives, exactly. Just their property."

"Why are you looking for their place?" the Chicano asked.

"Well, my cousins—" *Had he said anything about cousins?* He hated getting caught up in the quagmire of another lie. He tried to at least steer back to something he could talk about convincingly. "With your new ski area opening up—"

"Angel's Gate," Manny inserted, "going to be a real fancy place."

"Yes. My relatives are wondering how it will impact their property. I'm a land developer."

"Oh?" Now the Navajo leaned forward. The old guys seemed friendly enough, but both were looking at him with such keen interest, that it caused the barbers to pause and study Greg as well. He got the feeling these men hung out in this old barber shop a lot, chewing the fat, bored and in no particular hurry, practicing the old marine habit Gramps had often voiced, *Observe everything within sight or hearing.*

"Their place is supposed to be out toward Switchback Road, but I'll be darned if I could find it yesterday." Greg fished for information that might lead him to the Coleman place.

"Switchback's a bad old road," Manny allowed.

"I figured that out," Greg said, remembering his dizziness and nausea from driving the treacherous, twisting road. It was one hairpin turn on top of another, with no guardrails in most places.

"Manny lives out there," the Navajo supplied. "Raises horses."

"Really?" Greg was genuinely interested. "What kind?"

"Andalusians."

"Andalusians!" Greg did not have to fake being impressed. "I've always had an interest in them. I raise Thoroughbreds myself."

Manny looked pleased that Greg appreciated the rare Spanish breed. "I'm not a big trainer or anything," he said. "My farm is very small." His manner was humble, but he favored Greg with an engaging smile. "But it's forty acres of the most beautiful land in the Sangre de Cristos."

"And he's got a prize stallion. Encantado is quite the beast!" Elkhorn grew excited, boasting on behalf of his friend.

His barber said, "Daniel, please hold still."

Greg smiled, warming to his favorite subject. "I'd like to see this Encantado sometime."

"I'll show him to you anytime," Manny said generously. "Whereabouts do you raise horses?" he inquired politely.

"I've got a piece of land up on Colorado's Big Sandy."

"Oh, ho, ho!" Manny hooted. "I know about the

rancheros up there! You got a pretty big *piece of land* up there, eh, anglo?''

"Enough to raise a few horses," Greg allowed. It was close to a thousand acres, but why get into that? He figured these guys had dealt with more than one wealthy stranger in their midst and wouldn't be impressed.

The men all shared a knowing chuckle at his cryptic answer, and the conversation about horse farming continued while the barbers finished up their work on their three clients. Greg didn't find an opportunity to directly ask where the Coleman place was located.

Manny's haircut was the first to be finished. "Always feels good to get my ears lowered." He chuffed at the backs of them while the barber used a whisk to brush stray hairs from his collar. The barber removed Manny's cape and the old man hopped down from his chair with surprising agility.

"It was nice talkin' to you." He walked over to Greg and extended his gnarled hand. "Come out and see Encantado."

Greg shook the man's hand. "I will," he said, and meant it.

Manny smiled. He seemed like a nice, sharp old man, and there was a peacefulness about him that Greg liked. It was a quality that reminded Greg of the grandfather who had raised him.

"Mine's the first place on Switchback after you

cross the little bridge. It will be worth the drive, I promise you. Encantado is a beautiful creature.''

As Manny settled his battered hat on his head, Elkhorn picked up the topic of Greg's ''relatives'' again. ''Maybe my grandson Miguel knows those relatives of yours. He's a local cop.''

''Yeah.'' Manny seemed to agree with this idea. ''What's their names again?''

Greg hesitated. Eiden had warned him to lay low. But if these guys reported his inquisitiveness to the cop—and why would they?—he could always argue that they had brought it up. And while he was trying to keep his pledge to protect Ashleigh Logan's privacy, Eiden was sympathetic to Greg's cause, as well. ''Uh, it's Coleman.''

The old man shook his head. ''Don't know the name,'' he said. ''But there's two big old cabins built way back up on Switchback, way up on the mountain. Monstrosities. Vacant most of the time. Could be one of those.''

NEXT, GREG PAID A VISIT to the chamber of commerce, which was in the same building where Eiden had detained him when he had first arrived in town. At the opposite end of the dim hallway, he entered the double glass doors and tried to discretely determine if this Coleman cabin was one of the two ''vacant monstrosities'' Manny had referred to, and if so, exactly where it was located.

''If it's that far up on the mountain, it's probably

a private vacation home," the woman behind the counter explained, "and they don't get mail delivery. There's a lot of new construction, what with the new ski resort going in. But we really don't keep track of the seasonal people."

The woman had weathered skin, a friendly demeanor, and chic silver-and-turquoise jewelry. She smiled at Greg. "You could go down to the county seat in Taos and make a check of the tax records, I suppose. They might be able to tell you who owns a particular piece of property, that is, if you knew the exact location."

That was the trouble. He didn't know the exact location. He wasn't supposed to. All he knew was that the cabin where Ashleigh Logan was hiding was somewhere up on Switchback Road.

As he walked out he shot a glance through the glass door, toward the double doors down the hall that had Enchantment Police Department stenciled above an official-looking logo. He didn't want to be too openly aggressive in his search and risk alienating his only ally, but he couldn't just do nothing. Greg Glazier despised idleness.

He went back to his room and made some pointless business calls from his cell phone—he'd already delegated every task in Denver to his partner. He took another look at the tape of Ashleigh Logan, finding her more captivating each time he watched, and finding the sound of the deranged caller more disturbing. And he waited, and waited, for word of this woman…and the child she carried.

CHAPTER SEVEN

AFTER SIMON HAD SEEN Ashleigh at the clinic that first day, he'd driven out of town and then doubled back, looking for a cheap place to stay...and to hide. He'd lucked out and found a For Rent sign in the trailer park at the edge of town. The place was pretty bad—broken glass and the smell of propane—but the owner didn't ask a single question. Just took his cash and handed him the key. The baby would never have to come to that dump, anyway. Simon was prepared to leave Enchantment the minute he got his hands on the child.

He felt no guilt about what he was doing to Ashleigh Logan. She would simply go to the "bank" and withdraw herself another baby.

Ashleigh Logan was the kind of brazen woman who was ruining this country, destroying the very citadel of motherhood in her selfish, unthinking wake. Women like skinny little Ashleigh Logan thought they were so smart. They thought they could play with life itself, with God's holy plan. Well, God punished people who flaunted His ways. Ashleigh Logan would have to be punished. And that poor little artificially made baby would have to be raised somewhere far away from the public eye, far from the cruel publicity its mother seemed to thrive on. Simon had been prepared, all those years ago, to take care of his own baby when it arrived. But his wife, the selfish bitch, had destroyed his chance at fatherhood. Sharon had already been planning to divorce him, he realized later, the minute she finished her doctoral degree.

But now, Simon would have himself a baby. A baby who desperately needed him. It would be no problem for him to disappear and to care for a baby in some isolated place as if the child were his own. He had few real friends, no family. Simon would see to it that the child would never know of its terrible beginnings, its unholy conception. Maybe it was good that the place where Ashleigh Logan had chosen to give birth was so isolated. It shouldn't be impossible to kidnap a baby from a remote midwife's clinic, if he could find a way to get Ashleigh Logan alone with her baby for a moment. The Birth Place, he was sure, wouldn't have tight security like a big city hospital.

THE DAYS TICKED BY and Maureen Logan still did not call. Not for a week. Greg's only conduit to her was Miguel Eiden, and though he was doing what he could, each time they spoke, he had nothing to tell Greg.

"This isn't really a police matter, Greg," Miguel

explained one day when they'd met for coffee at the Silver Eagle café again.

"But the stalker is a police matter. I've got a tape I want you to look at."

Miguel frowned.

"It's Ashleigh's last show. The stalker's talking on it."

"Okay. Get it to me right away."

"Will you do one other thing for me? Will you contact me if there's any trouble out at their cabin? I'd like to do everything I can to keep the mother of my child safe."

Miguel nodded his understanding.

Though he'd met some people in town and found some ways to stay busy, Greg's thoughts were never far from Ashleigh after the incident at the clinic. He kept seeing her face going pale as the man had pushed toward her. He wondered what life had been like for her in the last few years. Horrible, undoubtedly. First the woman had buried a young husband. Then she'd somehow found the guts to salvage what she had, forging ahead with an artificially inseminated pregnancy, and enduring the stinging publicity. Before he'd left Denver he'd searched the Internet for media coverage and found an article blasting Ashleigh for glorifying single motherhood. *Man.*

And now she had been forced into hiding in this remote mountain town, in fear of some unstable stalker. His gut tightened with guilt over the turmoil he himself had caused these women. Nice move, Glazier, jumping out of the bushes that way.

But how else would he meet Ashleigh if he didn't catch her in town? He still hadn't found the Coleman cabin. What was the alternative to encountering her in person again? Contacting some shark of a lawyer to show up and browbeat her? Without sacrificing any of his own rights as a father, he wanted to approach this whole thing as gently and quietly as possible.

Greg turned onto Paseo de Sierra, still deeply absorbed in his troubled thoughts. He thought he'd get to know the town a bit, check out some of the local businesses. The square was crowded and he had to park in a narrow alley.

He'd been to the hardware store, Elkhorn's, once already. Greg smiled as he remembered Kendra saying that hardware stores were like a homing beacon for men. The place was a rustic combination sporting goods–feed store with a weathered boardwalk out front, a fogged display window crammed with ancient implements that would never sell, and closely spaced aisles overflowing with everything from thermal underwear to posthole diggers.

The man behind the counter today was the aging Navajo gentleman he'd met in the barbershop, Daniel Elkhorn. He gave Greg a silent nod of recognition, and then went back to his conversation with another old guy, whom Greg recognized from the barbershop as well. What was his name? Manny

Cordova? The two of them were haggling over a shiny new electric space heater, the kind that had a thermostatically controlled cutoff mechanism.

The Hispanic man pushed his beat-up hat back on his stiff gray hair and sighed. "I don't got that kind of money, amigo."

"Then I will just give it to you." The Navajo shoved the stove forward. He reached under the counter. "I got the box right here. Warranty and all."

"No way, man," protested the old Hispanic. "It can wait till I get my next social security check."

"But you got to have it now, old man. It is going to snow up on that mountain, maybe even tonight, and them pipes in that old shack of a pumphouse of yours is gonna freeze again for sure."

"I got my old kerosene burner. It works fine."

"Yeah. Like when you forgot about it last year, man. I saw that scorched feed sack. You gonna burn yourself up out there on that dilapidated farm, you stubborn old coot."

Greg had wandered up and down the cluttered aisles, all the while listening to the exchange.

"Come on, take the stove," the shopkeeper insisted.

"Naw. Better not," Manny said with stubborn restraint. Greg poked his head around the corner to see the Navajo shaking his head as he set the stove up on some high shelves behind the register.

Manny was fingering a horsehair lariat that was hanging on a post.

"Mr. Cordova," Greg smiled. "Remember me?"

"Oh, hello there," Manny said. "You're the guy who's checking out land up by Angel's Gate."

Greg wondered how he was ever going to keep his growing list of lies straight. "Yes. Greg Glazier." Greg put out his hand and they shook hands again, renewing their acquaintance.

"Hello, Mr. Elkhorn." Greg turned his smile on the man behind the counter. "I didn't realize you work here. I guess I should have made the connection to the name. You the owner?"

"Used to be. My nephew bought me out a few years ago." Elkhorn nodded at a large young man stocking shelves near the back. "I just come once in a while and do my best to get in the way."

"And give away the merchandise," Manny mumbled.

"What's that you say, old man?" Elkhorn put a mocking hand to his ear.

"Nothing. Having any luck finding that Coleman cabin?" Manny asked Greg.

"Haven't found it yet. I was wondering if the offer's still good to show me around up there, and I'd still like to see that Andalusian."

"Anytime. My place is the first turnoff on Switchback after you cross the narrow bridge."

"How about this evening?" Greg said.

"Sure. I'm headed home now. Come on up before

the sun goes down so you can get a good look at Encantado. I got him running in the front pasture. You'll see him right away. I won't move the horses to the barn until dark.''

''Great. See you in a while, then.''

The bell on the shop door clanged as the old man left.

''Now, what can I do for you?'' The shopkeeper spread his palms on the counter, giving Greg his attention.

''Oh, I was just looking around. That space heater…'' Greg pointed up at it.

''Yes?''

''Your friend needs it?''

''He sure does.''

''Why wouldn't he take it?''

''He's just stubborn. Manny don't let nobody help him, not even his own kids. Them boys would have a fit if they came home and found out their dad was using an old open-flame kerosene heater in his pump house.''

''His sons don't live around here?''

''No. Two are in the military, marines like their dad. One of them is getting close to retirement, I think. I can't keep track of where the other two live, exactly. One's a doctor out in L.A. Manny goes to see them once in a while, but the boys don't make it to his place that much. It's not, you know, the most comfortable house on earth, especially since his wife passed on.''

"He lives out there alone? Out on Switchback Road?"

"Yeah. All alone since his Rosa died. He's got his horses, you know, and lots of friends. He says he likes his old place the way it is. But he shouldn't be too proud to take a little help now and then, especially when it's a matter of safety."

"I agree." Greg pulled his billfold out of his hip pocket, rapidly extracting twenties. "How much?"

"The stove?"

"Yeah."

"You buying it for him?"

"Yeah."

"But why, man?"

"Why not? I have plenty of money, and it sounds like he needs it."

"But…this is kind of strange," the old Navajo muttered.

"Not really." Greg laid four twenties on the counter. "Does that cover it?"

"Sure."

Greg put a palm on the stove. "Would you put it in the box? And throw in that lariat?" Greg pulled three more twenties loose.

"That fancy horsehair one?" The Navajo expressed further surprise.

"He likes it, right?"

"Manny…he won't take no fancy gift. He's very independent. He stays up on that mountain for a reason. He doesn't want to owe no man."

"He won't owe me anything. It's just a way to pay him back for taking the time to show me around the mountain," Greg said, smiling.

AS SOON AS GREG LEFT the store, Maureen emerged from the aisle where she had been concealed. Part of her had to admit that watching Greg Glazier buying gifts for the sweet-looking old man had touched her. But part of her still wanted Greg to go away and not cause any more problems for her daughter. She sighed. But the more she saw of Greg Glazier, the more she realized that wasn't going to happen.

"Did you find everything you need, ma'am?"

"No, actually I didn't. Where would I find one of those intercoms people use for babies?"

The man scratched his head. "I wouldn't have anything like that. I imagine you'd have to go to the Wal-Mart down in Taos."

"Oh." Maureen cast about for a solution, something that would let Ashleigh summon her in the huge cabin without having to climb the stairs.

"Do you have a bell, then?"

"Yeah." The man frowned, seeming unable to make the connection between a bell and a baby monitor. "I got some bear bells over in the sport goods. And I got these cowbells." He pointed to the shelves behind him.

"A cowbell will do. And I'll take these light bulbs." She shoved them forward on the counter. "Do you know that man?" She turned her head toward the display window. Across the street, Greg Glazier was rounding the corner into an alley.

"You mean the fella who just left?"

"Yes. I heard you talking to him."

"We've met." The old Navajo proceeded to punch the register keys, his face as impassive as the stone cliffs rimming the town.

The locals around here were so closemouthed, Maureen thought. Their reluctance to talk or volunteer information was something she had valued because she felt that would help protect Ashleigh. At least she had valued their reticence until this moment. "But you seemed to know *about* him," she prodded.

"I met him at the barber shop a while back. Nice guy."

"I see. Who is he?"

"Says he's here to check out property. We get a lot of those."

"I see." So Glazier was telling the townsfolk he was looking at property.

"That'll be four eighty-nine."

Maureen dug out the money. "I heard your friend mention the Colemans. Do you know them?"

The man frowned at her, then he put the light bulbs and the bell in a small brown paper bag. "No, I don't. And I thought I knew just about everybody around here. But with the new ski resort going in, we are seeing more new people all the time. That Anglo—" he nodded toward the window "—he claims the Colemans live out on the Switchback Road. Do you know them?''

"No." Maureen snatched up the sack. "Thank you."

She rushed out to the Suburban. When she got inside she quickly slammed the door, staring pensively out the windshield.

Ashleigh looked immediately alert. "What's wrong, Mom?"

"Nothing." Maureen wondered if Ashleigh had seen Greg Glazier going into the alley.

"Mom, is something wrong?"

Maureen realized Ashleigh must be worrying about the stalker. Sooner or later they would have to end this charade with Greg Glazier. "No. Everything's fine. I, uh, I just heard the men in the hardware store talking about a snowstorm coming in. Well…" She altered her tone, becoming falsely bright. "Only one more stop and then we'll get back to the cabin. You must be getting tired."

"Actually, I was enjoying being down in the town for once. The doctor just said I'm okay."

"Yes. You told me that."

"The midwives haven't seen any activity on my monitor strip since I got to Enchantment, and my uterus is nice and soft. I think this place is exactly what I needed."

"Yes." Maureen wondered what would happen to her daughter's health when she found out the truth about Greg Glazier.

"I think the whole preterm labor thing was all a false alarm," Ashleigh continued. "It was probably just a reaction to all that stress back in Denver. I have felt a hundred percent better since we got up here. This place is so peaceful."

"It may be peaceful," Maureen said, glancing out the windshield and surveying the fading sky as she fired up the engine, "but, according to the men in that hardware store, the weather can change pretty fast this time of year." She pulled the Suburban away from the curb. "We'd better get to a grocery store and then go back up the road before that storm blows in."

CHAPTER EIGHT

THE HUMBLE HOME OF Manny Cordova rested in a verdant trough of land surrounded by towering pine trees and overshadowed by the sheer, high cliffs at the base of the Sangre de Cristo mountains.

Greg found the narrow turnoff easily. It was exactly as Manny had described it, a rocky, rutted drive that rose to pastures fanning out behind weathered corrals, a sloping old barn and a tiny, graying cedar house.

Greg bumped up the winding drive, taking it at a creep and wondering what tire traps lurked beneath the dry grasses that brushed against the high underbelly of the Navigator.

Almost immediately he spotted the Andalusian. A magnificent white stallion, galloping in graceful circles in the far pasture that rose behind the old house. Tail and head high, eyes wild, the horse had been spooked, perhaps, by the sudden appearance of the noisy SUV on the peaceful premises.

Beyond the stallion's solitary paddock, other calmer, quieter horses shared a sloping split-rail-fenced pasture high on the mountain.

Greg pulled up alongside the old man's dented, rusty pickup and climbed out.

He slammed the door of his Navigator and called out, "Hello!"

No sign of human life.

But at the sound of Greg's voice an elderly-looking mongrel trotted around the corner of the house and barked a belated warning. The dog looked like he was part blue heeler and part Border collie and every bit as elderly as his master.

"Hey, boy." Greg put the back of his hand down for a test sniff, and the dog slinked forward and obliged. "Where's Manny?"

Greg knew he'd driven up to the right place. There was nothing else that even resembled a drive-way coming off Switchback Road, not for miles. He studied the house. It looked as if it had been listing gently to the right, for, oh, the last century or so. A small addition with a sloping roof was tacked onto one side. In the shelter of an arbor styled out of shaved aspen beams crossed with grape stakes, an array of clutter—pots and rusting signs and old tubs and deer antlers and farm implements—littered a cluster of low battered tables. Old Manny, Greg decided, as he studied the fascinating jumble, must have the soul of an artist.

And, of course, there was that horse. How many perfect specimens of white Andalusian stallions could there be galloping around on this mountain?

The dog followed as Greg crossed the weedy lot

and hitched a boot up on the fence, waiting patiently until the stallion stopped galloping long enough to eyeball him. He summoned the horse with a soft whistle. The horse gave his head a rebellious toss but trotted over to Greg, nonetheless.

When the animal got close, Greg dug in his pocket and held his palm forward with a bit of the trail mix that he had nibbled on during his trip from Colorado.

The stallion took the bait, eating from Greg's hand as Greg reached over the fence and patted the horse's forehead.

He heard a noise coming from the vicinity of the barn and turned. The dog lumbered toward the sound, and presently Manny appeared around the corner with a floppy straw hat shading a knowing grin. "He is too easy, you see? Just a big old pet."

Greg smiled as Manny crossed the yard.

"A big old baby," Manny chuckled as he approached the stallion. "That's what you are, Encantado." He reached up to scratch Encantado's forelock. "How did you know he would not bite, eh? A stallion cannot be trusted."

"I know horses," Greg said with confidence, because he did. "He's a very fine animal."

"So did you find your uncle's place yet?"

"No luck yet." Greg hedged while he tried, unsuccessfully, to remember if he'd called his fake relative an uncle or a cousin.

"I got to thinking." Manny ran a gnarled, nut-brown hand over the horse's cheek and muzzle with expert ease. "It's odd, you know, how your *onk-kul*—" he said the word with that hint of Spanish accent people in this vicinity adopted when they were a bit skeptical of something "—how he asked you to come and look over his land, but didn't give you directions to his cabin. That's a leetle *extraño*— strange—is it not?"

"He didn't know I was coming through Enchantment." Greg wondered if his nose was actually getting longer from all this lying. "He's in Europe and I don't know how to contact him." Greg jammed his hands in the back pockets of his jeans and tried not to look like a liar. "And it's my cousin's place, not my uncle's."

"I see." Manny's gaze panned the endless sky, which was decidedly grayer and darker than it had been an hour ago. "The wind is kicking up." He took a big draught of air. "Smell that air. I think it will definitely snow tonight. Want to come in and have a cup of coffee? I don't get much company out here."

"Sure. I need to get some things out of my car first." Greg went to get the stove and the lariat. When he tapped on the small window set in the door of Manny's house, Manny signaled him inside.

The interior of Manny's place was as humble as the outside. What Greg could see from the front door was one long room—kitchen at the far end, living room at the near, and a short hallway that shot off toward bedrooms. The kitchen was U-shaped with a back door—the screen was patched with duct tape—next to a rounded old fridge. The counters were hideously cluttered, still bearing evidence that a delightful woman had once cooked happily at the old wood-burning stove. At the center of the narrow space was a little square table with a worn oilcloth clinging to it and four bentwood chairs pushed up around the sides.

The focal point of the living room was a spanking new TV facing a sagging rust-colored couch and a threadbare Herculon recliner with a joystick at the side. Impressive Native American–style paintings of horses dominated the brown paneled wall above the couch, and a lineup of graduation, military and wedding photos of Manny's boys, with smaller photographs of grandchildren stuck haphazardly into the frames, marched along the opposite wall. Beyond the TV, a picture window framed a glorious alpine meadow flanked by towering ponderosa pines with the Sangre de Cristos as a massive backdrop.

"Have a seat." Manny, working at a newish-looking Mr. Coffee on the worn Formica countertop, beckoned Greg toward the table. Greg put his gifts on the floor beside one of the chairs and seated himself.

"You have a great place," he said in all sincerity, and Manny took his meaning well.

"It's peaceful," he said, keeping his back to Greg while he poured water into the coffeemaker. "So quiet in winter you can hear snowflakes ticking on the shed roof. There's a stream a ways up back—real good fishing. And at night, you can see every last one of God's stars.''

The aroma of coffee immediately started to fill the small space.

When Manny turned his smile fell. He looked at the box beside Greg's chair. ''Did that old Indian at the hardware store tell you to bring that thing with you?''

''No, sir. It was my idea. I overheard your conversation and I told Mr. Elkhorn that I wanted to purchase it for you—as a gift,'' Greg explained quickly because Manny's mouth had started to draw down with disapproval. ''I wanted a way to show my appreciation for the time you're taking to show me around—and a fella has to stay on the good side of the only man with a prime Andalusian stud for five hundred miles around.'' Greg carefully laid the coiled lariat on the table. ''I hope you'll accept this, as well.''

Manny's black eyes flicked to the lariat for one instant, then he shrugged and turned back to the coffeepot. ''Okay. But you didn't come here to give me gifts,'' he stated. ''And you don't got no uncle up here,'' he added as he poured the coffee into two heavy mugs. ''And no cousins, either.''

Greg didn't even try to deny it. ''How'd you find me out?''

"Miguel Eiden is Daniel Elkhorn's grandson. He knows a lot about you."

Greg looked out the window at his isolated surroundings. Of course, the old man had checked him out before he'd given directions to this place. "Eiden. Figures. What did he say?"

"He said you were okay. A real successful businessman, and that you really are a horse rancher."

Greg accepted one of the mugs, suddenly ashamed of himself for lying to this kindly old man. "It was decent of him to give me his seal of approval, considering that he, uh, hauled me in for questioning on my first day in town."

Manny nodded and grinned as he brought his mug to his lips. His eyes twinkled as he sipped. "I know that, too."

Greg smiled into his mug. This old man appeared humble with his short stature and his baggy pants hitched up by worn suspenders, but under his bushy brows, his black eyes were assessing Greg carefully, sharper than an eagle's.

After Manny sipped his coffee again he touched the horsehair lariat and said, "Thank you. It's a nice gift. So? The truth is?"

"The truth is I'm looking for a woman."

"A woman? Miguel didn't mention no woman."

"That's good. I think the fewer people that know about her, the better."

"Then why tell me, amigo?"

"I have reason to believe she's staying up here in the Coleman cabin."

Manny gave him a suspect frown. "This woman— she running away from you?"

"No. She doesn't know me. Not yet. Not that she'll be exactly happy to meet me. At one time I thought she *might* be running from me, until I found out about the stalker."

"The stalker?" Manny's piercing old eyes grew wide.

"Yeah, some guy's been threatening her back in Denver."

"Why? I mean, who is this woman?"

"She's a television personality. Her show comes out of Denver, but it's on a nationwide cable network. People everywhere watch her. Apparently some weirdo started threatening her, threatening to harm her baby."

"She's got a baby with her?"

At the question, Greg felt a great heaviness in the vicinity of his chest. An ache. For his child. Ashleigh Logan had a baby *with* her, all right. And not just any baby. His baby. "She's pregnant."

Manny's brows shot up, then compressed into a frown. "*No comprendo.* Why are you looking for a woman who's pregnant? Unless…"

There was a sweetness about Manny Cordova, Greg decided, something innocent and old-fashioned. But at the same time his keen old eyes radiated a sharp comprehension of human nature, or maybe of everything in life, with an unflinching wisdom. "Unless…are you the father?"

"Yes."

Manny scratched his jaw. "But I thought you said she doesn't know you."

"She doesn't."

Manny shook his head, barely concealing his disapproval. "I heard of this stuff. The one-night stand, they call it. I try not to judge, but this is not my way, not *my* family's way." Manny's eyes flitted to a dusty crucifix nailed above the front door.

"It wasn't like that. We never…we were never together like that. This was an artificial insemination."

At this, Manny's eyes grew truly huge. "*Ay, Chihauhau.* I done that a few times with Encantado's seed. But I never met a real person who done it."

"It was not my choice, believe me."

Manny cocked his head and frowned at Greg. "I don't get it. If it wasn't your choice, how did she get your…?"

"It's really complicated. Let's just call it a scientific mistake. But I am absolutely positive this baby is mine and I intend to raise it as mine, to be a real father."

"I see," Manny said, although he was scratching the back of his head as if he didn't. "I *think*. So, how do you plan to find this woman?"

"I have no idea. I've already met with her mother down in town. Thanks to Officer Eiden."

"Miguel's a good boy." Manny aimed his mug at Greg.

"Yeah. I like him. But the mother only seems interested in protecting her daughter. She doesn't think this is a good time to settle this. And she's keeping me away from the daughter."

Manny scratched his head again, then hooked one thumb under his suspender and the other hand around his mug. "There ain't no good time for such a thing."

"I agree. So I'm going to have to find her on my own. Somehow. I'd appreciate it if you'd keep your eyes open. They're driving a red Suburban. You haven't noticed one traveling up and down the mountain by any chance?"

Manny shrugged with a palm up, as if to say *sorry*. "I wouldn't mind helping you find this woman, but I don't see many people out here. My horses and old Guapo over there are my only company."

Greg smiled at the old dog that came tottering forward at the sound of his name. Guapo. *Handsome* that dog was not.

"I appreciate that, Manny," Greg said as he scratched the old dog's ears. "Don't worry. One way or another, I'll find her," he vowed quietly. "Somehow I will find her."

GREG HELPED MANNY MOVE the horses to the barn, and by the time he left Manny's place, the sky was as dark as slate, and a gray veil of mist had shrouded the mountainside. Icy pinpricks of rain specked Greg's windshield as he rounded the first hairpin turn coming down. On the third curve, sudden dizziness assaulted him again, and a pair of headlights coming toward him intensified the effect. Suddenly, everything pitched off kilter. Disoriented, Greg jerked on the wheel and the Navigator slid sideways on the slick road.

Greg fought for control, but it was too late. He felt the heavy vehicle skidding toward the cliff side of the road, where there was no guardrail. Greg rammed hard on his brakes, but the Navigator tilted sickeningly and then hurled over the edge, slamming to a halt against a pine tree.

IN THE CAR THAT HAD VEERED toward Greg, Ashleigh Logan and her mother both screamed as they watched the vehicle careen into a skid and go bouncing over the edge. Maureen stopped the Suburban on the road's rocky shoulder.

"Mother, look!" Ashleigh pointed. "They hit that tree down there. I can see the headlights in the fog!"

"Oh, my God!" Maureen's first thought was to pray that the people in that car were all right. "I think I may have crossed the center line!" Her next thought was of her daughter, then of her grandchild. "Ashleigh, are you okay?"

"Yes." Ashleigh tugged her seat belt from below

the globe of her tummy. ''I think everything's okay.''

''All right. Stay calm. Think of your baby.'' Maureen unbuckled her own seat belt, reached in front of Ashleigh, opened the glove box and pulled out a flashlight, then opened the car door. Her limbs froze when she recognized Greg Glazier's Lincoln Navigator.

''Where are you going?'' Ashleigh reached across and clutched her mother's arm. ''That's a total stranger. You don't know anything about him! Remember that we're hiding from a stalker up here!''

''I do know him. I'm afraid that's your bodyguard.''

Ashleigh stared down at the vehicle where through the broken passenger window they both could make out the profile of a young man slumped forward into the inflated white air bag.

''And he's also someone who needs our help. Here.'' Maureen handed Ashleigh the cell phone. ''Call 9-1-1. And try to stay calm.''

CHAPTER NINE

OUTSIDE THE VEHICLE, the foggy air felt frigid. Maureen tugged her hood up against the spitting sleet and felt herself slipping on the fresh coating of crystals as she descended the steep rocky slope toward the tilting Navigator—the Navigator that belonged to the man who claimed to be the father of Ashleigh's baby.

Halfway down the slope, she saw Greg Glazier's head moving in the shattered window. She could make out a dark trail of blood on his face. Then the crumpled door of the Navigator scraped open. He stumbled out, his movements jerky and disoriented. He appeared to be dazed, in danger of wandering away from the vehicle, down the mountainside, away from her.

''Mr. Glazier!'' Maureen called out to stop him. ''Wait! We're here! Help is here.'' She waved her arms and scrambled down the rough, slippery slope as fast as she could.

She reached him before he got far. ''Mr. Glazier,'' she wheezed, out of breath, ''wait!''

At the sound of her voice coming near to him, he

made a clutching motion toward the door of the vehicle.

She clasped his arm. "Greg?"

"Mrs. McGuinness? Is that you?" His breath came out in halting white puffs.

"Yes. Are you all right?"

"Were you driving the car that was coming at me?"

"I'm afraid so."

"Are you...?" He seemed woozy. "Is Ashleigh with you? Is she all right?"

"Yes, she's fine. But you aren't. Your head is bleeding. Is anything else hurt?"

"I don't...I'm not sure." Greg touched his temple and swayed. "I can't...I don't think I can..." He blinked rapidly. "I can't seem to see anything."

"You can't *see?* But..." For the flicker of an instant Maureen considered the bizarre possibility that he could be faking, in order to somehow win her sympathy, or to insinuate his way, somehow, into the car with Ashleigh. But that idea was too hideous to even consider. For one thing, he did not seem like that kind at all, and one look at his eyes, even in the dim evening light, convinced her that, indeed, he could not see.

"Sit down. Greg—" she came around him "—sit down. Please." She grasped his shoulders as he started to stagger away from her. It was then that she noticed that the huge bump on the left side of his temple seemed to be getting bigger. She realized his head must have shattered the driver's side window.

She guided him to sit on a large rock nearby. His breathing was unsteady, rapid.

"Let me look at you, please."

When she did, his eyes had the glazed quality of someone looking but not seeing, and the bump on his forehead was definitely mushrooming into a nasty-looking purple knot. The cut there was bleeding down the side of his face, but Maureen knew that head wounds often bled excessively. Still, it looked like it would need stitches. "Can you see anything?" She shined the flashlight into his eyes.

"A light. I think," Greg replied.

"Mom!" Maureen jerked at the sound of her daughter's voice up on the roadside. Ashleigh was sticking her head out of the open window of the Suburban. "Is he okay?"

"I'm helping him, dear. Now, roll up that window before you get chilled."

"Is that Ashleigh?" Greg's voice sounded rapt, as his sightless eyes followed the direction of Ashleigh's voice.

"Yes, it is," Maureen said. Turning away from her daughter, she kept her voice low, "and I hate to have to remind you of this now, when you're hurt, but she doesn't know the truth about you yet. As far as she knows, you're just her bodyguard. Now, tell me, can you see me at all?"

"No."

"Lord. Well, I don't know if that's related to this bump on your head, but you need to see a doctor right away."

Greg touched his fingers to the wound, exploring, then wincing.

"We must get you some help," Maureen said, taking charge. "It's a pretty steep incline back up to my Suburban. Can you make it?"

"Yes." Greg stood. "My gun," he said.

"Your *what?*"

"My gun. It's in a lockbox under the driver's seat. The key is the smallest one—" he swayed "—on the key chain. Never mind. Just pull the whole lockbox out from under the seat and bring it with us."

"You have a *gun?*" Maureen, revising her assessment about his kind eyes and his dimples, wondered what manner of man Greg Glazier really was.

"It's legal. I'm a deputy sheriff." He seemed suddenly more lucid. "And I'm not about to leave a firearm registered to my name in a vehicle on the side of the road where any idiot can come along and find it."

Maureen found the lockbox. It was a bit heavy and awkward, but she preferred lugging it up the slope to touching a *gun.* She got a firm grip on the handle of the thing with one hand and on Greg Glazier's arm with the other, and they struggled up the embankment with Maureen guiding the big man.

When they got to the Suburban, Ashleigh leaned around and opened the back door.

"He can't see," Maureen explained to Ashleigh as she helped Greg into the back seat.

"Oh, my God. That's terrible." Disembodied, Ashleigh's voice sounded every bit as warm and rich in the confines of the Suburban as it did on TV. The smoothness of it slipped over him like a wave of silk. "He's bleeding! You poor man," she crooned. "Let me help you." He could have listened to this woman talk forever.

But right then he banged his injured head on the door frame, which hurt mightily, and it made him feel as awkward as a drugged bear. "Careful!" Ashleigh Logan cried. Then he felt a pair of delicate, gentle hands framing his brow, gently pressing a wad of tissue over the cut.

With Ashleigh's touch, Greg felt a strange thrill ripple through his gut.

She moved one hand to his arm and guided him into the seat while with the other she pressed his shoulder back. Again, the warm pressure of her hands seemed to have too great an impact on Greg; he reasoned that it was because he hadn't seen her reaching for him. He jerked. He certainly didn't expect to feel her fumbling at his hip next.

"Here we go," she said as if she'd found something, and he realized she was going to fasten his seat belt for him.

What with her girth and his blindness, the task

proved a bit awkward. Their arms and hands—and a few other parts Greg was determined to ignore—brushed and bumped in the fumbling effort. She leaned so close that he could feel her warm breath on his cheek and he could smell her perfume—light and flowery and clean.

"There," she said when she finally got the seat belt buckled. "I'm so sorry I didn't come down there to help you, but my doctor doesn't want me to do anything strenuous." She pressed her hand to his arm again, and he felt more warmth, more unwelcome stirrings. "It's me, Ashleigh, by the way," she added. "Here. Keep these tissues pressed to your cut." She guided his fingers up to the wad. "Sorry."

"It doesn't hurt."

"You did tell me your name was Greg…Glazier?" The silky voice sounded wary.

"Yes." *The father of your baby,* he added in his min With that thought he again worried about how they were ever going to resolve this thing. How could two total strangers ever find a way to raise a child together?

Greg heard the driver's side door open.

"What on earth is that?" Ashleigh said.

He heard the clank of his lockbox as Maureen tossed it onto the floorboard beside him.

"His gun," Maureen said.

"His *g-gun?*"

"The man is a deputy sheriff," Maureen said,

slamming the door. "And your bodyguard," she added as if reminding herself of the lie.

"Of course."

Greg couldn't tell if Ashleigh was looking at him or not, but his instincts told him she was.

"Mother," she said pointedly while he heard Maureen settling into the seat and buckling her seat belt. "I called the *police*." Her voice seemed a little loud, a little stressed to Greg. "And the 9-1-1 dispatcher said to call her back as soon as you'd checked on the victim."

Greg heard the engine start.

"They said," Ashleigh continued, "they can have help here in approximately twenty minutes. She's expecting us to call."

"That's too long," Maureen replied.

Greg heard the crunch of gravel and felt the Suburban bumping up off the shoulder back onto the road.

"I think we should call back and then wait for the police to arrive," Ashleigh argued.

"I don't," Maureen countered. "It's freezing out there, and that bump on his head is swelling rapidly."

"I know a man who lives right down the road," Greg inserted. He blinked and tried to focus his eyes again, unsuccessfully, though now he could make out a bit of dim light on the dash. "We could go there. He's probably got some ice I could put on my head." As Greg said this Maureen was already executing a bumpy turnabout in the road. "I could lie down for a while and see if my vision clears."

"Absolutely not," Maureen said decisively. "I think we'd better take you straight to the hospital."

"We're taking him to the hospital *ourselves?*" Ashleigh sounded unsure, as well she should, Greg thought. She shouldn't trust anyone, not if there was a stalker out there somewhere, looking for her.

Greg heard Maureen give a huge sigh, as if she couldn't quite get her breath. "Yes, we are. He's your bodyguard, Ashleigh. Your dad sent him here. Everything is all right."

Greg felt the force of gravity and clutched the door as they rounded a sharp turn.

"Trust me," Maureen repeated as she accelerated. "Everything will be all right."

THE DOCTOR WHO HAPPENED to be in the emergency room at the Arroyo County Hospital, a Dr. Ochoa, told Greg he was an obstetrician but that he had also done some family practice. Greg wondered if he was qualified to treat a traffic accident victim, but he sounded to Greg as if he knew his stuff. However, what he had to say was not very reassuring.

"You have a low-grade fever, and your dizziness was because of an inner-ear infection," he said after carefully examining Greg. "I'm not too concerned about the cut above your eye—we'll stitch that up. And your head injury is a simple contusion, but this loss of vision…have you recently had laser corrective surgery, Mr. Glazier?''

"Yes. About a month ago." *Right before I found out about Ashleigh Logan.*

"I recently read about accidents like this, where the impact from the air bag temporarily blinded someone—''

"Temporarily?'' Greg's voice lifted with hope.

"Yes, in most cases. The visual impairment usually clears up after a week to ten days. Of course, to be on the safe side, I want you to see an ophthalmologist in Albuquerque right away.''

"What happens if I don't go to Albuquerque and just wait to see if it clears up?'' Greg was already thinking that he wasn't about to leave Enchantment when he'd just now found the woman he'd been looking for all this time.

"Nothing dangerous. It's just that the sooner you are evaluated—''

"I want to stay in Enchantment,'' Greg said decisively. "I *need* to stay in Enchantment.''

OUT IN THE WAITING ROOM, Ashleigh had been enduring a tense vigil with her mother. Truth be told, she'd been tense ever since she'd looked down that slope and seen the pale-colored Lincoln Navigator. Megan had said her visitor's name was Greg Glazier. When Ashleigh put the two facts together, she decided that something about this guy didn't add up.

And something about the way her mother was acting didn't add up, either. She cut a glance at her mother's face again. Normally as unruffled as freshly pressed linen, Maureen's brow was as furrowed now as Megan's usually was. She was actually nibbling on a hangnail.

"Mother, what gives?" Ashleigh said.

Maureen startled. "What do you mean?"

"You are acting very weird."

"I'm just worried about that poor young man and this whole stupid accident. And I'm worried about you. You certainly don't need to be sitting here like this."

"I checked out fine. Dr. Ochoa reassured me the accident had no effect on me, or the baby, and I can still be up and about some, so sitting here for a while isn't going to hurt me."

"You're still on restricted activity, that's what he said," Maureen argued. "Which does not include sitting in a hard plastic chair for hours in an emergency room. You should be back there in one of those beds," Maureen fretted. "Where is that doctor?"

"Please stop worrying." Ashleigh studied her mother. She knew how Maureen thought. Like Megan, Maureen was a magnet for worry and guilt. But Megan's way of coping was to fret and Maureen's way was to control. During Chad's illness Maureen had worried about every bite Chad ate, every little cough. "The accident was not your fault, if that's what you're thinking."

"If only I hadn't had my bright lights on!"

"You didn't know they were on. You're not used to the rental, at least not in the dark. Mother, listen. I want to tell you something about this Greg Glazier—"

Dr. Ochoa swooped into the room, lab coat flapping.

"How is he?" Maureen stood, and when Ashleigh did, too, Maureen applied a gentle push on her shoulder, urging her daughter back down.

"Mother, please." Ashleigh stood her ground. "I'm fine. How is Greg?" she asked the doctor. She couldn't fathom why this Greg guy had shown up at Megan's house, looking for her. *Holdings in common?* But her mother certainly didn't seem concerned about him.

The doctor was still talking, so she decided to ask her mother about the whole thing later, when they were alone.

"Mr. Glazier's head injury is only a soft-tissue contusion," the doctor explained. "The swelling should go down in a few days. But the visual disturbances are another matter. He has what we call flap folds along the cornea with a little swelling in both the cornea and retina. It's an injury caused by blunt trauma from the air bag. They've been reporting it in medical journals for about a year. Seems it happens in patients who have recently had surgery to correct their vision."

"Oh, my." Maureen covered her mouth with her

fingers and Ashleigh squeezed her mother's shoulder in support. "I feel just horrible about this," Maureen mumbled.

"According to Mr. Glazier you didn't cause the accident, Mrs. McGuinness. He reported that he felt dizzy right before he lost control of his vehicle. He's been under the mistaken notion that he was suffering from altitude sickness. But we ran some tests and discovered the culprit was a chronic inner-ear infection."

He glanced at Ashleigh's girth and put up a reassuring palm at her concerned expression. "Nothing contagious. And just to be safe, I ran some blood tests. He's totally healthy, except for the ear infection which is probably secondary to allergies. I gave him a fairly strong antibiotic and in a few days he should be just fine."

"But what about his vision?" Ashleigh asked on behalf of her mother, who was biting that hangnail again. "He's supposed to be my bodyguard."

The doctor frowned. "I gave him the appropriate medication to reduce the inflammation. My hope is that with a few days of complete rest his vision will automatically return to normal. I'll need to see him in a week to remove the sutures on his forehead. At that time I'll determine if it's necessary to reposition those corneal folds. If it is, he'll need to see an eye specialist in Albuquerque. The immediate problem is he doesn't know anyone here and he needs a place to stay and rest—someone to watch over him until we see if his vision improves. His condition does not warrant a hospital admission, but obviously he can't drive, and he'll need help with meals and so forth. I don't want him ambulating—walking about—too much at first.''

"He can stay with us,'' Maureen injected quickly.

Ashleigh gave her mother an incredulous stare. Had she lost her mind? "With *us?*''

"Yes.'' Maureen kept her eyes on the doctor, as if he was the one who needed an explanation. "We're... he's from Denver. And I know Greg's family.''

"You *do?*'' Ashleigh looked at her mother in utter disbelief.

"Tell Mr. Glazier we'll take him home with us,'' Maureen said, plowing ahead. "We have plenty of room in a big cabin up on Switchback Road. I feel responsible for him, being our employee and all,'' Maureen added quickly. She turned on her stunned daughter with a defensive air. "This is the least I can do.''

"Good,'' the doctor said before Ashleigh could protest further. "Officer Eiden is in there asking him a few questions about the accident. I'll tell Mr. Glazier about your offer as soon as he's finished. His vehicle has been towed to a repair shop in Taos. I've given him a light sedative and I'll release him to your care if he agrees to that.''

"We'll wait here,'' Maureen said. She shot Ashleigh a look. "He is not the stalker, okay? So quit worrying.''

Ashleigh sat down, stunned. Her mother was bringing a man she'd barely met home so she could play nurse? And the worst part of it was—Ashleigh swallowed as she admitted this part to herself. It had been so long since she'd genuinely felt this way that she wasn't at all certain of it, and, of course, when one was pregnant, life was one crazy emotion after another. But the worst part was...she thought she might actually be attracted to this Greg Glazier.

CHAPTER TEN

THE LIGHT, MURKY AND DIM, but *light* nonetheless, informed Greg that it was morning. Thank God. It had been a long, dark, dreadful night. Perhaps he should have taken the doctor up on the suggestion to be admitted into the hospital for overnight observation. But when the man had told him that Maureen had offered to take him out to their cabin, Greg couldn't believe his good fortune.

How could he refuse the opportunity to get close to Ashleigh Logan?

It wasn't until later that night at the darkened cabin, when he realized he'd need assistance to find his way to the john, that he began to question his own judgment. He'd practically crawled to the bathroom instead of using the cowbell Maureen had given him. Then he'd lain awake most of the night, fighting a drugged haze and wondering what in the hell he'd done. Worse, he kept wondering what he would do if his sight didn't return.

But now the faint rays of morning light gave him some hope. His loss of vision was only going to be temporary, like the doctor said. How long would that give him to get to know Ashleigh Logan? He tried to look around the room, with little success. It seemed the light was coming from a long, high bank of windows opposite the hard bed where he lay. He had the impression the room was large, the carpet dark—blue, or greenish—with wood paneling running halfway up the walls. The place smelled musty, shut up, as if no one had slept on these sheets in a while. He tried to focus on details, to see what the woman had done with his clothes, but the effort of his inventory caused his head to throb in a queasy rhythm and he was forced to lie back on the pillows, eyes closed.

He heard steps on the stairs. He had a memory of negotiating turning steps and a couple of narrow landings. There was a tap on the door.

"Come in," he croaked. It must be the medication that was making him so dry.

"Greg?" It was the mother's voice. "It's Maureen. It's late. I assume you slept all night. I never heard the cowbell."

"The cowbell?" He pretended not to remember.

"Yes. I put it by your bed. Are you hungry? I can bring you up a tray."

"No." He tried to sit up as he heard the door of the room creak open farther. He could make out a fuzzy form gliding across the room. "I can make it downstairs," he added. *Where Ashleigh was, he hoped.* "No need to keep running up and down the stairs, Maureen. I know you've already got a lot on your mind."

"Well then, at least let me help you get down to the kitchen. I'm putting your clothes beside you on the bed. We stopped by that bed-and-breakfast to get your bag last night. I don't know if you remember—you were pretty groggy. Let me know when you're dressed."

As quickly as his condition would allow, he pulled on his jeans. Getting his T-shirt over his swimming head was torture. He should probably stay in bed, but that wouldn't get him what he wanted—to be with Ashleigh.

"I can just stay on the couch today," he told Maureen as she guided him down the stairs. "Unless that's where Ashleigh needs to rest."

"There are two large couches in the great room."

The air downstairs smelled of pancakes. A radio or TV was on somewhere. As they came out of the narrow stairwell, the fuzzy light seemed painfully bright—dazzling, in fact.

"Did it snow last night?" He blinked.

"Oh! Does that mean his vision is returning?" This was Ashleigh's voice. That deep, sultry, clear, broadcast-professional's voice that was already becoming familiar to him.

"It just seems unnaturally bright in here." Where was she?

"There are a lot of windows down here," Maureen explained. "It did snow, but it's melting fast."

With a little awkward bumping around, Maureen managed to get him seated at a table. He turned his head toward sounds from a kitchen and made out the blurry lines of a long structure, like a bar. Beyond it, something moved. Something feminine and blond and…rounded in the front. Then the figure was gone.

"You have no business cooking," he heard Ashleigh's mother say. "Go sit."

The figure swathed in pink floated into Greg's hazy vision and slid into place at the table. "It's me," she said. "Ashleigh." Then in a whisper she added, "We're in the same boat, you know. Both trapped in the care of Nurse Ratched, I mean, McGuinness."

"I heard that!" came the cheery retort from the kitchen.

Greg leaned forward and caught Ashleigh's scent again. Right now she exuded the most incredible, delicious, woman-in-her-flannel-robe scent. "Why are *you* trapped?" he asked in a low voice, so that her mother, who knew the deal, wouldn't get suspicious about what he was doing. And what *was* he doing? Feigning ignorance now would get him in a lot of trouble later when he had to come clean with this woman. But he wanted to hear that voice again, and he wanted to hear it talking about his baby. But the next words the voice said were a shock.

"Preterm labor. Oh. I forgot. You can't see me. But of course, you know I'm pregnant. Out to here."

He saw the shadow of her hand sweep in a graceful arc down her front while his chest remained

crushed in the vice of two words: *preterm labor.*
"You're having preterm labor?" he croaked out.

"Not really. It was all a big scare. A false alarm.
It's just that I'm way too early to deliver and I
started having these fake contractions. They call
them Braxton Hicks contractions, or false labor, but
believe me, a first-time mommy can't tell them from
the real McCoy, especially when that mommy's
wound up tighter than a cheap alarm clock. Not that
anybody wouldn't be strung out in my shoes. You're
from Denver, right?"

All he had to do was nod and she was off and
running again. She sure was a talker. Well, of
course, she was. She was a *talk*-show host. Maybe
that was a good thing, since he was definitely not
feeling chatty himself.

"Maybe you saw something about it on the news.
Or maybe my father told you about it when he hired
you. I'm the host of the *All About Babies* show."
She said this so matter-of-factly that he realized
there was no I'm-a-TV-star egomania going on here.
She was merely trying to establish her identity for
him.

"He only told me you have a stalker." Greg
didn't know what else to do besides go along with
this fairy tale Maureen had concocted.

"Yeah, well. It all started when I got this baby
by artificial insemination. Big flap. Honestly, people
can be so cruel. Anyway, that's not your problem.
The upshot is, the publicity and all, the whole thing

upset me to the point that now I have to put up with a home monitor and all this homebound, resting junk. But it's okay. I'll do anything to protect my baby."

So would he. Protecting them would be easy now that he was up here, that is, if he ever got his vision back. But how was he going to handle the rest of it? And how long should he keep up this charade? What had her mother already told her? He rubbed his forehead in consternation, wondering if he should politely inquire about the baby's father now, wondering if that would be downright cruel when he knew the truth.

"Mom has assured me that we can get along for a few days with half a bodyguard." She chuckled. "Mom's already altered the authorities in Enchantment to keep a close watch on anyone suspicious hanging around the town. Do you feel okay?" she asked kindly.

"My head hurts a little."

"I'm sorry." Her warm palm pressed around his arm and again he felt that crazy thrill. Incredible. "I should *not* be talking about my problem when you're in this condition. You must be so frightened, about your eyes and everything."

"No. It's okay. Listening to you talk actually helps get my mind off…this." He passed a hand in the vicinity of his eyes. "I'd like to hear more about…your pregnancy and everything."

But right then Maureen swooped in and set a plate

of fragrant breakfast food in front of him. "Here we are," she sang out.

Greg felt the touch of Ashleigh's slender fingers again as she wrapped his hand around a chilled glass of orange juice. "Can you manage?"

"Yes."

The three of them ate. Ashleigh and her mother kept up a steady stream of distracting chatter, mostly upbeat cooings about the prognosis of Greg's eyes, while Greg bent low, feeling his plate with his hands and staring intently at each painstaking bite of food, trying not to embarrass himself. Greg felt as if he was probably making a mess, groping for his juice glass and missing his mouth with a forkful of pancakes.

"Now," Maureen pronounced when the meal was done, "I'm going to put each of you on one of those opposing couches near the fireplace and you are going to rest. I have laundry and dishes to do."

"Oh, goody goody," Ashleigh said. "More rest! Come, Greg, and I'll show you how to rest! I'm an absolute expert at it."

She touched him again, taking his arm, and Greg let himself be led to a low couch that felt of cool leather. He could see the orangish glare of flames in a fireplace, but he preferred instead to fix his watery gaze on the pink mound that came around right in front of his face as she lowered him to the couch. It looked huge, and all he could think was that his child was in there.

"There you go," she said, then crossed the space between the two couches. She sat down and put her feet up on the opposite couch. She settled back, a pink blimp with blond hair at one end and red house slippers sticking up at the other.

"I take it you're sick of resting." Greg kept his voice low, because Maureen was banging around in the kitchen.

"That's all my mother says all day long, *rest, rest, rest.*"

"Is that because of your pregnancy?" Greg marveled at his ability to introduce the topic every time they turned around.

"Yes. Because of that episode of preterm labor or whatever it was. But like I told you, now they've decided they were Braxton Hicks contractions."

Hearing it repeated, Greg felt somewhat reassured. He'd never even thought about the possibility that she might lose the baby. There seemed to be something new to worry about every minute with this woman.

She sighed. "Anyway, my doctor says I shouldn't even be having those yet. It's so hard to tell anything for sure at this stage. So I have to *rest* a lot. I'll be so glad when I get a little further along."

"But your baby's okay?" His heart drummed with the import of his question.

"Oh, yes. I heard the heartbeat again yesterday at the clinic. It was wonderful."

Greg imagined it was. How he yearned to hear

that heartbeat for himself. "How far along are you?" He knew, exactly.

"Twenty-eight weeks."

"Have you had an ultrasound?" He hoped he wasn't getting too personal, but someday, Ashleigh Logan would understand the meaning of his questions. Someday. "I mean, people usually know what they're having. Is it a boy? Or a girl?" Either would be fine with Greg; he just wanted to know. His heart hammered while he pretended to lie still, waiting to hear if there would be a son or a daughter in his future.

"When I had my ultrasound, the little dickens crossed its legs, so we couldn't see—" he heard an abashed smile in her voice "—anything."

"Oh." Disappointment muted his voice.

"Hey, enough about me and this baby." Now her voice carried a forced cheerfulness.

Undoubtedly she was mistaking the reason for his quietness. Undoubtedly she thought he was a big bore.

"Tell me about yourself," she urged. "Let's see." The pink blimp shifted to its side. "I already know what you do for a living, deputy slash body-guard. Mother filled me in on your background some. Said you also have a ranch. So, um…how old are you?" She raised her arms and he could tell she was running her fingers through her long golden hair, a gesture of the very bored…and the very feminine.

He wanted to see her face, up close, to study her features, to try to imagine the baby she was making inside of her. "I'm thirty-four," he said.

"Oh. I'm thirty-five. So. Tell me about horse ranching. Is it fun?"

Talking about the horses wouldn't normally be a chore—ranching was Greg's great love. But with this woman, he wanted to discuss only one burning topic. He heard Maureen starting up the dishwasher in the kitchen. He had to find out if she had told Ashleigh anything, and soon. He wasn't going to let Maureen McGuinness control the situation forever. But for now, he reminded himself that as far as Ashleigh was concerned, they were just two strangers in the getting-acquainted stage. So Greg forced himself to make small talk.

WHILE GREG GLAZIER TOLD her a little bit about life on his ranch, Ashleigh eyed the long, lanky, undeniably good-looking man stretched out on the couch parallel to hers. Life was so unfair.

Now, when she'd made her fateful decision, now, when she was, in fact, over six months into that fateful decision, now at long last, here was a man she was genuinely attracted to. A man who was, in fact, her physical ideal.

She loved his face, his voice, his hair, the shape of his handsome head. Lord, it made her heart pound with gladness just to *look* at him. She squelched the guilty thought. Was all this excitement good for the baby?

Oh, life was unfair, all right. Now, when all she wanted to do was focus on her baby, now, when she should be resting as calmly as a cow instead of getting all excited and infatuated, *now,* she finally meets the man that she was sure she would never, ever meet. Not in a million years. A man who could pull her out of the past and into the future and help her put the loss of Chad into healthy perspective.

Greg Glazier. Oh! If only she'd never heard his deep voice. Watched his powerful movements. Seen the straight line of his wide mouth, his firm jaw with that enticing morning stubble. Because this thing could never work out.

But there was no help for it. Now that she was lying on a matching couch not six feet away from him, she could hardly take her eyes off the man. She was glad he couldn't see the way her gaze constantly trailed back to his reclining form, as if drawn by some huge magnet.

He fell silent and shifted on his couch. She found herself absolutely gawking as he moved. His legs were long, lean, very muscled. He had a cleanness, a solidity, about him that was incredibly appealing. He was wearing only jeans and a white T-shirt this morning, so that she could clearly see the proportions of his body. Everything bulged and dipped in all the right places. His chest was broad, curved with muscles. And as he lay on his back, his abdomen looked incredibly hard and flat. She cut a glance at her own bowling-ball front.

Oh well. Back to Greg Glazier.

She had no idea what he'd just said.

He crossed his arms over his broad chest.

His hands and arms were especially beautiful, especially masculine. Not overly hairy, they were veined, sculpted and tanned—she presumed from all of the outdoor work on that ranch of his. He had long fingers with blunt, clean nails and thick pads of muscle supporting strong thumbs. All of it was just right.

"Well, it doesn't matter. Gramps is gone now." His deep-set gray eyes were aimed in the vicinity of the fireplace, as if he was lost in thought. She realized he'd been talking about his grandfather, and she wished she'd been paying better attention because "Gramps" was someone he had obviously loved a great deal.

"I'm sorry to hear that."

He closed his eyes and laid his head back on the cushions, and her gaze fixed for one instant on his magnificent neck. He repositioned his arms over his chest and she could imagine, with no effort at all, being held in those arms. He stretched and let out a deep sigh that was almost a groan. The sound of it did funny things to her insides. She could have sworn the baby stretched at the same time Greg did.

"Are you okay?" she said.

His head jerked up, turned in her direction. "Fine."

"Still thinking about your grandfather?"

"Yeah. But I try not to dwell on the fact that he's gone."

"How long has he been dead?"

"Six months."

"And you were pretty close?"

"Very. Gramps kind of raised me. My mother left my father when I was young. He never remarried. I think he was too cantankerous for any woman to stand him for long. All my dad did was work. He was a sheriff. Then my old man got killed in the line of duty when I was barely out of my teens. That was hard on both me and Gramps. Gramps and I have kind of stuck together ever since."

"Your father was killed in the line of duty?"

"In a high-speed chase running down some cattle thieves. They're in prison now."

"Oh, my. I am so sorry."

"It was all a long time ago. Except for losing Gramps. That's been recent and...hard to accept."

"Yes, I expect it is..." Her voice trailed off.

"Are you okay?" He suddenly seemed more concerned about her welfare than his own sad history, which touched Ashleigh. She was a stranger to him, after all.

"Me? I'm fine. Just a little bored."

"You've got a pretty active life in Denver, with a TV show and all."

"I love my work. Well, I did. It got a little crazy right before I left."

"What will you do when the baby is born?"

Ashleigh thought it was a little odd that he didn't want to know why her work got a little crazy. Instead he wanted to talk about her life after she had the baby. "You mean about work?"

"Yes. Will you stay home and take care of the baby?" An odd question also, she thought. Most men didn't get too wound up with such topics, unless it was some weirdo like that Simon creep. She studied Greg Glazier. Perhaps he was just trying to get his mind off his own troubles.

"Well, the actual taping only takes a couple of hours a day. I'm going to convert a corner of my dressing room at the station into a nursery and I'll hire a nanny to come to the studio with me. The rest of my day usually consists of research for the interviews. I can do my preparation at home, while I take care of the baby."

Greg Glazier was frowning, as if in his mind he were really weighing her plan, which was none of his business. Honestly. Why were people such busybodies when it came to single motherhood? It bugged her that everybody felt free to express an opinion about the welfare of *her* baby. And, handsome or not, she suddenly remembered that something about this man bothered her in other ways. What was he doing here? And why was her mother acting so weird? Last night, when Ashleigh had confronted her mother again about taking in a stranger like this, her mother had become as defensive as an old badger.

"He is not a stranger," Maureen had practically shouted, then she lowered her voice to a whisper. "I told you, I know his family. And besides, it's in our best interest to take good care of him."

When Ashleigh asked her to explain that line of reasoning, Maureen had made a transparent dodge— "Omigosh, his medicine"—and ran up the stairs where he was staying.

Something about her mother's behavior was so odd that Ashleigh held off on telling her that Greg Glazier was the man who had shown up at Megan's house with some story about "holdings in common." Ashleigh wondered if this guy didn't have something to do with her father. Something…fishy. A risk-taker of the first stripe, Ashleigh's hard-charging father had been peripherally involved in some pretty wild, quasipolitical money-making schemes. She eyed Greg Glazier again. He didn't look like the shady type, but something about him sure didn't add up. Years of doing television interviews had taught Ashleigh how to read people loud and clear. This guy was hiding something. And she would get to the bottom of it, or her name wasn't Ashleigh Logan.

"It won't be easy," she went on, "raising a baby alone. But I have lots of friends and family for support."

"Sounds like you've got it all worked out," he said. "That's good. Right now, I imagine it's really hard, having to lie around like this all day."

"Well, I imagine it's really hard not being able to see."

He sighed. "I'm trying not to think about that."

"I could turn on the TV," she offered, "and you could at least listen to the news or something."

"That'd be nice."

"CNN okay?"

"Sure."

She picked up the remote and found the channel. He turned his eyes in the direction of the flickering big screen located next to the fireplace.

The first thing she'd noticed about him, in the dim light on the roadside last night, were his eyes. She supposed that was because of her mother's shocking announcement that he had been blinded. She had looked right at his gray eyes and felt a jolt that had nothing do with learning of his injury. Because Greg Glazier's eyes were incredible—intelligent, thoughtful. And kind.

She looked at those eyes now, fiercely hoping that the blindness was only temporary. Wouldn't it be awful if they could never look into each other's eyes, if he could never *see* her? She wondered where such thoughts of the future were coming from. But Ashleigh Logan had been through enough in life to know not to question it when fate did finally smile on her. For so long she'd wanted to feel the desire for love, connection, intimacy, and now here it was, here *he* was. *Now,* when she shouldn't be having these feelings. Life really was so unfair.

The second thing she'd noticed, as she'd buckled his seat belt after the accident, was that he was not wearing a wedding band. And her mother had confirmed it last night—Greg Glazier was not married. Although Maureen said she couldn't recall if he was widowed or divorced or what.

"Why don't you just ask him?" Maureen had said, knowing that her daughter wasn't the least bit shy about asking questions.

From her side of the entertainment pit, Ashleigh shot his profile a wry grin. She wondered what he would think of her if he could see her *now*. Well, she certainly made a fetching little sight these days. Unstyled hair that had grown out too long, baggy old pink robe cinched over a T-shirt left over from the days when she'd done a charity run about once a month, and a pair of fat supersize black exercise pants. Thick gray ski socks and old red slippers. She glanced at her ankles—so *swollen*—and then to top off the critical self-inventory, she gingerly palpated the massive zit that had bloomed on her chin. She was even wearing her big black-framed glasses to complete the homely picture. Well, he couldn't see her right now, thank goodness. Horrified at her own self-centeredness and vanity in the face of his blindness, she bit her lip and flapped her hand once as if to rebuke herself. There were more serious things to think about here than hair and clothes and how very fat and bloated one was. She glanced at Greg Glazier again and sighed. Poor, poor man.

He crossed his graceful bare feet at the ankles, causing her to stare. Even his feet seemed perfect! Oh, this was bad, what she was feeling. Very bad. She hardly knew this man, but the minute he'd ducked his dark head into the Suburban, she'd realized that here was a man she could really fall for. Which was a perfectly stupid thought. How could one know something like that in an instant? The very idea was insane! But the idea was there—that's the way she already felt, and there was no use kidding herself about it.

Maybe it was a good thing she had the baby to consider so she wouldn't actually *act* on these crazy feelings. But she hadn't felt this way about a man— not once—in the five years since Chad had died. Another wave of giddiness rippled through her, followed by a crushing letdown of guilt.

What about Chad? Here she was, pregnant with Chad's baby, in absolutely no position to fall in love, and she was actually thinking about it. Oh, life was really, really unfair. Because here he was at long last, right in front of her. Greg Glazier. A man she could actually fall in love with.

CHAPTER ELEVEN

GREG COULD FEEL ASHLEIGH Logan sizing him up. He tried to look at her and thought his vision might be clearing a little more. He could make out the outline of her mounded tummy more sharply against the dark leather of the couch. Draped in *pink*. Again, he wondered if the baby was a boy or a girl.

He wanted to grope his way past the small table that separated them and press his hands over her belly and keep them there until he felt his baby kick. He wanted to press his ear to Ashleigh Logan's swollen abdomen, listening for any faint sound from within, anything that might be his baby, moving, growing, alive.

Today, it looked like she had thick, black-framed glasses dominating her face, and a riot of blond hair. As a fuzzy profile, Ashleigh Logan looked vulnerable, like a messy little girl. The idea of some creep threatening to hurt her made him want to punch something.

"Your mom and I were talking earlier—" it was not a lie, though it had been quite a bit earlier "—and she said you don't know anything about this stalker except that he called in to your show a couple of times.''

The air in the room became still. Ashleigh muted the TV. From somewhere nearby in the house came the sound of Maureen humming as she did household chores.

Slowly, Ashleigh turned her head in his direction. Something about her pose made him regret what he'd said. He could imagine Ashleigh's fears, and that by mentioning the stalker, he'd just fanned them. He wished he could just come clean and tell her who he really was, but he had to talk to her mother first, find out what Ashleigh knew, what kind of mental state she was in.

Finally she said, ''Yeah. The cops think he's a fan of the show.'' She said it very flatly, as if suppressing anger over the whole situation. Then her tone became incongruously light, defiant. ''That's when you know you're really getting famous. When a fan becomes a stalker.''

Unprepared for her flippant attitude, he gave her a confused frown.

''Look,'' she said, her tone softening. ''For my baby's sake, I'm trying my best not to freak out here. I'm trying to stay calm, you know? I'm trying to trust that the police can take care of the problem. Even though about ninety percent of the time the stalker wins. I'm sure that as a deputy you're well aware of that.''

''It'll be okay,'' he said. It sounded inadequate,

but he couldn't say what he was really thinking, that he'd die before he'd let this creep get anywhere near Ashleigh and his baby.

"It's just hard, lying around all day with too much time to worry about this stuff."

"I can imagine." He tried to look at her again, squinting, with poor results. He could make out that she had folded her arms across her belly in a protective pose. He had to admire her guts. Most people would buckle under the strain of Ashleigh Logan's situation, but what he'd seen of her basic disposition seemed as solid as the mountains outside the window, as tranquil as the New Mexico sky. He tried to see her better, and when he couldn't, he rubbed his eyes.

"Didn't the doctor tell you not to do that?"

"Uh. Yeah. Thanks for reminding me."

He lay his head back on the throw pillows and let his fuzzy gaze drift up to the ceiling. "That's good—that you're letting the police handle things. Could he possibly be someone you know? An old boyfriend? The baby's father or something?" He knew who the baby's father was, even if *she* didn't. It was weak, but it was an opening to discuss what was really on his mind.

From across the space came a cynical-sounding little "Humph."

"Did I say something wrong?"

"I don't have an old *boyfriend.*"

"But you're single, right?" Why was he doing

this? His duplicity was only going to make her hate him more intensely later on.

"I'm single and haven't had a relationship in years." She was extremely candid, he'd give her that.

"Then, if you don't mind my asking, who is this baby's father?" He turned his head on the pillow and wished to hell he could read her facial expression clearly. He wanted to see her reaction to this topic, wanted to test the limits of her candor. But there came another long, disturbing silence from her side of the room.

Finally she said, "This is my late husband's baby." Now her hands appeared to be stacked on top of her abdomen in a protective gesture.

"Oh. Your *late* husband. I'm so sorry." What else could he say? He was beginning to feel like a creep, pretending ignorance this way. Then he saw a way to press on. He arranged his face in the confused frown again. "I don't understand."

"Don't you watch the news?" She sounded a little irate now. "The story was all over the place."

"I guess I missed it. What story?"

"The story of how I used my long-dead husband's banked sperm to get myself artificially inseminated with this baby. That story."

Greg hoped he was doing a good job of looking properly astonished. He wasn't much of an actor, but he assumed that was the effect she wanted from that blunt tone of hers.

"I see," he said.

"Do you?" Now her tone became sarcastic. "Well, that's just amazing, because hardly anybody else does. They all think I'm nuts."

"I don't. I can see why you'd want to have some part of your husband with you, through his child. And I understand how hard it is to let go of someone. I'm widowed myself."

"You are?" Her voice softened with awe and she pushed her awkward girth up straighter on her couch.

"Yes. Three years ago."

"Chad's been gone five years." Her voice conveyed a newfound compassion, a connection. "How did your wife die?"

"Renal failure. Kendra was getting dialysis and was on the transplant list, but they couldn't find a match in time. It was actually a massive stroke that killed her." He worried about telling a pregnant woman such upsetting facts, but Ashleigh Logan seemed strong enough to handle anything that was thrown at her. She'd survived a similar ordeal with her own husband, hadn't she?

"How incredibly sad. Did the two of you have any kids?"

"No. She couldn't have children. Her kidneys had always been bad, so bad that a pregnancy would have killed her."

"Oh, my." Her voice became softer. "And then she died, anyway. I'm so sorry."

"How did your husband die?" His private detective had already told him all of the details, exact dates and everything, so that he could credibly confront the owners of the sperm bank. But it would seem insensitive if he didn't ask her.

"He had cancer."

"I see."

Her pose was still alert, with her head craned forward from the couch cushions, as if she was really interested in him now. "I've never met anyone as young as I am who is also widowed."

"Oh, I have." Greg rolled his eyes. Had the doctor told him not to do that, too? His grogginess and his head injury seemed to be making it hard to think clearly.

"Doesn't sound like it was a great experience."

"It was at a singles group at a big church in downtown Denver. I let some friends talk me into going to one of the dances. A Halloween thing. Adults in ridiculous costumes doing the chicken dance in a big circle."

"It wasn't fun?"

"No. *Hell no.* The whole event reeked of desperation."

"Ouch."

"I was twice as depressed after that so-called party. That one drove me right back to the ranch."

"I know what you mean. I tried dating for a few months myself, mostly to get my mother and my sister off my back. It was a charming parade. One guy wanted to show me his scars—the emotional variety. One told me the price of practically everything he owned before the salad had even arrived. One, I think, was an ax murderer.''

Greg chuckled. He liked this woman. A lot. She had enough class not to complain that every one of the men had also tried to get in her pants, but Greg had seen her once or twice on TV—before the pregnancy. He imagined that sort of thing was a given in her life.

''Since then, I've sort of distracted myself with my work.''

''I can understand that,'' he said, smiling. ''And I really do understand why you're having this baby. I think it's your right to have a baby any way you please, and to have anyone's baby you please.'' He wished he hadn't added that last part, since she was eventually going to find out that she wasn't having a baby with whomever she pleased. She was having a baby with someone she didn't even know.

''I wish to hell this stalker agreed with you.''

''Is that why he's stalking you? Because your baby comes from a sperm bank?''

''My baby comes from *Chad*.'' Her resonant broadcaster's voice took on a determined edge that told Greg she was not about to relinquish that cherished notion easily. ''But yeah, this guy is some kind of deranged fanatic who thinks any interference with the natural process—whatever that means—is an abomination. He's clearly unbalanced. He has made it clear in a series of creepy messages that he thinks my pregnancy should be terminated...or that I should be terminated, if necessary.''

Greg couldn't stay in a supine position during this kind of talk. He bolted up, curling his shoulders forward, like a panther wanting to strike. ''Somebody needs to terminate *him*,'' he muttered, and felt every one of his muscles tighten.

''Watching a little TV, are we?'' Maureen said as she came bustling into the room. ''Oh, dear. I'm sorry, Mr. Glazier. I shouldn't have said that.''

''It's okay.''

''It's time for your pills—the ones to reduce the swelling.'' She took his hand and pressed two tiny tablets into his palm. Then she handed him a glass of water.

''Thank you.''

''How's your headache?''

''Better, I think.'' Actually it was throbbing, but he'd already taken all the pain medicine he wanted to. Any more, and he was afraid he'd go to sleep and miss his opportunity to talk to Ashleigh.

''Ashleigh, can I get you anything, dear?''

''No thanks, Mom.''

Maureen started puttering around in the great room, stacking magazines, fluffing pillows. Greg could sense Ashleigh's impatience and tension over her mother's presence. It was as if Ashleigh wanted to continue to talk to Greg alone. Her next words confirmed that hunch.

"Let's go out on the deck," Ashleigh said. "There are a couple of chaise lounges out there. What do you think, Greg?"

"Sure." He would go anywhere she took his baby.

"Do you think that's wise, Ashleigh? It's a little chilly out there. Maybe you should just rest on the couch."

"Mom, the doctor said I am fine. I can be up and about now."

"Within the house." Maureen's tone was condescending.

"I'm supposed to *ambulate* a little bit, so that when the midwife comes to see me the day after tomorrow, she can *assess* how I *tolerated* it."

Greg had to smile. Ashleigh was a bright woman, and obviously sick of the role of patient.

"The sunshine and fresh air will do me good." Ashleigh pushed herself up. "We'll take some blankets."

Greg could make out the bright patterns of a couple of Navajo blankets as Ashleigh grabbed them off a nearby chair.

She tucked them under her arm and crossed the room to him. She reached down and took his hand. "I'll help you get settled out there," she offered.

He took her hand and stood up and let himself be led, all the while enjoying the feel of her warm skin and thinking, *This is the mother of my baby.*

Out on the deck, they settled onto the chaise

lounges with the Indian blankets wrapped around them. It was not as windy as it had been the night before, but there was enough of a breeze to make the aspens seem alive as the sunshine twinkled off the branches framing the second-story deck. Thick stands of the glistening yellow trees trailed up the mountainside, their color mingling with the deep green pines. Beyond the nearer view, three peaks rose high, facing the morning sun. During the chilly night, they had taken on a fresh cap of snow.

"Baldy, Wheeler and Touch Me Not." Greg pointed out each summit without thinking that he didn't want her to think his sight was clearing up too fast. He wanted to buy a little time near the mother of his child.

"I only knew of Wheeler." Ashleigh's voice held a note of heightened curiosity. "You can see them?"

Greg didn't want to tell her he'd been up here before, and he certainly didn't want to tell her why. Again, he wondered how much her mother had told her.

"Well, I can see the outlines, yes." He squinted into the distance. "I think a bit of my vision is returning."

"Maybe this Southwest sunshine is too harsh for your eyes." She struggled to push her rounded girth up off the chaise. "I've got some sunglasses."

"No." Greg reached across the small space between the lounges and grabbed her wrist. "I'm fine.

I like it out here. The aspens provide plenty of screening.'' He motioned at the tops of the trees fluttering at the perimeter of the high deck, framing it with moving golden color.

"Okay.'' There was a skeptical tilt to her head and he felt definite tension in her arm. A pulling away. He thought he felt her pulse racing as he dropped her wrist.

"What are you doing in New Mexico, exactly?'' She adopted a casual tone. ''I mean, I'm aware that you don't know anyone in town. Mother says that's why she wanted to help you. And she still thinks she was partly responsible for your accident. It's amazing that she knows your family in Denver. Isn't it a small world?''

"Yeah. Small.'' The lying was getting to Greg, and he longed to tell Ashleigh the real reason why he was here, but he wanted the timing to be right. Once he dropped his bomb, there would be no turning back. It would be better if she could get to know him first.

ASHLEIGH WATCHED GREG GLAZIER, trying to keep her face neutral. She feared that even with his bad vision, he might sense the penetrating quality of her gaze. Something about this deal had her red flags flapping in the wind. What family in Denver, exactly, were they supposed to be talking about? He'd just told her his whole family was dead. Somebody—this man, her mother, or *both*—was lying, and she would get to the bottom of it. She could be disarming, she knew. After all, it was her frank, non-judmental manner that encouraged her guests to talk about such personal matters as birth and sex on her TV show.

She eyed the man next to her again. She figured he could barely make out the hot yellow of the fluttering aspen trees beyond the deck and nothing smaller than a mountain in the distance, but he was leaning forward as if studying the view.

"Do you see a white stallion anywhere on that old farm in the canyon below us?" Greg suddenly asked her.

She allowed this diversion and pushed her girth forward, bracing on the arms of her chaise. "Yes, as a matter of fact, I do. He's right out there." She pointed.

"That's a rare horse. A purebred Andalusian. I went there to check him out. Eventually I hope to get the owner to sell me samples from the stallion."

"Samples?"

"For breeding."

"Oh." That word, from this man, made her feel strangely warm. "Is that where you were coming from when you had the wreck? That farm?"

"Yes. I'd just seen the horse for the first time. He's a fine specimen."

"I see." She tried to keep her voice from sounding skeptical, but what was her bodyguard doing out horse shopping?

She tried to sort out whether her urge to spend more time with this man was about her attraction to him or finding out the truth. But it was no good. The man was a complete enigma to her. A very handsome, very intriguing enigma, who, she was certain, was keeping something from her. Something important.

"What were you doing at my sister's house?"

Before he could answer, the patio door to the deck rolled open. "Time for your antibiotic, Greg!" Maureen sang out.

She swept up to Greg with the pill and a glass of water, seemingly oblivious of the tense current running between the couple.

"Thank you," Greg said, and took the pill.

Ashleigh was unable to read his facial expression. She had no idea what he could be thinking.

Her mother certainly was acting strange, as if this man was some kind of adopted son or something. She was actually smiling at him.

"Greg, if you want to be first in the shower, I'll help you get to the upstairs bathroom. The one drawback at this cabin is that the water gets cold rather quick. The hot water heater is totally inadequate. We'll have to space out our showers."

"Uh. Sure. I understand. I'll go first." Greg threw off the Indian blanket and pushed to his feet.

From her chaise Ashleigh watched in pensive silence while Greg took her mother's arm and was led away into the house.

CHAPTER TWELVE

WHEN THEY GOT UPSTAIRS, Greg said, "Maureen, what, exactly, have you told your daughter about me? I mean, besides the bodyguard bit."

The woman had actually led him into the bathroom. He heard her turning on the shower.

"Nothing." Her tone was crisp, decisive. "And that's the way it's going to stay. My daughter's condition, both physical and emotional, is fragile. I will not have you upsetting her with some story about mixed-up sperm."

"She has to know the truth sometime."

"Not yet, she doesn't. If Ashleigh can make it to thirty-seven weeks' gestation, she can have a home delivery with a midwife. I'm sure you can see why that would be a safer alternative as long as this stalker is on the loose. So until she reaches thirty-seven weeks I won't have anything upsetting her."

"She was asking me questions out there." Greg jabbed a thumb toward the deck area one story below the bathroom window.

"Then maybe you shouldn't be alone with her again. Look," Maureen continued, "give her some time to at least get used to you. I told her that I know your family. That's enough for now.''

"Well, maybe not." Greg tried to lean a palm against the counter and missed. It was pretty difficult to try to play this game on his terms when he needed assistance in the bathroom. "Maybe if we're going to keep up this little charade, I should tell you something about myself."

"The water's hot now. You'd better get to it while it lasts. Here's a towel. I'll put it right here on the counter.''

"I don't have parents."

Her face, blurry-looking because of his vision, came around to confront him. He could make out the white towel clutched to her front. "What do you mean, you don't have parents?''

"My father's dead. My mother hit the road practically the minute I was born."

"I'm…I'm so sorry. I had no idea. But you have some sort of family, don't you? Someone I might plausibly know in Denver?''

"Not really. My grandfather passed on a while back. That makes me the last of the Glaziers. Me and—'' he jerked his head in the direction of the deck ''—Junior out there.''

"I didn't realize…'' Maureen breathed, clutching the bath towel to her chest.

"I told you. This baby is the only person I have left in this world.''

FOR ASHLEIGH, THE ENSUING days took on a surreal quality. It was as if they were a little pretend family, all together on fall break in a remote mountain cabin—enjoying hearty breakfasts together, taking turns at showers, lounging by the fire. But all the while the secrets simmered below the surface, ready to erupt at any moment.

A couple of times Ashleigh had started to ask Greg about the visit to her sister's and she noticed that her mother was always Johnny-on-the-spot to change the subject.

Maureen seemed determined to involve Greg in charming conversations about his business success, his horses, his lovely life in Denver and out at the ranch. Ashleigh got the feeling her mom was doing some kind of hard sell, trying to convince Ashleigh that Greg was a good guy.

But Ashleigh didn't need convincing. She sensed Greg was a man she could trust—it was obvious that her mother did, judging from a conversation Ashleigh overheard.

"Let's see what the midwife says about her condition first," Maureen had whispered while she changed the dressing over Greg's stitches. "Let's get her past this danger zone of her pregnancy."

Her pregnancy. Ashleigh released a quiet sigh at those words. She would try to corral her growing fascination with Greg and focus on her baby— Chad's baby.

On the third day, Katherine Collins, the midwife from The Birth Place, showed up for her scheduled home visit.

The plan, Greg had gathered, was for Ashleigh to deliver in the secluded cabin, away from the prying media and the threat of the stalker. To qualify for a home delivery, Ashleigh had to reach thirty-seven weeks' gestation, and for a while that possibility had been in question, so she had continued under the supervision of Dr. Ochoa.

When Greg heard the midwife's Jeep start up the cabin's rocky drive, he claimed he needed to lie down and disappeared behind the closed door of his upstairs room. He waited a few minutes, then quietly crept out to the landing that overlooked the great room and stood behind the wall. From there he could hear what the midwife had to say about the well-being of his baby.

"Everything looks good," the midwife said cheerily. "Let's listen to the little one's heartbeat with the Doppler, then, shall we?"

Greg's chest tightened in anticipation and he leaned toward the corner, listening intently. A hollow rushing sound, like static on an untuned radio, filled the expectant silence of the great room. Then it became a faint, rapid *kawoosh, kawoosh,* and Greg knew, without a doubt, what he was hearing.

His own heart seemed to change its beat in answer to the little one's. Tears stung his blurred eyes as, for the first time, he listened to his child's heartbeat. *Little baby,* he thought, *your daddy's up here, and he loves you. He loves you very much.*

A magnetic force pulled at him as he tilted his head around the corner. If one of the women looked up and saw him there, sneaking about on that walkway, he would have some fast explaining to do. But his eyes were drawn to Ashleigh's orb of an abdomen, exposed where the midwife had drawn her dark sweatpants down and her top up. Although his vision had almost completely returned in the last few days, the scene was still a bit hazy to Greg. But he knew one thing. *There,* just below Ashleigh's luminous, tautly stretched golden skin, lay his child. A living person. His son or his daughter. The name of the nearby town came to Greg again, as he remembered his thoughts when he'd arrived here, looking for this very thing. *Enchantment.*

His eyes traveled slowly over Ashleigh's gravid form. He was fascinated, looking at her. Her face appeared to be stretched in a smile, with her chin tucked down, as she, too, seemed to be fixated on the place where the midwife held the Doppler and the sound came rapidly, steadily: *kawoosh, kawoosh, kawoosh.* As he stood there with his back pressed to the wall, the precious heartbeat of their baby filled Greg's heart and mind as nothing in his life ever had. Hypnotizing him. He smiled. He was enchanted, all right.

AFTER HEARING THE BABY'S heartbeat, everything changed for Greg. He had thought himself determined before, but now his purpose became laser sharp. This child was *his*. And he knew he would never rest until he held *his* child in his arms. And he was going to do everything in his power to protect that child and its mother, whether Ashleigh was aware of it or not. He asked to use the phone in the Coleman cabin and cleared the decks of his business dealings until after December 19, the baby's due date.

A week later, Maureen and Ashleigh took Greg to Dr. Woodgrove, the local G.P., to get his stitches removed and have his vision checked. While the two women sat out in the waiting room, the doctor told Greg the good news—his vision was almost normal.

"I can't keep up the lie," he told Maureen when they got back to the cabin. "If I stay up here like this, I'll end up telling your daughter the truth sooner or later."

Maureen had actually acted disappointed when Greg asked to borrow her Suburban so he could pay a visit to Manny Cordova.

"I'd like to make a deal with you," he said, coming straight to the point after the old man invited him inside. "I'll help you do some fixing up around this place in exchange for room and board."

"You found her, didn't you?" Manny's voice was kind, not accusing. "The young woman who is pregnant?" Manny had not seen Greg since his accident.

"Yes."

"Miguel told me and Elkhorn about your accident, and that you've been staying up there in that cabin."

"I see."

"What is she like?"

"She's…she's a very pretty girl, in a pregnant sort of way." Greg smiled. "And she's fun. Very bright. Talks a lot."

"What does she think of you?"

"I have no idea."

"So. You want to stay here with me now. Why? So you can be close to her?"

"I figure it can't hurt. They're still waiting on a part for my Navigator down in Taos. She thinks I've been hired as her bodyguard. If I'm this close, I can at least keep an eye on that cabin."

Manny nodded. "Ah. The stalker. Miguel told me and Elkhorn about that, too. We keep our eyes open for trouble whenever Miguel tells us these things." Manny's eyes softened as if he were taking pity on Greg. "I can see why you worry about her. I guess you could stay in the boys' old room. It ain't the Ritz or anything."

"I don't care."

"No. I expect you don't."

The boys' old room was a bare, functional dormitory with a linoleum floor, high, narrow windows without curtains, a bare light bulb in the middle of the low acoustic-tile ceiling. Four twin beds were still crammed against the walls—''Take your pick,'' Manny said. That very afternoon, Manny followed Greg back to the cabin in his rusty old pickup and they moved Greg's things down to the farm.

As Greg looked out the clouded rear window of the truck, thinking of his child, thinking of Ashleigh, he felt as if he was leaving his family. He craned his neck and looked up at the towering gables of the Coleman cabin, and there, on the high deck, stood Ashleigh, her rounded belly clearly visible as the wind whipped her flowing white lawn dress against her form. She looked like a princess, trapped in a tower, watching her true love bumping away down the rocky drive in an old pickup. Greg knew the idea that she cared for him was a fantasy, as this whole odyssey had been. He wasn't her true love, but he sure as hell wanted to be.

MANNY AND GREG SPENT THEIR days working outdoors, which was exactly what Greg wanted to do. Being out in the brisk mountain air, free of the dizziness and malaise of his inner-ear infection, Greg felt his real strength returning. And with it, his resolve. He wasn't going to let the mother of his child sit up there in that cabin alone and scared. Even if Ashleigh didn't realize it yet, she needed him. He would find a way to fix this. Greg was good at fixing things.

And Manny thought that was just great. Together, they worked hard, sharing their mutual love of horses, the outdoors and the endless, rhythmic work of a small ranchero. Greg liked repairing things, tackling the stuff held together by Manny's all-purpose duct tape first.

Their days were long, their meals were simple, and their sleep was sound. Each morning Greg awoke to the smell of wood smoke and bacon frying. And each night, as he went to sleep looking at the moon floating over the pines, his last thoughts were always of Ashleigh, high on the mountain, sleeping beneath that same moon.

The days passed and Greg watched Ashleigh's pregnancy progress. During this time, he tried to find ways to perform the kindnesses that would show Ashleigh he cared, beyond being her bodyguard. He knew it was a risk, but he couldn't seem to help himself. He took her interesting books to read and CDs to listen to. Whenever he went to town, he brought back little treats for her—muffins, scented candles, a stained-glass bobble for her window. He hung a bird feeder on the deck outside the master suite and filled it with winter seed. He gave them Manny's phone number and told Ashleigh and Maureen to call if they needed anything. Anytime. For any reason.

Every day, he walked the perimeter of the property, just checking. Then if anything needed fixing at the cabin—from the plugged-up garbage disposal to a broken window lock—he was there to do it.

When he wasn't up at the Coleman cabin, he was

working with Manny. Manny had his rituals, and Greg tried to be respectful of his host's lifestyle and go along with them.

One ritual was to attend mass every Wednesday at noon, as well as on Sunday. Though not especially religious, Greg went along with his elder friend and sat in the back pew of the tiny, old Holy Cross Church in Enchantment. The quiet time soothed him, cleared his mind, let him make his plans. Greg's mind and spirit had not felt so focused in all the years since Kendra had died. Manny's companionship, his humble and sincere devotion, touched Greg in ways that he couldn't explain.

On the third Wednesday of Greg's stay, Manny had agreed to take Greg down to Taos to pick up the Navigator, which was supposed to be repaired.

But it wasn't.

"Your part still didn't come," the man at the Ford dealership explained.

"Well—" Manny shrugged "—so that the trip won't be totally wasted, how about we run into the Ranchos de Taos church." Manny smiled. "They have a nice little mass at noon."

"Fine." If Manny wanted to stop and go to mass, Greg wasn't going to argue with the simple man who had taken him in and made this tortured time of waiting more bearable. Greg had heard of the venerable St. Francis of Assisi Church. The place was as serene as the paintings portrayed it, essentially unchanged in two hundred years.

Halfway through the mass, Greg grew strangely restless.

The old church, with its thick adobe walls and fortresslike mission feeling, had a peaceful quality, but Greg couldn't shake a sense of unease.

Today, the small space was peopled by uniformed schoolchildren up front and a smattering of old-timers like Manny. The atmosphere grew quiet as communion began. Greg had sat patiently in the back with his head down and his elbows propped on wide-spread knees, just thinking, about Ashleigh mostly, when something made him look up as the singing started.

With the gut instincts he'd acquired as a deputy strumming, Greg surveyed the front of the church. The line of worshipers inched forward as the priest doled out hosts. Everything looked normal.

On one side of the altar, a statue of the Madonna and infant Jesus stood frozen in a timeless pose of serenity. Greg stared at it, thinking, trying to figure out where this strange sense of warning was coming from. Manny was coming around to the side aisle by then, his gnarled hands folded in front of his chest, his gray head bowed. Greg watched him for a moment before his eyes were drawn back up to the statue.

Suddenly, he remembered the story of Mary, having to hide from evil men to save her baby. She couldn't have done it without Joseph. Greg's eyes traveled to the statue at the other side of the altar, the one of the strong carpenter who had protected Mary and the baby. Joseph, he thought, must have experienced the same sense of frustration he felt. Facing an unseen enemy who wanted to hurt his baby. *The life of a child had been in his hands.* Suddenly, a spinning sense of foreboding washed over Greg.

He was overcome with the feeling that he shouldn't be down here in Taos, so far from Ashleigh and the baby.

Manny was sidling into his pew. He knelt stiffly, just as Greg took three long strides up the side aisle. An old woman frowned at Greg as he pressed against the adobe wall and let her pass.

"Let's go," he whispered, bending down toward Manny's bowed head.

Manny didn't hesitate. Quickly he made the sign of the cross, grabbed his hat off the pew and followed Greg out.

"What is wrong, amigo?" he said when they got outside the doors of the church.

Greg whipped out his cell phone. "Good. I've got a signal." He punched the cabin number.

"Ashleigh? Hi. It's Greg. Everything okay up there?"

"Yes." Her throaty voice sounded tinny with the distance, but she sounded relaxed and happy, though a bit surprised. "Everything's fine. We're just having a good old boring day."

"Oh." Greg did not know what he had expected

to hear. The sense of warning inside the church had been so strong. "I just wanted to check. You're sure you're all right? Feeling all right, I mean."

"I'm great. Katherine came up for a home visit. Everything checked out great. She brought me some tapes and childbirth books and baby catalogs from the clinic. At last I have a reason to get up in the morning." Ashleigh's voice was joking, happy. "You'd be *amazed* at the baby stuff you can order from catalogs these days. All delivered straight to your door. I was just getting ready to place an or—"

"Don't have it sent straight to your door," Greg interrupted with sudden insight. "You don't want delivery trucks coming up to the cabin. Someone could spot one, put two and two together."

"Oh. Right. I hadn't thought of that."

"Give them directions to Manny's place. When I get the stuff, I'll bring it up to you. Okay?"

"Okay."

He loved that idea—taking her pretty baby things that would cheer her up.

"Would you like a visitor later today?" He'd gotten in the habit of having a cup of herbal tea with Ashleigh after he made his rounds. "I'm down in Taos with Manny, but we should be back in about an hour. We tried to pick up my Navigator, but it wasn't ready."

"That's ridiculous. They've had the thing almost three weeks."

"They're having trouble with one part. They

should have called me. Miscommunication, I guess.'' Greg would have been perturbed about such a screwup two months ago. Now it seemed like such a small thing.

''I guess.''

''You're sure you're okay?''

''I am fine.''

The long drive up to the mountains over the high desert plateau, with the Rio Grande Gorge winding continuously on their left, allowed Greg time to think, to settle down.

''I don't know what got into me back at the church,'' he apologized over the whine of the old truck engine. ''I guess I just don't feel comfortable being away from Ashleigh for long.''

''It's okay, amigo. That church—it's a funny place. The Spirit whispers there sometimes, you know?''

Greg shook his head. Manny the mystic.

''And you got to do what you got to do.''

Halfway to Enchantment, it started to snow.

''Ah,'' Manny sighed with satisfaction as fat flakes hit the windshield. ''Here comes the first big snow of the season. I thought I could smell it coming. This one'll stay on the ground for sure.''

The hushed quality of the snow drifting down and sticking to the blackish-green junipers and the reddish rocks on the canyon walls seemed to invite contemplation. Greg gazed off in the distance, catching glimpses of silver water rippling in the deep gorge below.

They rode along in silence for a very long while, enjoying the beauty.

"How long has your wife been dead?" Greg asked suddenly. He'd been thinking that his over-reaction back in the church had something to do with his own demons, with his old feeling that, somehow, he had failed Kendra.

"Oh, many, many years."

"You still miss her?"

"Yes, of course. Do you still miss your wife?"

"Sometimes. For a long time, I didn't think I'd ever love anyone again."

Manny's sharp old eyes assessed him, then returned to the gently winding highway. "Love is a funny thing, eh? We all want it. We all need it. But none of us can make it happen. Love is the magic between two people, and one person alone can't make it happen. But when it happens, it just happens, and there is nothing we can do to change it."

"I suppose." Greg smiled at Manny' profile. The old man drove hunched over, both hands gripping the wheel, steering the rickety truck as intently as a stock-car-race driver. Manny the romantic. Greg had grown very fond of his new friend's simple ways, his artist's heart and his oh-so-true bromides. "Anyway, I definitely think it's happening to me."

"Ah." Manny's walnut of a face crinkled into a

knowing little grin. "I think I seen that one coming."

"Oh? It's that obvious, huh?"

"Amigo, a man in love, he's like a bull elk, sniffing the wind." Manny chuckled, enjoying his metaphor. "It's the way you look up at that cabin when you stop to catch your breath while we're working. The way you run up to that cabin at the drop of a hat. The way you say her name."

Greg released a forlorn sigh.

"What's wrong, amigo?"

"I just wish I knew she felt the same about me. She sure as hell isn't gonna feel great about me when I tell her the truth about the baby. The longer I delay, the worse it's going to be, but her mother keeps insisting that if Ashleigh hears the truth, it will upset her so much that it will jeopardize the pregnancy. She wants me to wait until Ashleigh's far enough along that if she goes into labor, the baby can be born safely at the cabin."

"When is that, amigo?"

"Not until after Thanksgiving."

"Whew." Manny gave a little whistle. "That's a long time to be keeping a secret that's going to change everybody's lives."

Greg sighed again, staring out at the endless landscape of snow-dusted buttes and canyons. "I came here thinking that's all I wanted—to make sure my child was born safely and to forge some kind of relationship with him. But now…"

"Now you have fallen in love with the child's mother."

"Yeah. It's a real mess."

"Oh, now. Not such a mess. That's the way it's supposed to be. *La madre, el padre, el bebé.*" Manny ticked off three fingers. "A family is a family, however it gets made. Besides, life's usually messy, one way or another. That's the fun of it, eh? You got the mess. I got the mess. It's how we clean up the mess that counts."

Greg folded his arms across his broad chest, convinced that his particular mess would never work out. "Am I nuts? Falling in love with a pregnant woman?"

"'Course not." Manny's compassionate gaze swept over Greg's dejected posture. "When my Rosa was pregnant, that's when I loved her the most. And pregnancy is a great time to get a woman to fall in love with you. The way I see it—" Manny scratched his chin "—a woman, she needs attention, and lots of patience, all of the time, but especially when she's pregnant. It's not unlike training a horse, amigo. You got to give them plenty of rope, plenty of sugar, plenty of gentling with the hands."

"Gentling with the hands?" Greg cut Manny one of those insider-guy grins. "I haven't gotten close enough to use *the hands* yet."

"Some are more skittish than others," Manny said, grinning back. "Just like the horses."

"Skittish, huh? I guess this particular woman has got her reasons," Greg allowed, "for being skittish."

ASHLEIGH'S REASONS BECAME frighteningly real two days later. She was brushing her luxurious hair, staring absentmindedly out of the windows of the master suite, when she thought she saw something move in the trees. With the brush still suspended above her head, she stood stock-still. And there it was again. The movement had not been from her reflection! She stifled a cry and hurried to the bedside lamp, switching it off. She tried to control her panicked breathing as she stared toward the dark woods outside the windows with wide eyes.

A shadow in the trees shifted. Her stalker had found her.

"Mom!" she cried as she snatched up the cowbell off the bedside table, clanging it as if house was on fire.

WHEN MANNY'S OLD WALL PHONE jangled, Greg was out working by the light of the moisture-ringed full moon with Manny. They were putting up snow breaks along the fence in anticipation of another huge snowfall, predicted by morning. By the third ring, Greg had dashed to the house and snatched up the phone. He stretched the cord to the window and looked in the direction of the Coleman cabin.

"Yes?"

Manny came in the back door and stared up at the cabin with him, listening.

"Greg." It was Ashleigh, and the fear in her voice made his chest tight. "Can you come up here? There is something or someone outside my window. We called Miguel, but he's nine miles away on a domestic violence call. The other officers are all tied up as well."

"I'll be right there."

Manny went, too. He took a rifle. Greg took his gun.

"Keep your safety on," Manny advised while they drove up. "We got a lot of teenagers running around in these mountains, especially when the moon is full. Sometimes they take this road up north to an abandoned mining town."

"Let's hope it is just kids," Greg said.

"If it is I'm going to scare the pee out of the little dickens and teach them a lesson about trespassing. I've half a mind to make them think I'm the ghost."

"The ghost?"

"A teenage boy fell down the mine shaft a long time ago. Must be thirty years now. The kids say he haunts the mountains when the moon is full."

"If a bunch of kids have been harassing Ashleigh, I'll do more than *scare* their little asses."

They parked down on the road, killed the headlights and approached the cabin in the dark, climbing the rocky, sloping lot on foot.

Greg halted in the pines, putting a hand up to

signal Manny, coming up behind him. The two men stood as still as statues in the dark mist. A few minutes passed in silence, and then, they spotted him. A deer emerged from the trees, a huge buck wagging an impressive set of antlers. The deer halted and gave them a bold, hostile stare and then slipped off into the woods.

"That old buck," Manny said as he came up beside Greg. "I seen him around this mountain before. Tricky fella. No hunter can get him. Antler clacking don't even fool him."

"Would he venture that close to the cabin?" Greg asked.

"Oh, sure. He's not afraid of anything. I expect that old devil would do whatever he wanted."

Convinced they had discovered Ashleigh's prowler, Greg and Manny circled the perimeter of the cabin again, anyway, sweeping the surrounding area with their high-powered flashlights.

Ashleigh came out to the railing of the lower deck and called out to Greg. "Do you see anything?" She was wearing a plaid flannel nightgown and had thrown a pale shawl over her shoulders. Her blond hair shone in the moonlight.

"Get back inside," Greg commanded.

The men finished their search, finding plenty of deer tracks in the trees, but no human footprints. They decided to go inside to calm the frightened women.

They cut through the trees, and just as Manny was

pushing a large pine limb out of the way, Maureen slammed a door on the upper balcony. Manny jumped and the limb whacked backward at Greg, knocking him off his feet.

"Amigo!" Manny cried.

"I'm fine." Greg immediately got up and fingered the clean rip that the limb had left in the leather sleeve of his jacket. "Just got a hole in my jacket." But where the limb had scraped his recently healed forehead, it was starting to sting. He touched it and felt a wet stickiness.

"Amigo, I am so sorry," Manny said. "Hey. Your head—it is bleeding."

"Oh, dear!" Maureen called out. She had apparently rushed to the rail when she heard the commotion. "Come inside and let me check you." She disappeared from the balcony.

When he got inside, Greg saw Ashleigh, standing beyond the foyer. Her long hair tumbled over her shoulders and her eyes were locked on him with an expression of gratitude. She was irresistibly feminine. His eyes traveled to her front, as always. He wondered if she noticed how he was always looking there. He took two steps toward her. "Are you okay?"

"I saw a shadow move," Ashleigh said. "Right outside my window."

"Apparently it was only a deer." Greg led her to the great room and sat down beside her at the table, rubbing his hands up and down her arms, then gently over her shoulders. He couldn't help himself. If Manny and Maureen hadn't been looking on he would have crushed the woman against his chest. This stalker ought to be shot. Damn the creep to hell. Who would frighten a pregnant woman this way?

"You're bleeding," Ashleigh said.

"I startled him and he ran into a limb." Maureen came up beside her, looking at Greg's bloody temple with concern. "I'll get the first aid kit."

The mere movement of stripping off his jacket hurt like hell. That limb must have been bigger than he thought.

Maureen came in and put the first aid kit on the table. "I feel awful. What was I thinking, slamming that door like that when you men were out there looking for a prowler?"

"No. It was my fault." Manny took off his hat and sat down on the bench opposite her.

"It wasn't anybody's fault," Greg said.

Maureen bit her lip.

"I'll take care of him, Mother." Ashleigh stepped around in front of Greg and bent forward, examining. "You'll have to take your shirt off, too. It looks like your shoulder's been cut."

Greg sat there, stripped to the waist, facing Ashleigh's magnificent belly again, smelling her wondrous in-a-nightgown-at-midnight smell, while she dabbed antiseptic on his flesh wounds.

"Oh, sorry," she cried and Greg realized he was clenching his jaw.

"It doesn't hurt that much," he said.

"Then relax. I'm almost done."

He couldn't relax. Not when her full body, only inches from his face, begged to be touched. He turned his head to the side, craning his neck away, trying to lessen the impact of her presence, when out of the corner of his eye, he thought he saw a movement in her abdomen! "God!" he cried and snapped his head back, staring.

"What?" Ashleigh stopped with a cotton ball in midair. "Did I hurt you?"

"No." He looked up into her face, then straight at her belly again.

"Then what's the matter?"

"It…the baby." He swallowed. "It just moved." Involuntarily his fingers came up, poised over the area where he'd seen it.

"Yes," she chuckled, every bit the serene Madonna. "There's a baby in there, and from time to time, the little creature moves."

"No." Greg frowned at her. "I mean it *really* moved. It looks huge! How can you stand that?"

"It's not painful." She smiled. "Would you like to feel it?"

Ashleigh didn't know why she said that. Something about their pose already seemed so full of trust, so tender and close. So intimate.

Suddenly, she felt painfully aware of the other two people in the room. She glanced at her mother.

"Will you help me put on some hot chocolate?" Maureen said to Manny.

The old man looked puzzled, but he followed Maureen into the kitchen.

"Do you want to feel it?" Ashleigh repeated. Again, she couldn't imagine why she was trusting him like this. But something in his eyes looked almost…hungry. There was no other word for it. Hungry to feel this baby.

"Yes," he croaked.

"Go ahead." She held her hands aloft, one holding a gauze dressing and one holding a tube of antibiotic ointment, giving him a moment of trusting access to her front.

Greg looked up into her eyes, then gingerly, reverently, he framed his palms on her. They felt surprisingly warm through the flannel fabric and suddenly the whole moment felt slightly forbidden. Ashleigh was suddenly aware that she was in her nightie, albeit a matronly one, standing right in front of this man, with her abdomen practically pressed against his face. And him with no shirt on, his muscles flexing with apparent restraint.

With his hands on her, they waited for the baby to do something. Ashleigh felt strangely solemn, looking into Greg's eyes.

"Oh, God," Greg breathed as her baby's tiny body flexed. "It moved!" he exclaimed in disbelief, in awe. Beneath his gentle hands, the baby rolled, powerfully, like a young animal, testing its muscles, testing its bounds.

Ashleigh looked down into his eyes. "Yes." Beneath the muscles of his chest, she could actually see Greg's heart pounding.

Some seconds ticked by while Greg kept his hands where they were and his eyes locked with hers. She was certain something unspoken passed between them as Greg pressed his hands more firmly into her flesh, scrunching the gown up ever so lightly. Her arms came down and she rested the butts of her full hands on the thick muscles that tapered from his neck to his back. She leaned into him with her mouth slightly open. Their breath mingled for one instant and then abruptly, they turned away from each other.

In the same instant he dropped his hands, balling them into fists on his knees.

What the heck was that? Ashleigh thought. There was some undercurrent here that she didn't understand. She cleared her throat.

"Would anyone like some hot cocoa?" Maureen said a little too loudly as she and Manny came back into the room.

"No," Greg said. "I think we'd better go."

Quickly Ashleigh finished applying the dressing. She wondered if Greg could feel her fingers trembling.

Not in a million years would she have ever

guessed she could have these feelings again. And while she was pregnant! She wished she'd never let him touch her like that.

But it was too late. Now Greg Glazier had looked in her eyes and seen it plainly. Desire. Pure, undiluted, burning desire. For him.

MAUREEN AND ASHLEIGH STOOD at the front door of the cabin and watched as Greg and Manny faded into the darkness, walking down the rocky drive toward the road.

Greg turned and looked back once.

Ashleigh closed the door and avoided her mother's face. When Greg Glazier had looked into her eyes with his hands on her like that, she'd felt...well, she wasn't real sure what she'd felt, but it was the strangest, strongest feeling she'd had in a long, long time. It went way beyond mere physical attraction or infatuation. A pregnant woman had no business feeling this way about any man other than the father of her baby. She simply *had* to get a grip on herself.

CHAPTER THIRTEEN

A FEW DAYS LATER, MANNY'S old wall phone jangled loud enough to wake the dead. Greg dived into the back door and snatched it up, breathless, for the millionth time cursing the fact that cell phones did not work in most parts of these mountains and that Manny was too frugal and too old-fashioned to own a portable unit.

"Yes?"

"Greg, it's Ashleigh. Come up here quick."

"What's happened?" He gripped the phone. Before he went charging up the mountain, he had to know how to prepare. "Tell me!"

"It's my father, he's had a massive heart attack."

Thankfully, Greg had retrieved his vehicle from Taos the day before. When he got to the cabin, Ashleigh answered the door, noticeably shaken. "We just got off the phone again," she told him, leading the way to the great room. In there, Maureen sat perched on the edge of one of the leather couches, obviously in a state of shock, dabbing a tissue at her eyes.

"It's bad," Ashleigh told Greg. "Daddy's in the

ICU at the Mile High Medical Center. He's going to have to have open heart surgery right away.

"My sister Megan is with him." Ashleigh looked like she'd been crying, too. "We're waiting to hear when the surgery will happen."

Greg reached out to run a reassuring hand up and down her arm and was relieved when she allowed it. Her skin was soft as silk but felt chilled. "Let's sit down," he said, wanting to enfold Ashleigh in his arms and warm her.

Greg spent some time reassuring the women as best he could, not sure what he was called upon to do here. This was something he couldn't fix. But he did know one thing. It was no good for Ashleigh to be upset like this. All he could do for now was listen, and be grateful that Ashleigh had thought of him in her time of need.

Ashleigh told Greg that her father had never had heart trouble before, but he had led a stressful lifestyle. He smoked and he drank too much alcohol, but he was getting the best of medical care.

"I told mother she has to go to him immediately," Ashleigh explained. "That I'll be fine here. He's her first priority now."

"How can I leave you here alone!" Maureen protested. "Unless…" She looked up at Greg over her soggy tissue. "Ashleigh, could you get me something for this headache, please?"

Ashleigh got up and started for the kitchen. "I

need the Tylenol, dear. Upstairs in my overnight bag.''

As soon as Ashleigh ascended the stairs, Maureen turned to Greg.

''Greg, I must get to my husband as soon as possible.''

''I agree. How can I help?''

''I have an idea. Ashleigh already thinks you've been hired to watch over her. Why don't you come up here and stay in the cabin with her?''

''I don't know, Maureen. Do you think she'd go for that?''

''I think she trusts you. She's certainly had enough time to observe you from a distance. I even caught her up on the balcony, watching you with binoculars the other day.''

''Watching me?''

''You were out working the fence line with Manny. She seemed very intent on your every movement.''

A strange electrifying thrill shot through Greg at the idea of Ashleigh covertly observing him with the binoculars.

''Listen to me.'' Maureen seemed to sense that she no longer had his full attention. ''I would feel so much better with someone right here in the cabin, not just down the road.'' She gave him a pleading look. ''You've got that gun—and it will come in handy now. You understand that I must go to my husband.''

Greg nodded.

"If we both present this to Ashleigh, she'll accept the idea."

Maureen fretted for a moment, wringing the tissue. "We can say Marvin wanted you to come into town undercover at first because he didn't trust the local cops, but you've checked them out and we have their full cooperation. Oh, I don't *know*. It's not like Marvin will contradict what we say, anyway. After all he's—" She broke off and pressed the tissue to her mouth.

Greg felt sorry for her, but even so, he couldn't help giving his head an incredulous shake. "We're making this too complicated, don't you think? Why don't we just tell Ashleigh the truth now?"

"Now? When's she's already so upset about her father?"

"Maureen, I don't know how long I can keep up this charade."

"Oh, for heaven's sake! Do you want to help her or not?"

Of course he wanted to. He'd do anything that put him in closer proximity to Ashleigh. And she did need him now—more than ever.

"If you do it my way, I can go to my husband immediately, without waiting until I find someone to take care of Ashleigh. And we won't have to come right out and tell her the awful truth about the baby. We can hold off until she gets past thirty-seven weeks."

"The awful truth?" Greg made a face. Here he had thought Maureen was starting to like him.

"You know what I mean. The shocking truth. Promise me you won't tell her yet. She's too fragile. She's had too many setbacks. Now there's this horrible news about her father—" Maureen pressed the tissue to her mouth again.

"I won't tell her," Greg promised. He couldn't make himself the cause of any more of Maureen's grief.

"Good." She sniffed. "Then I'll tell her that you've agreed to stay here and watch out for her and that Marvin will give you a big bonus for your trouble later. You can stay in that upstairs bedroom where you stayed before." Maureen looked sideways, distracted, as if she were trying to think of everything at once. "Thank God you have an all-terrain vehicle. And a gun. Lord. Who knows how long I'll need to be with Marvin. I better start making my plane reservations now. Can you come and stay tonight, if necessary?"

Greg listened while Maureen rattled on, but when the real implications of her proposal began to sink in, he interrupted. "Stay the night? You want me to stay right here in the cabin, alone with her? Tonight?"

"Why, of course. She needs help, and protection. She's still not supposed to be on her feet too much. She can't do the laundry and the cooking and the grocery shopping. Besides, she would be terribly frightened up here in this big isolated cabin all by herself, even for one night. Ashleigh is a city girl.''

"Can't you hire a lady or something? Someone from the clinic, perhaps? One of the midwives, maybe?''

"Greg, I would think you'd jump at this chance. The more she knows about you, the easier it will be for Ashleigh to accept the truth later on. Besides, as I said, she trusts you. I know my daughter.''

Greg was trying to picture this scenario—the two of them alone up here—and the images in his mind made him swallow hard. "You honestly think she'll agree to this?''

"Ashleigh's father does controlling things like this all the time. He's always hiring people to get things done for me—it's a way of making up for his constant absences. It's a habit that infuriates Ashleigh. You'll have to be convincing, though, and keep acting like a bodyguard. But you can do it. I trust you, Greg.'' She patted his arm, the way a mother would encourage a favored son. "I trust you to keep Ashleigh safe. That's because I know what this baby means to you.''

Greg nodded, turning his thoughts from Ashleigh, and thinking about his child. Surely he could stay up here with Ashleigh and ignore how attractive she was, if it meant keeping his baby safe. At least he could do it until the baby came.

"Mother.''

They jumped at the sound of Ashleigh's voice.

She had come out and was looking down at them from the upstairs walkway. "I'm sorry. I can't find your Tylenol."

"It's okay, dear." Maureen kept her poise. "I'm coming up there."

She turned to Greg and said under her breath, "Are we in agreement, then?"

He gave a tight nod.

Maureen went upstairs to pack her things and tell Ashleigh their newest lie.

SIMON FISCHER CONGRATULATED himself on his excellent detective work. Sometimes all one had to do was read the papers with an eagle eye. Every day Simon checked the *Denver Post* online at the library. He used the same key words every day: Logan, Ashleigh; McGuinness, Marvin; All About Babies.

So. Ashleigh Logan's big-shot father had had a heart attack. Avidly, Simon read the entire article, top to bottom. It was apparently a slow news day because the reporter had dug for facts to fill every column inch. Which was good for Simon. He could practically smell something buried in this piece. Something useful. And here was something: Marvin McGuinness's daughter, Megan, was the only person permitted to see the Denver entrepreneur at the hospital. He kept on reading. The daughter refused to comment to the press on her father's condition. His wife, Maureen, an anonymous nurse was quoted as saying, was expected to fly in from Santa Fe, New Mexico, later that night.

Would Ashleigh be left alone in Enchantment? That would be almost too good to be true.

GREG RETURNED TO THE CABIN later that day with his things. Maureen had already taken off in the rental Suburban to catch a small connecting plane in Santa Fe.

Ashleigh greeted him at the door of the cabin. With a big smile, she said, "This should be interesting. Where is your gun?"

"Right here." Greg rattled the lockbox.

Maureen had been right about one thing. It was going to be up to Greg to put on a good act.

Greg put his things back in the room he'd occupied when he'd been blinded. He stood out on the walkway, satisfied that he could see the door to the master suite from up there. And then the two of them settled in for a strange afternoon.

"Well, here we are," Ashleigh chirped as she sat and put her feet up on one of the leather couches.

"Yeah. Here we are." Greg noticed that she'd dressed in real clothes for once. A pair of skinny little black leggings and tiny black flats revealed feet that were still delicate and legs that were still pixie trim. Her big red fleece maternity sweater looked new…and it dipped to a subtle vee over her womanly cleavage. Her glasses were gone. She'd washed her hair and blown it out to flow over her shoulders, straight and shiny. She was wearing makeup, which she could apparently apply like an expert. Part of her TV-personality package, he supposed.

The gussying up made him tense. He liked her better in her ratty pink robe and faded red house slippers. At least then he wasn't reminded of how incredibly beautiful she was, pregnant or not.

"I hope this setup doesn't make you uncomfortable," he said sincerely, because the situation sure as hell made *him* uncomfortable.

"I'm all right. Apparently, my father trusts you."

"I'll try to respect your privacy."

"No problem. You're in your part of the house. I'm in mine."

Another beat passed and Greg let his eyes travel around the room as if he'd never been here before. He'd never noticed what an exotic, sensual setting this was. The massive fireplace sat cold today. And it would stay that way, he decided.

"So." Ashleigh's voice startled him. "Can I get you something to drink?"

"No. I'm supposed to take care of you, remember?"

"Oh, yeah." She looked him up and down. "The bodyguard."

Greg was certain her smoky voice had carried an underlying note that said, *I don't believe it for a minute.* He wished to hell they could just have it out, right now. Get the cards on the table. But then he had a vision of Ashleigh running, hysterical and crying, to the master suite. Slamming the door. Sobbing her heart out. Going into premature labor. Delivering a damaged baby...

He snatched up the remote. "Let's see what's on." He focused his eyes on the big screen.

"Yes. Let's."

They watched TV. They ate soup and sandwiches. And after dark, they admired the reflection of the outside lights on the newly fallen snow. Greg stood at the high windows with her, four feet away, with his hands jammed in his pockets.

Somehow, they made it through the first day without touching. That evening, she spent a lot of time on the phone with her mother and sister, getting updates on her father's condition.

Greg felt conflicted about the fact that Ashleigh absolutely refused to let him assist her with any personal tasks. It made it easier on his libido, but as the days went by, he worried that he wasn't doing enough to help her. What if she needed him in the night? What if she slipped in the shower or something? A dozen times a day, he'd have a pulse-pounding false alarm, thinking he'd heard the damned cowbell.

Before the first week was out, the tension erupted into a silly argument about her going up and down the short flight of stairs to the long mudroom where the washer and dryer were. He was washing the breakfast dishes and, out of the corner of his eye, saw her floating by with the empty laundry basket propped against her side.

"Where do you think you're going?"

"To the mudroom to get my *underwear*."

"Your underwear? I didn't put in a load of underwear." Greg had been congratulating himself for at least keeping up with the laundry pretty well since he'd arrived, or so he thought. Now, he realized he hadn't seen any of her underwear among the clothes.

"I know you didn't. I did. I don't want *you* washing my underwear."

"And I don't want *you* going up and down those stairs."

"Oh, for crying out loud! It's six little steps."

"Ashleigh. I'm supposed to take care of you." They had been going round and round like this for days. Greg felt as if he was walking a tightrope between keeping this willful woman safe, and keeping his raging hormones tamped down. It didn't help that every time he tried to do something for her, Ashleigh treated him like an overbearing barbarian.

"My father hired you to pack a gun and patrol the grounds," Ashleigh said in her typically blunt way, "not to wash and dry my anti-man panties."

Greg had to grin. "Your *anti-man* panties?"

Ashleigh blushed at her verbal slip, but her attitude was cheeky. "Yeah, that's what my sister and I call them. They're anti-man, all right." She bit her lip and tossed her ponytail like a tough girl. "Maternity panties are the best birth control on earth, it's just that, unfortunately for some women, they're a few months too late. I sure don't want some *man* looking at them.''

Greg laughed out loud. Ashleigh was such a case. ''What if I promise not to look at them? What if I just scoop them out of the dryer and throw them in the basket and scurry up the stairs with my eyes closed?''

''*What?* Then *you'd* have another accident.''

''Come on, Ashleigh. Stay away from the stairs.''

''Oh, stop it.'' Ashleigh tossed him an ornery grin as she defied him and headed down the stairs.

No sooner had she gone around the corner than Greg heard her give a yelp. Followed by a sickening series of bumps.

His heart pounded in terror as he ran to the doorway. He leaped down the six steps to Ashleigh, who was on her side, pushing herself up on one arm, with her legs twisted under her.

''Dammit!'' he said, grabbing at her with his wet, soapy hands. ''Are you all right?''

''I guess I slipped on a step. But I…I caught myself on the rail.''

''Dammit to hell!''

''Will you please stop cursing? The baby will hear you.''

He was running his hands all over her, returning his palms to a circular pattern over her abdomen on each pass. ''Does anything hurt?''

''Nothing but my pride.'' But her flippant attitude

didn't fool Greg, because when he touched her lower leg, Ashleigh's breath caught and she winced.

"What's wrong?" he said.

"My ankle." She bit her lip. Straining, she turned herself to sit squarely on her buttocks with her legs straight out in front of her. "I think I came down on it pretty hard."

He ran his hands lightly down each of her legs. "This one?"

She winced again. "Yes."

ASHLEIGH WAS MORTIFIED as Greg carried her back up those steps. He took her to the bedroom and laid her on the bed. He put her ankle up on a pillow and arranged two more behind her back.

"Lie still," he said, and left.

Ashleigh's ankle was truly starting to hurt and she was so mad at herself she wanted to pop. She should have let him help her wash her underwear. She should have let him help her all along, instead of being so proud and stubborn about everything. Tears stung her eyes as fear gripped her. Had she harmed Chad's baby?

Greg came back in with a plastic bag of ice. He wrapped it in a hand towel from the bathroom and gently positioned it around her ankle. When he glanced up at her, his eyes softened with pity. He knelt next to the bed, facing her, and stroked her hair back from her face. His touch sent a wave of longing through her so strong that it pulled her eyes closed.

"Now, listen. Don't cry," he said, misreading her emotions. "We're going to get you checked out right away."

He went to the closet and came back with some loose warm clothes and a pair of huge yellow sweats. Ashleigh allowed him to help her get the bulky robe out from under her hips. The thin cotton gown underneath did nothing to conceal her lush curves, her large, dark nipples. "Where are your bras and panties?" he said with absolutely no hint of embarrassment. "All down in the dryer?"

"There." She pointed to the bureau drawer, finding that her own embarrassment was so acute she could hardly speak.

He came back with the underthings. Without asking, he looped the panties over each leg and inched them to knee level under the gown. "Can you get these the rest of the way up?"

She nodded, feeling her cheeks flame.

He laid her functional cotton—and *huge*—bra beside her on the bed. "Holler if you need help. I'll be right outside the door."

She struggled to get out of the gown—in addition to her injured ankle, one shoulder felt a little sore— and then into the bra and panties. The sweats, unfortunately, were across the room on the chair. She pulled her gown over her front and called out, "Greg?"

He came in immediately.

"I need my clothes," she said.

He crossed the room, snatched the sweats up and turned, eyeing the thin gown clutched to her front.

"Ashleigh, let's be honest, okay? I know I'm a man. I know you're a woman. You know it, too. But we've got an emergency here. Think of the baby, sweetheart."

Sweetheart? Was it her nakedness that encouraged such sudden familiarity? But she found the endearment comforted her, made her relax and believe that he would never hurt her, or even so much as embarrass her if he could help it.

She remembered taking care of Chad when he was sick, recalled the tenderness and love, and how unimportant little vanities seemed during those times. Ashleigh dropped the gown and let him assist her into the sweats. He put one athletic shoe on her uninjured foot and tied the laces with the briskness of a daddy getting a little girl dressed for school. "Okay, let's go." He clutched the ice bag in his fingers and scooped her up in his arms again, and this time she had calmed enough to appreciate the ease with which he did it. Even her enormous girth was no match for his strength.

He stopped at the front door, lowering her gently to the rough-hewn bench there. He snapped her coat off the hook and helped her wiggle her arms into the sleeves.

"Stay here," he commanded, and Ashleigh

wouldn't have moved off that bench for anything. She sat with her palms on her front, praying for the baby to kick. *Just one kick, little one. Please. Tell your mommy you're okay.*

Greg pulled the Navigator right up to the front door, scooped her up again and loaded her gently into the vehicle, positioning the ice pack on her ankle. Then off they went down Switchback Road to Arroyo County Hospital.

CHAPTER FOURTEEN

DR. OCHOA TOLD THEM everything was fine. This news brought a fresh spate of tears to Ashleigh's eyes and a fresh spate of comforting from Greg.

He had stood right by the exam table the whole time, squeezing Ashleigh's hand when the nurse picked up a heartbeat with the Doppler, stroking her forehead while Dr. Ochoa was examining her. When the doctor pronounced Ashleigh and the baby's health sound—except for Ashleigh's mildly sprained ankle—Greg had given Ashleigh a glad hug without bothering to wonder what the doctor might think of them.

Dr. Ochoa kept his face perfectly neutral while he made a note on Ashleigh's chart. "So, Greg. I take it your vision is back to normal these days?"

"Yes. It's fine, thanks." Greg was blinking back tears of relief.

"I still want you to see the ophthalmologist in Albuquerque."

"I promise I'll do that, just as soon as I can. Right now, I can't leave Enchantment."

"I understand." But the look Ochoa gave Greg said he didn't, exactly.

"It's going to be awkward getting around on that ankle for a few days." The doctor turned his attention to Ashleigh. "I don't want any weight-bearing on that leg. Should we see about hiring you some help?"

Greg looked at Ashleigh expectantly, communicating his desire to do whatever she asked.

"No. I'll be fine. Greg can take care of me." When Ochoa frowned, she elaborated. "Besides being an old family friend, Greg was hired by my father to be my bodyguard," Ashleigh explained, as if hiring bodyguards was an everyday occurrence. The overly casual way she said it made Greg think, again, that Ashleigh had her suspicions about this whole setup he and Maureen had cooked up. And he wondered, again, why Ashleigh never voiced those suspicions.

Ochoa gave Greg a last skeptical look, which Ashleigh did not see. Greg only hoped the doctor wouldn't share this bizarre story with anyone in town, but he wasn't too optimistic. His days at the Morning Light had convinced Greg that a person couldn't so much as take a poot in this town without everybody else knowing about it.

ASHLEIGH'S TWISTED ANKLE required that Greg help her constantly. The hospital had dispensed crutches, but in her condition, they proved useless. Worse than useless, because in Greg's opinion, with the cabin's multiple floor levels and many area rugs, crutches were downright dangerous. So he helped Ashleigh get out of bed, go to the bathroom, get seated at the table, get settled on the couch.

He didn't mind the nursemaid duty—he had been Kendra's chief caregiver in her final days—but having his hands on Ashleigh's soft, healthy body all day, every day, was driving him wild. Even watching her lean forward while he propped an extra pillow behind her back was a torment. Her cleavage had become more and more lush as the pregnancy progressed, totally feminine. Would she breast-feed the baby? Did he have a right to ask? Of course he had the right! But Ashleigh didn't know that.

The midwife had loaned Ashleigh some educational tapes about breastfeeding, delivery and such. He hoped the tapes might provide a way for him to broach the topic, but Ashleigh refused to watch them while Greg was around.

Her guarded responses about her pregnancy frustrated him. If he was going to have anything to say about his child's beginnings, he would have to tell Ashleigh the truth soon. He wished to hell he hadn't promised Maureen he would wait.

One morning after breakfast, she put a tape in the player. That was her favorite trick—to watch the videos while he cleaned up the kitchen. He'd had enough of this. He quickly threw the dishes in the water to soak and went out into the great room. She hit the stop button on the remote the minute he came in.

"I think I should watch the tapes about delivery, too, don't you?"

"Why?"

"What if something happens, and you go into labor? Shouldn't I be prepared?"

"Suit yourself." She hit the start button.

Greg's eyes bugged at what he saw. It seemed like a little foal slipped into the world a lot more smoothly. This tape showed a woman panting, near exhaustion, pushing until her face was beet red. Really...suffering. Could he actually help Ashleigh do *this?*

When they finished watching the tape, Greg went to clean up the breakfast dishes and contemplate his inadequacies.

"I guess I'll need a little help...you know, getting into the shower." Ashleigh was standing propped against the kitchen door frame, with pink cheeks and hair that badly needed a shampooing. She still hated it every time she had to ask him for personal help.

"What are you doing, walking around without my help?" Greg dropped his dish towel and rushed to her side. "You're supposed to use the cowbell when you need me."

"I'm so sick of this whole routine," she moaned. "I feel so helpless."

"You are helpless." He looped her slender arm up over his shoulder. They were getting so used to the feel of each other's bodies that they didn't even hesitate when they touched. "You're big and pregnant with a sprained ankle. Besides, I like taking care of you. It's no trouble.''

"Of course it is. You didn't hire on to keep house and haul me around all day.''

"I said I don't mind.'' His eyes locked with hers, and it took all of his willpower not to tell her why. "Let's get you in the shower.''

Fortunately, Ashleigh's mother had already ordered a shower stool for her, back when their biggest worry was preterm labor. Greg would assist Ashleigh down onto the stool, still clothed, then he'd make sure the towels and her pink terry-cloth robe were within easy reach. After he closed the door, Ashleigh would undress, awkwardly, and toss her oversize T-shirt, socks, undies and sweatpants in a heap outside the shower. Later, when she was wrapped in her robe, he'd come back in and help her to the bedroom where he had her clean clothes waiting on the bed.

Then they'd trade spaces, as it were, and Greg would go clean up in the bathroom, with the door closed, while Ashleigh sat on the bed and got dressed.

But on this morning, something went wrong. The hot water, always iffy, abruptly turned frigid while Ashleigh had her hair lathered with shampoo. The sudden blast of cold water made her shriek.

Greg came charging through the door and was confronted by her full profile through the fogged shower glass. She had her arms up, grasping, unsuccessfully, for the faucet controls high above her head.

"Are you okay?" He jerked the shower door open and stopped the water.

"Greg!" Her arms slapped down over her front and she bent forward, trying to cover herself, but there was way too much of her for that. "Get out of here!"

"Are you okay?" he demanded. He snatched a towel off the bar and threw it over her.

"Yes."

"I thought you'd gotten burned by the hot water or something."

"H-hardly! There was no hot water!" Now he finally realized that she was shivering.

"Let's get you dry." He reached for the other towel.

"I'm *fine*," she said emphatically. "Now, please just g-get *out*."

Two minutes later she emerged, supporting her weight on the doorknob, wrapped in the robe and a head towel, looking thoroughly chilled. "G-got r-rinsed off o-okay," she said. But her teeth were actually chattering.

He rushed to her and wrapped an arm around her waist as he led her to the bed. It was a halting trip, with Ashleigh limping and leaning heavily on him. Greg threw back the covers and helped her get under them.

Her body was trembling so hard that he pushed

the covers up around her in a tight cocoon. Still, she shook and shivered. It was painful to watch.

Compassion, he told himself, was what drove him to climb into the bed behind her and spoon his body tightly around hers.

"Oh, th-thank you," she whispered as he wrapped his warm arms gently but firmly over her quivering middle. "Th-that feels so good."

He closed his eyes and tightened his hold, wanting to tell her that he'd do anything to make her feel good. Anything.

"Well, I guess you d-done gone and seen me nek-kid," she said, attempting one of her little jokes.

He squeezed her tighter.

Then the baby kicked, soundly, and Greg's eyes flew open in shock. "Did you feel that?" he breathed.

"Of course I did, silly. I guess this little guy doesn't like being ch-chilled, either."

"Little guy?"

"Yes. I'm having a boy." Ashleigh drew in a huge breath. When she released it, her shivers seemed to subside completely and her body relaxed. "Dr. Ochoa wanted me to have another ultrasound before I made the final decision to have a home birth. Dr. Hill—my OB in Denver?—he wasn't too crazy about that idea and they wanted to make sure everything looked normal. If I could possibly avoid it, I didn't want to risk a hospital admission or even going to The Birth Place, where the stalker might find us through computer records or something. I'll feel a lot safer if I can keep the baby hidden away up here until they catch that creep.''

"It's a *boy?*" Greg bit his lip, the secret he held in his heart almost too much to bear.

"Yes. Isn't that great? I hope he looks exactly like Chad."

At that, Greg bit his lip harder and made a small strangled sound, tipping his head forward until his forehead touched the back of her hair.

"What's wrong?" Ashleigh's voice was suddenly concerned.

"I just...I'm glad you're okay, that's all. I thought you fell again, when I heard you yelling in the shower just now. I thought...when I saw you at the bottom of those stairs—" He choked off his words, his half lies, and let the emotions come. The baby was not going to look like Chad. The baby, a *son,* might even look like him, like Greg.

"I'm okay. I just got a little chilled, that's all."

When he didn't respond, Ashleigh twisted around to peer into his face. "Greg? Did you hear me? I said I'm okay."

He kept his head down, feeling as if his emotions were spinning out of control.

She twisted more to get an even better look at him. "Are you choking up or something? What's wrong?" She sounded alarmed.

He *did* have tears in his eyes, but not for the reason she thought—that her fall had scared him.

"Nothing," he sputtered. Her fall *had* scared him, and with a fresh jolt of emotion he realized it was because he loved her, and couldn't let anything happen to her, not only because of the baby that was inside of her, but because she was Ashleigh, the woman he loved.

In his mind, it seemed as if Ashleigh and the baby were one now. Maybe they always would be one to him—his *family*. How the hell did some men ever let themselves get divorced? He couldn't imagine it, and he wasn't even married to this woman yet. All he wanted to do was protect her, make sure she and the baby were happy and safe. He wanted to hold her and...how in the hell would a man continue to protect his family if he was the head of a broken home?

"I'm just glad nothing bad happened when you fell, to you, or to our baby."

He felt her body go extremely still. "*Our* baby?"

His heart kicked once, then raced with fear at his mistake. "I meant...I meant *your* baby."

But Ashleigh was not so easily deflected. "Why would you say that? *Our* baby?"

Silence.

"Greg, you're not...are you getting attached here?"

More silence.

"You know," Ashleigh persisted, "to this baby...to me?"

He rose up and propped his head on the butt of

one hand so he could look into her eyes. "How could I not be attached to the two of you?" he murmured. "Being with you, taking care of you like this, day after day?"

She relaxed her head back against the pillow and let him hover over her, let their eyes speak to each other, heart to heart, soul to soul. "Oh, Greg," she breathed. "I knew it."

"Could I feel it—*him*—again?" Greg asked.

She smiled and nodded.

He placed a palm beneath the covers so he could touch her abdomen, but stayed on the outside of her robe so her privacy wouldn't be transgressed. He closed his eyes as he let himself touch her belly, intentionally, for the second time.

When the baby finally kicked again, they both smiled, and then grew solemn as the same wave of intimacy passed over them that had engulfed them that first time.

"This is so weird," she whispered, turning her face up to his again. "I don't feel strange at all, letting you touch me this way, having your hands on me."

Slowly, with the full gravity of his intentions, Greg ran one hand under the robe and over her belly as he dropped the other to loosen the towel and lace his fingers into her golden hair, something he had longed to do when he'd first admired it. "Do you wish these were Chad's hands...touching you now?" He had to know.

Ashleigh shook her head slowly. "No. I mean, of course, I wish Chad had never died. But I can't change that. And if feels so right for *you* to touch me. You're the man who's been taking such good care of me these past few weeks. I honestly couldn't imagine anyone else touching me right now."

Greg crushed a handful of her tangled wet hair as a powerful wave of desire sluiced through him. Their mouths drew closer. An inch, maybe two, and their lips would be touching. "Ashleigh," he whispered, his voice grown strangely hoarse. He swallowed. "I have to tell you something."

"Okay." She lay looking up at him, wide-eyed. Innocent, and totally honest. Could he really tell her the awful truth now?

Maybe he should deal with this on a first-things-first basis. After all, the mix-up at the sperm bank wasn't the most important thing anymore, at least not to him. The most important thing was that they'd found each other, even if it had been in a mixed-up, crazy way. Even if they went on through the rest of their lives with Ashleigh thinking that the baby was Chad's, he wouldn't care.

"Don't freak out, okay? I mean I know you've got a lot on your mind, but I just can't keep this inside of me any longer. Ashleigh, I'm…I think I'm falling in love with you."

She sucked in a little surprised breath, then threw her arms around his neck, urging him to press his torso across her lush body, and then she found his mouth.

Their kiss was not like a first kiss, not tentative, not exploratory, not awkwardly seeking for an initial fit.

It was the deep, connected kiss of ripened lust, of wild hunger finally turned loose.

She twined her arms even tighter around his neck, and he worked the fingers of one hand into her damp hair, grasping her head, turning it to accommodate his will, while with the other hand he grabbed her upper arm, forcing it higher and tighter around him.

To deepen the kiss any further would have been like melding them into one being, but still they tried.

Greg used his tongue the way he knew she wanted him to. She opened to him, drew him into her mouth eagerly—a promise of more.

With his mouth still fastened on hers, he released her arm and traveled down the length of her body, running his palm over her ample flesh possessively, no longer seeking with a reverent, privileged touch in order to feel a tiny baby's kick. But claiming now. Fondling with caresses that said, I want *this*. And *this*. And *this*.

Finally, they broke the kiss and looked into each other's eyes. Both surprised. Both on fire.

"Ashleigh…" He was breathing hard. "We'd better stop. I don't want to hurt you."

"Hurt me?" Ashleigh was as breathless as he was. "I haven't felt this wonderful in months. No, in years! I don't know if I've *ever* felt this good. I can hardly stand it! My God, Greg. Don't you see? I'm in love with you, too!'' She feathered her fingers through his hair at the temples. ''When I first saw you, I knew. It was like I recognized you or something. I thought you were so beautiful that I couldn't stop looking at you.''

He smiled. No one had ever called him beautiful. Kendra had said *cute* in high school. *Handsome,* when he became a man. But never *beautiful.* Thinking of Ashleigh secretly admiring his looks when he hadn't been able to see her doing it, made his heart feel strangely light.

''Oh, my gosh!'' Ashleigh slapped her forehead as if something unbelievable had dawned on her. ''I've fallen in love,'' she practically shrieked at the ceiling, ''with my bodyguard!''

He chuckled. ''Let me hold you, you silly woman. Let me hold you the way I want to…at last.''

He did. And after he'd held her for a while, after they'd marveled that they'd found each other, after they'd blessed their good fortune, Greg said it was time to get Ashleigh out of the damp robe and towels.

The level of intimacy between them seemed totally altered now. When he fetched the blow dryer and dried her hair, as he'd done before when she was too worn out from limping around all day, it felt more like languid lovemaking than a dutiful ministration. Now she understood the meaning of his touches, which had always felt more tender, more seeking, than they should have. Now she understood why.

She let him touch her that way the whole day. On the couch he hauled her legs up onto his lap. He rubbed her feet. He hooked a hand in her inner thigh. He laced his fingers in hers. And he kissed her. Over and over.

That evening, that very evening, Greg brought up the subject of marriage.

"We need to discuss something," he told Ashleigh as he set a bowl of chili onto the place mat in front of her. Next to it he had arranged crackers, carrot sticks, fruit and a glass of milk.

Ravenously hungry as always, Ashleigh grabbed her spoon and started eating before he had even seated himself. *"Yum,"* she said after the first heaping bite. "This is fabulous chili, Greg."

"Let's hope it doesn't give you heartburn."

"I'll take my chances." She took a quick gulp of milk. "What do you want to talk about?"

"I don't want to stop taking care of you once the baby comes."

That brought Ashleigh up short, with a spoonful of chili halfway to her mouth. "You mean you want to stay on with me, here." Even as she said this, she was wondering if instead he meant what she hoped he meant. "You mean as long as I'm still in hiding up here in the cabin?"

"No. I mean I want go back to Denver with you."

She put the spoon back in the bowl. "But..." She still wasn't sure what he was asking, exactly, though her heart had started to beat erratically with an irrational hope. "We don't...we don't really know each other well enough to commit to anything, to live together...or anything like that."

"I'm not talking about living together. I want to get married, if you'll have me."

When her jaw dropped at that, he added, "The baby deserves a father."

"Oh, Greg." His proposal had taken the breath out of her. She didn't know what to say. Although those were the very words she longed to hear, she wasn't sure she liked his reasons. She couldn't let him marry her in a hurry just for the baby's sake. She wanted their union to be about the two of them, and only about the two of them.

"That's so wonderful of you, but this isn't your baby. It's not your responsibility. You don't have to marry me just because of the baby." She grabbed a carrot stick, a distraction.

"I would want to. I want to take responsibility for this baby."

"That's really sweet of you, Greg. But it might make more sense if we let the baby get a little older, let me get back on my feet, then we can see where our relationship is going, all in good time." She picked up her spoon and scooped up another spoonful of chili, trying to get the conversation back on a rational track.

Only then, did she notice that he was not eating his supper. "Greg, what's wrong?"

For a long moment he sat looking down, with his hands bracketed on either side of his bowl of chili. Then he drew a huge breath and raised his eyes to hers. Very quietly he said, "Ashleigh, listen to me. This *is* my baby."

CHAPTER FIFTEEN

AT FIRST ASHLEIGH WASN'T sure she'd heard Greg right. But then she realized that, of course, he was speaking metaphorically. "I know you *feel* like it's your baby, Greg, but the truth is—"

"No." His interruption was harsh, like a slap intended to wake her up. "The truth is, *I* am this baby's father, not Chad."

She swallowed and, with a shaky hand, put her spoon down.

"I love you, Greg, and I know what you are trying to do," she tried again in a low voice. "And that is the sweetest thing anyone has ever said to me. But you know very well where this baby came from. And you know very well that this is not your baby. We don't have to pretend otherwise. We're both grown-ups here."

"You're not hearing me." He swiveled his chair toward her, with his legs spread wide, forming a vee around the chair where she sat. He grabbed her hands, and the seriousness in his deep gray eyes scared her. "This *is*—" he flattened one warm palm on her front "—*my* baby. They made a terrible error at the sperm bank in California. My sperm got mixed up with your late husband's."

"*What?*" She jerked her fingers free from his and put her palms on her sides, protectively. She stared at him, shaking her head slowly in denial.

"I deposited my sperm before I had a vasectomy about five years ago, right at the same time Chad did. We used the same doctor in Denver. When the samples arrived in California, they got them confused. All of mine stayed at the main site and all of Chad's got transferred to the backup facility."

"*What?*" she repeated, and pushed his hand away from her.

"They discovered the error when they had a brownout at the main facility," he explained in a rush. "All of my sperm was defrosted, destroyed during the power outage. But all of Chad's survived in the backup storage. You could still have Chad's baby if you want to, but *this* child is *mine.*"

As he talked she tried to twist away from him, but he maintained his pose, with his strong thighs bracketing her. "It's complicated." He pressed his hands around her shoulders. "But I've verified that it's all true. I know it's not what you want, but—"

"Complicated? It's insane! I don't believe you!"

"Don't you see?" He squeezed her upper arms. "That's why I'm here. That's why I came to Enchantment. I wanted to tell you all along, from the very start, but your mother thought—"

"*My mother?*"

"Yes, Maureen didn't think you could stand the shock in your cond—"

"Mother knows about this?"

"She has, for a while. When I first came to town, I talked to her. I think that's why she invented the bodyguard story, why she took me in when I got hurt. I think she wanted us to get to know each other a little bit better, before…before you found out the truth."

Greg stared at Ashleigh as a horrible apprehension built in his chest. He was scared to death of what she might do now, of how she might view their relationship. And he was scared for the baby because Ashleigh was starting to tremble, and what if Maureen was right? What if the shock…he mentally calculated the weeks of her gestation. Thirty six. Would the baby be okay if Ashleigh went into labor now?

"Listen, Ashleigh." Fear made his words too forceful. "Please. I debated and debated about telling you this. But I don't want to start our relationship with a lie between us. And you've got to understand, I want to be part of this baby's life, from the very beginning."

Ashleigh stood. She stared at him in disbelief. This man was the father of her baby?

Greg stood, too, blocking her way as if he was afraid she was going to leave.

"Being my bodyguard—that was all an act?" Greg was starting to feel like a stranger to her.

"Yes. And no. I mean, I *have* been protecting you. I *want* to protect you. And the baby. And I can do that. I *have* been doing that. You know I'm a deputy sheriff. Calling me your bodyguard was your mother's idea."

Ashleigh turned away with her hand protectively cupping the baby. *Chad's* baby. She closed her eyes tight. "So, do you...do you really love me, or was that all an act, too?"

"No! Ash! Don't even think that!"

He reached for her, but she whirled away, immediately crying, "Ouch!" because she'd landed on her ankle.

"Sweetheart!" He grabbed her arm.

"Don't—touch—me!" She yanked away and braced one hand against the table. Of all the lies she might have suspected, this was never one. Greg Glazier. The father of her baby.

"You've got to let me help you," he insisted. "You can't walk. You can't bear weight on that ankle."

"That's very convenient, isn't it?" she hissed. "You waited until I was totally dependent on you, until we were alone up here, to unload your horrible news on me."

He drew back, hurt filling his eyes. "Horrible news? Is it such a horrible thing that you're having my baby? I mean, I could understand why you'd feel that way before we knew each other. But now...an hour ago you said you were so in love with me you could hardly stand it.''

"That was an hour ago, before I learned…'' She was beginning to feel numb. "I knew it was something. I suspected you and my mother were keeping something from me. I was embarrassed because I thought maybe she was just matchmaking again or something. But *this*. Oh, my God!'' Her voice rose. ''*This* is hideous!''

At those words Greg felt his whole body become still—frozen. Even his breathing grew shallow, deathly quiet. How could she think having his child was hideous? And how could she think his love was a lie? But he couldn't blame her. He *had* lied to her, and now he was paying the price.

"I…'' She sounded as if she was going to cry. "I want to go to my room now.''

She allowed him to help her limp back to the master suite. She told him to put a flannel gown on the bed, and then she made him leave her there, alone.

He sat down on one of the leather couches in the great room, staring at the walls of night-blackened glass, trying to sort it all out, getting nowhere. He needed her. He needed to talk to her, to have her tell him it was all going to be okay. That they were going to be okay. He needed her to make one of her flippant little jokes. But an hour later, when he finally went back to the master suite and listened at

the door, he heard the sounds of her sobbing beyond it.

He tapped softly on the wood. "Ashleigh?"

No answer.

"Won't you at least let me hold you?"

No answer.

"Are you okay, sweetheart?"

"I'm not having any signs of labor, if that's what
you mean." The answer snapped back at him like
the crack of a whip. "The baby—" her voice rose,
sounding almost hysterical to Greg "—*your* baby,
is not in any danger."

SIMON FISCHER WAS AMAZED at how easily he could
remain hidden. For weeks he had done nothing but
eat and loiter. From his favorite hiding places he
watched the town, the people, and especially the
clinic. Especially the clinic. That was the key. The
midwives made home visits in the surrounding
countryside. He remembered Ashleigh Logan's fascination with that when she had the midwives on
her show.

"How quaint!" she had cried. "How adorable
and cozy and quaint!"

The trouble was, the midwives came and went
from the clinic several times a day, going in all different directions. One man couldn't keep up with
them. How would he ever figure out which one was
visiting Ashleigh Logan?

Then the answer had hit him while he was thinking about the noisy comings and goings of the trucks
out on the winding highway that ran near the trailer

park. A white FedEx truck had gone through town and up into the mountains once. A brown UPS truck twice. That's when it had dawned on him. Wouldn't Ashleigh Logan be needing a lot of baby supplies? Wouldn't a spoiled woman who had oohed and aahed over every silly baby accessory made for today's materialistic young mothers want all those things for herself when her time came? Simon had seen the logic of it in the clarity of a sugar rush after his third doughnut. Today, when the delivery guy came out of the bank, Simon was going to follow the big brown truck straight, he suspected, to Ashleigh Logan's hideout.

Simon did not tolerate frustration well. He understood that about himself. While he waited in the early morning frost, he stuffed a second gooey bear claw in his mouth, but felt little relief from the gnawing emptiness that chronically plagued him. Weren't these UPS guys supposed to be quick? The man in brown had been in that little bank for at least ten minutes.

Simon became even more frustrated after following the brown truck to a ramshackle little farm that looked as abandoned as a ghost town, except for some horses running around out back. Ashleigh Logan wouldn't stay *here*. He pulled the Ford off the road and watched as the UPS truck stopped at the gate. The driver hurried as he opened it. He roared up the drive, braked, hopped out and left a large package under the shed roof on the porch. Then the young driver trotted back to his truck, jumped in and roared back down the drive. He hopped back out

long enough to close the old welded-pipe gate.
When the driver turned the truck back onto the road,
Simon squeezed down across the bench seat in his
car. No point in being seen way out here. The guy
was probably in a hurry to get back to Taos or Ra-
ton. He would not report a broken-down old green
Ford stuck in the snow on the side of Switchback
Road.

Simon waited until the whine of the truck's engine faded around the bend. Then he drove up and
repeated the driver's procedure with the gate, except
Simon moved sluggishly—he was a big man after
all.

He walked up to the old house, certain that a
trendy urban princess like Ashleigh Logan would
not take up residence in such a humble abode. As
he stepped up on the porch, the sight of the box
made his phlegmatic heart speed up painfully. He
broke into a sweat. He should have been in the
CIA—that's how good he was at figuring stuff out.
What he could see of the label told him it was a
stroller, perhaps. A *baby* stroller.

He knocked at the door several times while a
mangy old dog stood his ground, barking a dry,
obligatory guard-dog warning. If someone answered, Simon planned to claim that he was lost and
needed directions. When he was satisfied that no one
was home he took his time examining the box.

Ms. Maureen McGuinness, the shipping label
read, *care of Mr. Manuel Cordova.*

CHAPTER SIXTEEN

FOR ALMOST A WEEK, Ashleigh had hardly spoken two words to Greg except when she initiated a tense conversation in which she grilled him about the exact details of the sperm bank mix-up. He had answered all of her questions as patiently and thoroughly as he could.

"Will you submit to a paternity test when the baby is born?" she asked at the end of the week following his admission.

"Absolutely."

He still took care of her, faithfully ministering to her like some kind of wary penitent.

Thanksgiving came. Ashleigh's sister called and they talked quietly for a long time.

Greg, busy in the kitchen, couldn't pick up much of what Ashleigh was saying. And maybe he didn't want to. She was probably telling her sister what a conniving liar he was.

Ashleigh had spoken to her parents often during that week—mostly about her father's condition, which had just recently been declared stable. Greg felt like a rat, listening in on her end of the conversations from the walkway above the great room. He was hoping she'd tell Maureen that she knew the truth about the baby. But when she only mentioned Greg briefly, once in obvious response to some polite inquiry from her mother, his spirits sank. She ended her chats without saying one word about the fact that she knew Greg was the father of her baby, or that Maureen had been in on the deception. Maybe, he told himself, she was just trying to spare Maureen additional stress. Or maybe she was rejecting the truth, rejecting *him*.

Manny was off visiting his son in Los Angeles for the holiday week. Greg had offered to take care of the horses, but Manny said Daniel Elkhorn would gladly do it, and that he would take care of Guapo at the same time. Greg missed Manny, and thought how comforting it would be to have the old man up here in the cabin for the day, maybe even with old Guapo in tow, a third party to soften the horrible tension between Greg and Ashleigh.

Manny had gone to town and stocked their groceries before he left, so Greg tried cooking a festive dinner with all the trimmings, hoping the aroma of roasting turkey would warm Ashleigh's heart, but when the feast was spread on the table, she picked at her food and made sparse, stilted conversation.

It was as if she thought the whole situation was so obscene that she'd given up and was going through the motions. He worried that she might be sliding into some kind of prepartum depression, if there was such a thing. He hoped that if he gave her enough space and let her rest enough, her battered emotions would somehow heal.

MANNY WAS GLAD TO BE BACK on his peaceful ranchero. The big city did not agree with him, though his son Robert and his dear wife did their best to make an old man comfortable.

He planned to go up to the Coleman cabin and take the box he'd found waiting on his porch up to Ashleigh and Greg. It looked like a baby stroller. He had a little surprise for them, too. Just a little thing he'd bought for the baby in Los Angeles. He set the tiny teddy bear on the kitchen table so he wouldn't forget it.

First, he wanted to start himself a nice big pot of pinto beans. Robert's Anglo wife was a good cook, but she didn't know beans about beans. Manny chuckled at his own little joke and started filling his old dented bean pot at the sink. A knock on the door stopped his preparations.

The man standing there was so large he blocked the sun.

"Hello?" the man said politely. Too politely.

The hair on the back of Manny's neck stood up.

"Sí?" Sometimes Manny found it was safer to pretend your English wasn't so good.

"Is there a Ms. Logan here?"

Manny was not one to judge on appearances. But the man's lower lip drooped so terribly it made him want to look away, and his thick eyeglasses were so dirty you couldn't see the color of his eyes. He did not look like the type of person who would have business with Ashleigh, unless he was this stalker Miguel was so worried about. Manny tried to search his memory. Hadn't he seen this fellow around town?

"*Quién es?*"

"I have some flowers for Ms. Ashleigh Logan."

Only then did Manny notice the sparse arrangement in a cheap glass vase.

"*Sí.* I take it." Manny reached for the vase, grasping it firmly at the neck before the man could stop him. There might be something here that Miguel could use—clues to where he got them, maybe even some fingerprints.

"Is she here?" the man demanded.

"You go. Gracias." Manny slammed the door and bolted it. Something he never did, way out here.

He went to the living room and looked out through the curtain. The tall man was lumbering toward a dented and dusty faded green Ford Crown Victoria. Old model. Perhaps 1985. Manny grabbed the pad and pencil beside the *TV Guide,* adjusted his glasses. When the man backed around, Manny wrote down the tag number.

Forgetting the beans, Manny hurried to the old black wall phone in the kitchen. First he called Miguel Eiden to tell him to intercept the battered green Ford at the bottom of Switchback Road. Then he called Greg.

GREG'S BRIEF CONVERSATION with Manny set him on edge. When he finally reached Miguel Eiden an hour later, he grilled Miguel about the man that had come to Manny's. Thanks to Manny's quick thinking, Miguel had been able to stop him.

"It's that character from the magazine again. I don't like the looks of him," Miguel sighed, "but he wasn't breaking the law."

"Hell, I wasn't, either, but you hauled me in."

"I followed him down the mountain and took him in for questioning."

"And?"

"And he claimed he was using the flowers as a ruse to find Ashleigh, of course."

"That's stupid."

"Yeah, it is. I checked him out. Nobody at *Reproduction and Sexuality* magazine ever heard of him. But lying's not a crime, either. I'll just have to keep an eye on the guy. Seems he rented a trailer out south of town."

"Morris Reed," Greg said with disgust, "is your perp."

"But we don't have any hard evidence that he's the guy who's been stalking Ms. Logan. Denver is working on that. At least I've got his pretty picture and his prints now."

"Good. Can we get a restraining order on this guy?"

"For what? Delivering flowers? Not exactly assault."

"Shit."

"I'll keep tabs on him."

"I appreciate that, Miguel, but you can't be everywhere at once."

"Which is why you will never leave Ms. Logan's side."

"Right."

KATHERINE COLLINS HATED Switchback Road. Everybody in the county did.

She rounded the first hairpin turn, shifting gears on the Jeep to accommodate the steep grade. As she climbed, she was glad to see that the strong sun had melted most of last night's snow off the road. Let it stay clear until this baby comes, she thought. Ashleigh Logan's pregnancy had been a tense one, for all of them.

Katherine would be visiting Ashleigh Logan more often, now that the baby's due date was approaching. Which meant she'd be climbing this abominable road a few times a week.

DURING SIMON FISCHER'S DAILY vigils, he had learned to identify each of the midwives' cars. Most of them drove four-by-four vehicles that could handle the mountain roads. He'd seen the dark green Jeep climb Switchback Road twice now, both times on a Wednesday, and that was significant because Switchback Road wasn't where the woman with the long graying braid lived. He'd followed her home twice, also.

Switchback Road was where the old man was taking deliveries of Ashleigh Logan's baby paraphernalia.

On the third Wednesday morning, Simon crept along the winding curves behind the midwife, the heavy rear end of his Ford occasionally sliding on a frosty patch. He ended up at the driveway of a huge cabin jutting from the south face of the mountain. He parked off the road and quickly, stealthily, crept up through the trees toward the house. The climb made him breathless, but it was well worth it. The midwife was standing at the high double doors of the cabin, stethoscope looped on her neck, black tote hitched over her shoulder, clutching a clipboard. So, she had a client in there. And Simon had a pretty good idea who that client was.

His breath came hard as he watched the door open, squinting through his thick glasses to see who answered. A tall, handsome young man. The one who had thrown him to the ground at the clinic. Ashleigh Logan's lover? The guy smiled and opened the door wide for the midwife. Their friendly greetings and laughter drifted through the trees and over the snow to Simon's hiding place. Then the door closed.

Simon crouched down while his heart drubbed maliciously in his chest. If the woman was going to sleep with some guy, why hadn't Ashleigh Logan created her baby in the natural way instead of condemning the poor child to be an outcast, a freak? Never mind. Simon would take care of this baby. He would protect this poor little baby from the world's judgment, from the cruel exposure that silly woman seemed to love. It would be just the two of them, Simon and his child, against a cruel, sinful, sick world.

Despite the chilly air, Simon was sweating. He turned and trudged back to his car, glad that the grade was downhill this time. Time to get out of here before he was seen. He had what he wanted for now, anyway. The next-to-the-last piece of his puzzle had clicked into place. Soon, his vigilance would be rewarded. Soon, he would save the baby.

WHEN KATHERINE HAD FINISHED Ashleigh's checkup, she was surprised when Greg Glazier followed her out to her Jeep. "Careful going back down that road," he said.

"Always," she said, smiling.

"Was the snow a problem this morning?"

"No. It's mostly melted by midmorning, usually."

"No patches of ice, either, I guess."

"No. There's usually not much ice by midmorning, either."

"What if the baby comes at night?"

"That's why we drive Jeeps, Mr. Glazier." She waited patiently at the door of hers. This kind of anxious, double-checking talk was common—among expectant fathers. But Greg Glazier wasn't the father in this case and Katherine wondered why he was behaving so anxiously. Perhaps it was the responsibility of guarding Ashleigh. Or perhaps Greg Glazier was falling in love with this woman, pregnant or not. Katherine thought she recognized the signs.

He looked back up at the house. "Do you think Ashleigh's doing okay?"

"Oh, yes. The fundus is the right height, though the baby hasn't dropped yet—"

"Dropped?"

"That just means engaged down into the pelvis. Ashleigh's baby is still floating high." Katherine made a chopping motion with her hand at the bib of her overalls. "That's not unusual for a first baby. Nothing to worry about. The fetal heart tones are strong. She's doing very well."

"I meant, do you think she's doing okay emotionally. She doesn't seem kind of down to you?"

Katherine studied him, again wondering why a bodyguard would be so emotionally invested in his charge. But looking at him, at his kind eyes so full of concern, she thought surely he had developed real feelings for Ashleigh Logan. Well, that was certainly understandable. Ashleigh was a very beautiful young woman. What did they call it? Star quality?

And maybe that explained Ashleigh's odd little question about intercourse at the end of pregnancy.

The final stages of pregnancy were a trial, even under the best of circumstances, even for stable married couples. But this couple had endured extraordinary stresses, not the least of which was being sequestered alone together in this cabin for weeks. That was the kind of stress that drove people into the shelter of each other's arms. Could this couple have fallen in love? It was starting to look that way.

"It could just be the inactivity." Katherine kept her answer neutral, professional, addressing only the concern Greg Glazier had voiced. "It's too bad the sprained ankle keeps her from getting around much. A little mild exercise would do her good. You know, just a brief walk in the woods or something."

Greg Glazier frowned. "I'm worried that her mental state is more serious than that."

Katherine had the feeling that there was something he was not telling her.

"Has something happened? Another scare with that stalker or something?" Miguel Eiden and Lydia had been in close communication about this case ever since that day when Miguel had picked up Greg Glazier at the clinic. Katherine felt her cheeks growing warm at the memory, though she knew she had done the right thing. Why hadn't Greg just told them that he'd been sent up here by Ashleigh's father to guard her? Something about this whole story didn't add up. But over the weeks, it was obvious that Ashleigh had come to trust Greg, especially after Mrs. McGuinness had to leave. And now it was a real godsend that he was here, what with that awful man in the old Ford running around town. It was almost as if Greg Glazier were a nurse's aide, bodyguard and surrogate husband all rolled into one.

Greg quirked a dark eyebrow at her. "You mean a new development with the stalker? Not since that weirdo showed up at Manny Cordova's."

"Well," Katherine started, wanting to be reassuring. "Ashleigh may have seemed a little quiet today, come to think of it. Toward the end of a pregnancy, some women do withdraw a bit. There's a lot to think about, even for a woman like Ashleigh, who knows *all about babies*." Katherine winked, smiling at her little play on words.

Katherine pressed a calming hand on his muscular forearm. "You're doing a very good job of taking care of her, Mr. Glazier. I'm sure it's just a little cabin fever." She smiled again, looking up at the luxurious cabin. "I mean that literally, I guess. We've only got a couple more weeks to go. Until then, just try to build a little diversity into her days if you can."

THE FIRST WEEK IN DECEMBER brought an unseasonably warm day. Though the temperature in the Sangre de Cristos was forty degrees, the blazing southwest sunlight warmed the chilly air until it felt almost like spring.

"How would you like to have lunch out on the deck?" Greg suggested.

"Fine." Ashleigh shrugged and laid aside the baby catalog she'd been perusing. She stood and pulled on a sweater, actually looking at Greg for the first time in days. His eyes, she thought, held some message—yearning, second thoughts, something like that. He'd been so kind. Had her sudden withdrawl hurt him? Undoubtedly it had.

He set up a small parson's table between the chaise longues and served a tray of soup, sandwiches and raspberry tea.

Ashleigh ate more heartily than she had in a week, and the sunshine relaxed her. When the meal was done and Greg started to take the dishes back into the cabin, she stopped him with a gentle touch on the wrist. "We'll do that later," she said. "I...I have to tell you something."

He put the tray of dishes back on the little table. "Sit down."

He lowered himself to the chaise, facing her, elbows propped on his knees, hands clasped in front of him, as if to control his jumpy nerves. Obviously, he feared what she might say to him. Maybe he was afraid she would say that she had decided she didn't love him, after all. But that would be a lie.

"You had the vasectomy because you were trying to save Kendra's life, didn't you?"

Greg swallowed, looking down at his clasped hands.

"You told me that her kidneys were so bad that a pregnancy would have killed her. That's why you had the vasectomy, isn't it? To make sure she never got pregnant.''

"It was all a long time ago." Greg glanced up as Ashleigh stared at him with tears in her eyes. Along with the tears she felt forgiveness welling up.

His apology tumbled out quickly. "Ashleigh, I'm so sorry for the pain I've caused you. You've had more than enough pain in your life."

He watched her face closely as he continued. "And I know that all you were trying to do was get past that pain and move on with your life by having this baby. Believe me, I get that. If I could have, I would have walked away and let you go on believing this baby was Chad's. But I couldn't do that, not after I heard the baby's heartbeat." She bit her lip and the tears she'd been holding back spilled over. "Ashleigh, I'm so sorry."

She touched him then, a fierce clasp of his forearm that she hoped clearly told him all was forgiven. Greg closed his eyes at her touch and pulled a deep breath of mountain air through his nostrils.

"Greg."

Greg opened his eyes and studied the woman he loved. In the surreal sunlight, she looked like a radiant angel to him. All golden skin and golden hair and silver tears sparkling down flushed cheeks. "I'm the one who should apologize," she choked out. "I've been selfish." Her voice got stronger and her tears poured freely as she continued. "I've been so caught up in my own shock and disappointment that

I haven't stopped to think what these last few weeks have been like for you. It must have been awful for you, wondering if you were going to ever see your own baby—the only baby you could ever have.''

Greg would have said anything to make her stop crying. Anything. But words wouldn't come. He looked down at his arm, where she still clutched him, and hoped she would always hold fast to him this way. He lifted her hand off of him, opening his arms, leaning across the small space between them, and she fell into his embrace, weeping loudly on his shoulder.

''I love you so much!'' she cried, and Greg's heart pounded with happiness as he held on to her. No moment in his life had ever seemed as wondrous as this. He held tight to Ashleigh Logan, while above them somewhere in the pines a bird flitted past, finding its new place and calling out something high, something sweet, something that to Greg sounded a lot like *Joy! Joy!*

CHAPTER SEVENTEEN

AT LAST GREG AND ASHLEIGH felt close, truly close, and they adopted a comfortable rhythm again; this one was far more domestic, far more intimate, than their previous careful habits. All was known now, all was decided between them, and Ashleigh let Greg assist her in the most personal matters with complete trust. Now they could talk freely about their future, about their baby, even disagree about some things. For example, what would they call him?

"Gemariah," Greg suggested. "That was my grandfather's name. It's from the Bible."

"And that's where it should stay," Ashleigh countered. "It sounds like some kind of ancient disease."

Greg smirked.

"I was thinking we might call him Cory."

"*Cory?*" Greg grimaced. "Sounds kinda girlie. The little guy's got a *penis,* remember?"

When they bantered this way, or when he gave her a back rub, or when Ashleigh asked him to hold her until she fell asleep, Greg felt as if he was al-

ready her husband, except for the one intimate connection that was temporarily denied them.

He refused to even broach that subject. *After the
baby comes,* he told himself when his physical frus-
trations reared up, *after the baby comes.*

In the meantime, he funneled his pent-up energy
into keeping the mother of his child plump and
happy.

Every day after he fed Ashleigh a nutritious
lunch, Greg settled her on the couch with a book or
the TV remote and then turned his attention to whip-
ping through his chores. He'd discovered that if he
ignored her at this time of day, Ashleigh usually
drifted off for a little nap. It pleased him to see her
sleeping peacefully, and to think of the little baby
curled inside her doing the same.

But the days weren't all blissful. One morning he
was carrying a basket of clean laundry across the
great room, toward the master suite, when a sound
stopped him in his tracks. From the direction of the
couches, he had heard a distinct sniffle. Sure
enough, Ashleigh had a fist pressed to her mouth
and her eyes were wet. Her nose was bright red, so
she'd probably been crying for a while.

Greg lowered the laundry basket to his thighs.
''What is it?''

As always, he'd kept his voice gentle, but pregnant women, he was learning, really were juicy little
things—seeping from every pore, as it were. He
could understand it when she cried about missing

her family, or the uncertain state of her father's health, or even from the sheer boredom and isolation out here.

But in the last few days Ashleigh had oozed tears over a TV show about unadopted puppies, over the fact that she couldn't find any of her hair scrunchies, and over his casual confession that he occasionally dipped snuff out on the ranch. Never mind that he didn't really care for the stuff.

He was trying, masterfully, to maintain his patience, but he wondered what trivial upset had thrown her gyroscope off kilter now.

But this time it wasn't so insignificant.

"I'm scared," she said.

"Oh, sweetheart." He dropped the laundry basket and crossed the room in two giant strides. He knelt by the couch and tried to put his arms around her, but she leaned away.

"What are you afraid of?" he asked. *The impending birth? The stalker?*

She twisted the tissue he handed her and blurted, "I'm scared that I've messed up my life. All I wanted was a *baby,* and now I'm hiding in this cabin with a stalker after me, my father's so ill and I can't even see him, and..." She let out a sob that tore at Greg's heart.

"Oh, sweetheart," he repeated.

"And now I can't even remember Chad's face. I...I f-forgot to bring a picture with me, and now I can't remember what he looked like, not really."

"Oh, Ash. Come here."

But instead of letting him comfort her, she turned her face to the bank of windows. "I swore I'd never forget him."

"You haven't forgotten him, sweetheart." He stroked her hair. Her forehead felt hot. "Maybe you've forgotten a few details, that's all. It doesn't mean you've forgotten how you felt about him. That's what counts—the love you shared. That'll never go away."

"That's just it. I *have* forgotten how I felt about him, sort of. All I can think about is how I feel about *you.*"

Greg's heart did a quick *thud-thud*. Was this going to be good or bad? Was she going to pull away from him again and retreat back into the losses of the past? Now, when they'd finally broken down all the barriers, when they'd finally stopped all the games and the lies and gotten truly close? "You don't want to think about me?"

"Of course I do! You're the father of my baby, and I love you. I mean, all I can think about is…being with you."

"That's all I can think about these days, too. Our life together."

"No. I mean *being* with you…making love to you. Every time I look at you, I think about that. How I'd like to feel close to you, to feel normal, like a woman again. But when I think that way, it makes me feel so guilty about Chad. Oh," she sobbed and rubbed her fevered brow. "I'm all mixed up."

Ashleigh kept rambling, but Greg's mind was snagged back on one fact. She'd been thinking about making love to him? Really? He didn't think pregnant women ever wanted that.

"It's like I'm in a whole new world now," she was saying, "and you're suddenly the center of that world. And the world I shared with Chad is way, way back there, not even real anymore. It's almost as if...I don't know." Fresh tears pooled in her eyes. "This isn't what I planned at all!" she wailed.

"Oh, sweetheart. This isn't what either of us *planned*. I didn't plan that stupid brownout in California, but it happened. I didn't plan to fall in love with you, but I did. Totally." He touched her again, this time pressing his warm palm possessively to her abdomen. "I didn't exactly plan on being a daddy, at least not this way, but I'm going to be. That's the reality."

Finally, she looked at him. "That's just it. I wouldn't change anything now, even if I could." Her voice fell to a whisper. "I guess that's the trouble. I'm *glad* I found you. And I'm...I'm so glad this is your baby, and not Chad's. And that makes me feel so guilty!"

"I know how you feel." He tried to wrap his arms around her again, but she held herself apart from him, still unyielding.

"For a long time—" Greg kept his voice gentle

as he spoke "—I felt guilty about Kendra, wondering if there wasn't something else I could have done. I think guilt kind of goes with the territory when you lose someone. But it won't do us any good to feel guilty about Chad, or about Kendra, for that matter. What's happening here is between the two of us now. This is our baby. And this baby deserves two parents who love each other, who are *happy* together, not guilty and sad. Ashleigh, we have to let the past be the past and stop looking back."

She pressed her knuckles to her lips, letting out a sob. He could see how mightily she was struggling with this final letting go of her husband. Though Chad had been dead five years and Kendra only three, Greg understood that he had managed to let go more completely. The human heart, he realized, did not heal on a set calendar.

Maybe part of Ashleigh's trouble had been this whole sperm bank business. He had not had any such lingering part of Kendra to hang on to. It seemed ironic beyond comprehension that it was Chad's banked sperm that had inadvertently brought the two of them together now.

Ashleigh had had so much to process and accept, and she'd had to do it all during the hormonal overload of pregnancy. He would have done anything to ease Ashleigh's pain at that moment, but only she could let Chad go. He couldn't do that for her. All he could do was try to comfort her.

"Can I just hold you for a minute?" he said.

"No!" She rocked miserably, locked in her guilt and her pain.

But her sharp denial told him how badly she needed him to do just that. He slid up onto the couch and took her in his arms.

Finally, she sank against him, sobbing.

Ashleigh pressed her cheek against Greg's chest, letting the full impact of his strong muscles, the sound of his strong beating heart, engulf her senses. Her longing for him and the hopefulness that the longing gave her welled up, bringing more tears. She let herself cry it all out. She cried and cried while he held her, until she felt cleansed, and when she calmed down, she felt suddenly light, as if she were an empty vessel. She clung to him fiercely and said, "Oh, Greg. I want you."

"I want you, too." He circled one arm around her hips, pulling her body up into a C on his lap. "And I'll have you. Someday soon."

"We belong together," she said. She rested her head against his shoulder as he cradled her.

"Yes, we do. And we will be together, for the rest of our lives. We'll get married as soon as we can safely take the baby back to Denver."

"No. I mean we belong *together*. Joined. Our bodies."

"Ashleigh—"

"Don't you want to feel that close to me?"

"Of course I do! But you...you're..."

"I'm nine months pregnant. Don't you think I

know that!'' she cried. ''But I'm also in love. I'm so in love with you right now. What if something happens to one of us—''

''Don't say that.'' He touched two fingers to her lips. ''Nothing is going to happen to anybody.'' He tightened his arms around her and pressed his lips to her forehead.

''We've been alone in this cabin together all this time,'' she persisted, ''and yet we've never even been together. Never once. Not once…not as… lovers.''

''But Ashleigh—''

''No!'' She pressed her cheek to his shoulder and cupped a hand over her mouth, drawing two gulping breaths, fighting for control, but it didn't help. Control refused to come, because nothing would help her now, except… ''I want—'' She swallowed hard and grasped the back of his shirt, squeezing her eyes shut. ''I want to make love. Just this once. I *need* that, Greg. Please, don't deny *us* this. Please. You would do what I asked, if it would comfort me, if we were married, wouldn't you? If we were married and having this baby and we were in love—''

''We are in love,'' he interrupted, and his eyes bore into hers as if to say, *Never question that again.*

She nodded solemnly. ''Yes. We are. And because we're in love, I want you. I want to feel like I'm yours.''

''We can wait until after the baby is born,'' he

said with conviction. But the tight muscles of his jaw told her it was an effort.

"I asked the midwife and she said it wouldn't hurt anything as long as it wasn't overly vigorous."

"You asked the midwife?" Greg looked stunned. Then slightly embarrassed.

"Please," Ashleigh begged. "I need this. It would…it would comfort me now. I can't…I can't explain it." She felt tears welling up again. "I need to be joined with you. Now. Not later." In her heart Ashleigh knew this need had something to do with letting Chad go and fully accepting Greg as the father of her baby, as her future husband…as her lover.

His eyes studied her face and she could see his resolve shifting. "If we…if we get physical, won't it hurt the baby?"

"Katherine said it's okay it we're careful. I'll tell you if something doesn't feel right, and we'll stop."

His eyelids closed again, slowly, as if weighing something of great import. "All right. If this is really what you want. But I'll…I'll only enter you—"

She nodded solemnly.

"Only enter." His eyes searched hers again. Determined. In control. "Only once. To join us—nothing more." Ashleigh could tell that he was indulging her emotions against his better judgment. He was going to give her what she wanted, but he was determined to safeguard their baby as well. She had no doubt that Greg Glazier could do this.

"Nothing more," she agreed, because what choice did he give her?

Slowly, gently, he started.

First, he raised her top and spread a palm on her naked abdomen. Instantly, the baby kicked and Greg bent forward and reverently kissed the spot.

Ashleigh smiled. "You see? Everything's all right."

But Greg didn't return her smile, as if the situation were too solemn, too intense for smiles. Keeping his eyes on hers, he shook his head. "Don't," he mouthed.

She sobered and nodded, understanding that he didn't want to diminish what they were about to do. Eyes wide, she kept still on his lap, silently, allowing him to touch her.

They had spent hours like this—Greg with his hands on her, feeling for movement from their child, adoring her body while he rubbed lotion on her, getting to know her through his fingertips as he massaged, comforted, warmed her. But now his touch was different. Now his hands felt as if he was, at last, *claiming* her. For himself. For them.

Those hands traveled up, marking her skin with his heat, encircling her full breasts. He stopped there and pushed her top out of the way, and held her breasts before him, just looking, again, claiming with his eyes.

"I love you," she whispered.

"I love you, too," he answered, and looked up

into her face. Then he lowered his head and pressed a kiss, wet and hot, between her breasts, at the apex of her very pregnant abdomen.

She lowered her head back on the pillows as the beating of her heart became wild, intense.

He raised his head. "Are you sure this is okay?"

"Yes. I'm just so in love."

"I won't do this if you're going to get over-wrought."

She smiled at the ceiling. *Overwrought?* She loved him when he said old-fashioned things like that. Greg Glazier had certainly proved himself to be a man unlike any other. Perhaps—well not *perhaps,* she was thoroughly convinced of it now—Greg Glazier was the only man, unique as he was, who could have drawn her out of her carefully built fortress of grief. Out of the darkness, into the dazzling light of his love. She closed her eyes as the New Mexico sun poured through the vast windows, washing over them, changing them.

"I'm not overwrought," she said. "I'm just happy. My body has never felt so alive, so womanly. I can't see how feeling this good could possibly be bad for the baby."

His hands stilled, gently cupping her breasts. "What if it makes you go into labor?"

She smiled and tossed her head. It was exactly as Katherine Collins said. Women welcomed labor. Men feared it. "I'm due, remember? Any day."

"Any day," he whispered, and pressed his lips to the crown of her swollen abdomen again.

"Greg." She spoke his name while the desire to be joined with this man—physically, emotionally, spiritually—grew deeper than any desire she had ever felt. It was, she knew, her soul wanting his soul. "I want you inside of me now. Will you do this for me?"

"Yes." He pushed himself away from her and stood. "But I'm taking you to the bedroom." He bent and gently scooped her up.

The master suite was awash with light at this time of day, so that everything in the room seemed lit from within. Ashleigh couldn't imagine a better time, a better place, for their first real intimacy.

After he laid her on the bed, he removed her clothes in silence. Her body, fleshy and sensuous, glowed in the slanting rays of the late afternoon sun. With his eyes boldly adoring her, Greg straightened and took his jeans off.

"Turn on your side," he said, his voice husky, low and solemn.

She did as he asked. He tilted her up slightly, and slid a flat pillow under her abdomen for support. "Comfortable?"

"Yes. But a little nervous." She closed her eyes and bit her lip.

He bent forward and kissed her lips lightly. "That's natural." His voice was deep. "It's a big step. Are you sure?"

"Absolutely."

He ran his hands down her front, bringing one palm down to cup the inside of her thigh. He urged her legs open, then molded his body against hers. He pressed her most sensitive part with his palm while he angled his hips sharply up to fit hers. That first impact of his hot, hard flesh right where she needed him most was a sensation Ashleigh knew she would never forget as long as she lived. "Oh, Greg," she gasped.

Despite his earlier intentions to simply be joined to satisfy Ashleigh's emotional needs, Ashleigh heard Greg's sharp intake of breath as he positioned them together for deeper contact.

"Greg," she whispered his name again, as his warm, strong hand gently guided one of her legs high on his hip.

"I know," he answered as his breathing grew heavier. "I'll be supergentle."

"No. I was going to say, don't…don't deny us anything."

"We can't do everything we want, Ash. I'm only going to be inside you, remember? Just barely inside. No…no thrusting or anything like that."

She tried to nod, but flushed with desire, ended up tossing her head aside in frustration.

"Ashleigh…" He took her face in his hands and turned it toward his. "I won't do this unless we promise to keep it gentle."

"Okay," she whispered. But her breathing became even more rapid.

And then slowly, so slowly, with his eyes holding hers the entire time, he entered her. As he filled her for the first time, Ashleigh couldn't control herself. She tilted her hips, opening completely to him, causing his muscles to ripple as he struggled for control. Despite herself, she writhed against him until, finally, he groaned and pushed to fit her, fully and completely.

It had been so long. So, so long, for Ashleigh. When he lowered his head and reverently kissed her mouth, a great wave of longing crested over her.

But with his strong hands, he held her hips still. "We promised," he reminded her, "nothing strenuous."

"I can't help it."

"Slow your breathing down. Try to match mine," Greg commanded.

Watching his face closely, Ashleigh could see that he had trouble controlling his own breathing. And inside her she could feel him—throbbing. When the day came for them to finally make unrestrained love…she closed her eyes in ecstasy at the thought.

Greg looked down at Ashleigh, at her quivering eyelids, at her soft, luminous flesh, and he realized that this exquisite creature was truly *his*.

He kept them joined, while they held their bodies absolutely still.

They did manage to slow their breathing, finding

an identical rhythm. Looking into each other's eyes, to Greg it seemed their very heartbeats were becoming synchronized.

When he was unable to bear it another second, Greg's eyes slid closed and he grasped the back of her neck, pulling her mouth to his, clasping it in a fierce kiss. She answered with a moan that tore unbidden from her throat. In response, his body bowed in an involuntary movement below, but immediately he checked himself.

But his sudden stillness only seemed to drive Ashleigh wild. She tried not to move, quivering with the effort, but then she cried out, "Ah!" as her own tremors started. He could feel them localized at first, then pulsing upward, outward, roaring through her whole body, unstoppable.

"No," Greg said, when he realized the intensity of what was happening to her. He held her tight, but it was too late. She had tumbled over an unseen cliff and was pulling him with her. With a low growl, he grasped her body against his and, holding tighter still, felt himself pumping into her.

He whispered against the pulse in her neck when their bodies had finally quieted. "Oh, Ashleigh. I'm sorry. I couldn't stop."

Ashleigh stroked the hair at his temples back. "Don't be sorry. I asked you to you, begged you to. I couldn't stop, either."

She threw her head back while love, joy, happiness, every emotion that a woman in love could feel, coursed over her face. She smiled. "*I* am *not* sorry. In fact, I'm overjoyed."

"We'll see if you feel overjoyed—" Greg kissed her upraised chin "—when our little experiment throws you into active labor."

CHAPTER EIGHTEEN

SURE ENOUGH BY THAT afternoon, Ashleigh began to have twinges of contractions. At first she waited them out in silence, knowing Greg would blame himself for precipitating something that was totally inevitable and natural. But after a couple of hours the pattern and the rhythm of labor became unmistakable…and harder to conceal.

Barely suppressing her flushing anticipation, she sought Greg out. He was in the cabin's kitchen, making their supper. "Don't get all excited," she told him just as a stronger contraction started, "but feel this."

Greg turned to face her fully, wiping his hands on a towel and swallowing the bite of carrot he'd been chewing as if it were a rock. He looked into her eyes and let her guide his hands to rest on her front. With his palms feeling her tightening uterus, his eyes grew huge. "You're kidding," he whispered.

"Nope." Ashleigh's breath caught and she held it as the contraction reached its zenith. "Sure feels like—" she let out her breathe "—the real thing. Doesn't it?"

"I'm calling Katherine." He guided Ashleigh to a kitchen chair. "Don't move."

Greg felt a wrenching sensation in his own belly as he spoke with the midwife. This was it. His child was going to be born.

"Katherine said to call her right back after we timed them," Greg told Ashleigh when he'd hung up.

He quickly turned off the burners under the food and took Ashleigh by the hand, leading her to the bedroom where he made her lie on the bed on her side until the next contraction came. He was ready with his wristwatch, counting the seconds. While they waited for the next one, Greg stroked Ashleigh's forehead and said things like, "I can't believe he's finally coming." And "You'll be okay." And "I'll be right beside you the whole time."

Ashleigh held his fingers nervously, occasionally kissing them and saying things like, "I can't wait to see him—to see what kind of baby we made." And "I'm not afraid." And "I'm so glad I found you."

"I found you," he reminded her, but she didn't answer because another contraction had started.

Her eyes closed and her breathing grew rapid. It had been five minutes.

"This is it," Greg pronounced after the third contraction in fifteen minutes. "You're in labor."

Greg called Katherine again, and then got busy getting the cabin ready. There wasn't really much to do. He'd been preparing for weeks. Ashleigh would deliver the baby in the queen-size bed in the master suite, which had its own bathroom, complete with a huge Jacuzzi tub in the sunny corner. In case she wanted to get into a tub of warm water during labor or even during the birthing process. Greg had wiped the entire bathroom down with disinfectant again that morning—right after their crazy lovemaking episode.

He still couldn't believe that had actually happened. Life with this woman would surely prove to be unpredictable. Life with this woman and their *son,* he corrected himself, and smiled. That thought propelled him to the bassinet and the changing table at the ready in the corner. He checked the baby's stack of things—a diaper, a cotton onesie, a long gown, a tiny knit skull cap, a supersoft receiving blanket.

The midwife would bring her oils for Ashleigh, as well as everything for clamping and tending the cord, but Greg jerked the top drawer of the changing table open, anyway. The contents looked like something out of a medical supply catalog. He had picked out each item himself—he didn't give a big green bean what Ashleigh and the midwife said about births being ''natural.'' He was going to be prepared.

He had procured his own sterile clamp at the hospital, sterile blunt scissors, too. He'd made a duplicate travel kit in a Ziploc bag. He took it out and put it on top of the changing table, just in case. He thumbed the disposable covers and snap-activated cold packs he'd bought for Ashleigh's perineum. He eyed the saline baby nose drops, a bulb syringe, blunt tweezers, baby-safe ear swabs, cotton balls, four-by-four gauze, petroleum jelly, a thermometer, baby wipes to refill the warmer up top, diaper ointment, tiny comb, tiny brush. He'd even found tiny baby nail clippers.

He jerked the next drawer open to give it the same once-over. Tiny diapers, tiny undershirts, tiny socks, tiny everything.

Third drawer. Burp cloths, crib sheets, big blankets, a humidifier.

Down in the living room they had a snuggly carrier, a car seat, a stroller.

Hell, between him and Ashleigh they'd bought the whole inventory of Babies ''R'' Us and had it shipped up to this mountain, via Manny's place, of course, in these last few weeks.

Ashleigh smiled and shook her head as he dashed past her, into the bathroom again. The supplies for the baby's first bath were lined up with military precision on a clean white towel next to a small plastic basin on the bathroom counter. A concave foam pad covered with another thick towel, just the size for a sweet little newborn—lay in waiting next to the little tub. Greg refolded the little knit hooded towel and rearranged the stack of baby washcloths next to it. *Okay. What else?*

He stepped out of the bathroom and jerked open

a drawer in the master alcove, frowning at the contents. Next to her nursing bras, he had three clean cotton nursing gowns at the ready for Ashleigh. Some anklets in case her feet got cold. A neat stack of freshly laundered "anti-man" panties and a supply of pads. *What else?*

The batteries in his flashlights were fresh. The gas tank in the Navigator was full. The pantry, the fridge and the freezer were bursting. There was a ham. Bottled spring water. Frozen bagels. Cottage cheese. Milk. Eggs. Orange juice. Whole wheat bread. Peanut butter. Prechopped salad in a Ziploc bag. A stash of Ashleigh's favorite treats.

He slammed the lingerie drawer shut and whirled to the bedroom again, dragging a hand through his hair as he headed toward the stairs.

"Greg." From the bed, Ashleigh's smoky voice halted him. "Where are you going?"

"To the kitchen." He frowned, assessing her for the first time since he'd started his galloping inventory. Still lying on her side, with pillows tucked all around, she looked perfectly relaxed, perfectly safe.

"Why?" She smiled indulgently. "Are you going to boil water and tear rags?"

"No, smart-ass. I was going to check the baby's bottles and binkies and stuff."

Ashleigh patted the bed with one hand and her big tummy with the other. "I'm breastfeeding this little guy, remember? And the baby and I happen to be over here, not down in the kitchen."

He crossed the room and knelt by the bed with his elbows poking into the mattress. He clasped her hand and kissed her fingers, then looked in her eyes, feeling slightly foolish. ''I just want to be ready,'' he croaked.

He pressed her delicate knuckles to his forehead, overcome with emotion. He could not believe the time had finally come, and soon they would see their child. The idea of the baby—*his baby*—suckling at Ashleigh's beautiful breasts made his chest swell, aching with joy. He found he couldn't speak, his happiness was so great.

''Stop obsessing.'' Ashleigh stroked his hair. ''We're all ready. Now, hold me. I'm starting another contraction.''

He eased himself onto the bed beside her and gently cradled her body from behind. He slid his palms around, under her top, over her abdomen, stroking her skin in warm, featherlight circles while she breathed through the contraction, and then through another. And another.

Between contractions, they touched and whispered to each other. Dreaming aloud about where they would live, how they would raise this child, what it would be like when they could finally make love with abandon. While outside the vast uncovered windows of the cabin, snow began to flutter down, at first in tiny, teasing specks and then, later, in great, gentle flakes.

NATURALLY, KATHERINE COLLINS thought as the flakes began to stick to her windshield, Ashleigh's baby would decide to come after dark—the sun was well behind the peaks now—and in a snowstorm. She flipped on her wipers, and as they raked away the first slushy flakes, she hoped the precipitation wouldn't get too thick. She downshifted as she climbed the first turn of Switchback. The midwife who was supposed to assist her had been called out to an emergency a few hours ago, and Katherine wouldn't be able to expect her at the Coleman cabin anytime soon. Well, first babies were usually slow to arrive. It would all work out. She'd faced this kind of stress before.

She flipped out her cell phone to make one last-ditch check at the clinic. Once she got in that cabin, tucked into the rocky south face, she knew that her phone wasn't going to work.

Their receptionist, Trish, always working late, always conscientious, answered the phone.

"Any hope for a backup for me out here at the Coleman cabin?" Katherine spoke fast, not knowing when she'd lose her signal.

"Oh, dear, let's see."

Over the static, Katherine could hear Trish's chair creaking as she got up to check the dry-erase board in the back room.

"Not much chance. Lydia's delivering the Dorhman baby back in a birthing room right now. She'll be tied up the rest of the evening. Heidi's out on a postpartum check near Eagle Nest.''

''What about Dawn?''

''Out of town. Skiing with her family up in Red River. I suppose I could try and raise her. It's not that far from you. I'm sure she'd come down if I can find her.''

''No, don't do that. This should be a normal delivery. Ask Heidi to come on up here when she's done.''

The signal was breaking up so badly that Trish had to shout her next words. ''I'll call her now.''

Katherine punched End. The snow was getting thicker, creating a blinding screen in front of her headlights. She raised the speed on her wipers and checked her speedometer. Eight miles to go.

GREG WAS PACING, JUST LIKE the nervous daddies in the movies. Ashleigh sighed as she watched him, long legs striding to the dark windows then back. She decided that looking at one's lover was a great way to distract oneself between labor pains. And her lover—soon to be her husband!—was a fine specimen of a man, indeed.

He raked one of his large, graceful hands through his disheveled hair and gave her a grin. ''Hang in there, sweetheart,'' he said. He'd already brought her ice chips and a warmed cotton blanket, rubbed her tummy, her back, even her feet. He seemed to have endless strength and energy. She sighed. What had she been thinking, planning to have a baby without a man?

Again, his heavy cowboy boots clunked from area rug to hardwood floor in a determined rhythm. Even his behind looked cute in his jeans. Ashleigh broke into a broad grin, but it was quickly drawn down by the gravity of a viselike pain compressing her middle.

Greg flew to her side, placed one hand over her rock-hard fundus, gauging. When the contraction was done, he frowned at his watch. "That was a long one. And did it seem really strong to you?"

Ashleigh nodded, blew out a cleansing breath. "They're getting much stronger now."

Greg swabbed her forehead with a cool washcloth, looking out into the snowy night. "Where in the hell is Katherine?" he said under his breath.

KATHERINE WAS STRUGGLING to see the road in the worsening storm. She slowed to a crawl around the next curve, unsure if she was even keeping to her own side of the road. This was shaping up into a dangerous snowstorm.

When the road straightened, she saw the blur of headlights coming up behind her. She hoped the driver wasn't going to be one of those idiot tailgaters, but even as she had that thought, the headlights closed in. He couldn't pass her in this mess, and he didn't try. He simply dogged her bumper, following her.

Around the next curve they went, Katherine keeping her traction going slow and steady. The driver behind, in some kind of old sedan that probably didn't even have front-wheel drive, fishtailed his way through the turn. He was probably getting impatient. *Too bad, buddy,* she thought. *I won't hurry through a mountain snowstorm for anybody.*

Katherine got so preoccupied checking the rearview mirror for her tailgater that she didn't even see the huge deer dart out of the trees. Instead she felt a massive thud. She screamed as her heart jolted and the Jeep careened into a spin, slamming into a boulder at the side of the road. She batted away her air bag just in time to see the car behind barely missing her rear bumper. Then it went spinning off onto a turnout ahead.

Shaking, Katherine got out of the Jeep and covered her mouth at the sight of the huge buck, illuminated by one shattered headlight, antlers entangled in her front bumper. The impact had killed the beautiful creature…and had completely disabled her Jeep.

Up ahead at the turnout the big boat of a sedan was righting itself. Her broken headlight was reflected off the eyeglasses of a massive man behind the wheel. She waved frantically. But when he pulled onto the road, he drove away from her, on up the mountain.

Of all the… Probably some zoned-out druggie.

There were a few strange types tucked back up in these mountains.

She climbed back inside her Jeep. Checked her cell phone for a signal. None. Checked her speedometer. Six miles to Ashleigh's. Too far to walk in this freezing snow. She dug out her emergency roadside kit, found the flashlight, the poncho, her Help-Call-Police sign and two chemical light sticks. She put the sign in the rear window, donned the bright yellow poncho, and climbed back out of the Jeep. She snapped the light sticks, shook them vigorously, and placed the greenish glowing wands strategically at the corners of her vehicle.

Then she climbed back inside and wrapped the blankets that she kept in the back seat around her shoulders and legs. She huddled, considering whether or not it might make sense to walk to the nearest house for help. On other trips she'd made up here during the day, she'd seen a turnoff to a run-down old place. But that could be where the coldhearted bastard who'd left her stranded out here was heading. No telling what kind of creep that guy was, and if he was, in fact, dangerous, she'd be out in the boonies with him, on foot.

She decided to lock up and stay put. *Oh, please,* she prayed, *let Heidi get finished quickly and drive up this road to find me.* And please, keep Ashleigh and the baby safe. And *please,* help Greg Glazier if he has to be the one to deliver this baby. Please give him the skills he needs and help him be calm and strong.

CHAPTER NINETEEN

Simon Fischer kept the old car moving up the steep road, but after witnessing the accident, he eased back on the gas. This road was slick! And dark. He peered through the endless shifting pellets of snow in front of his headlights. The turnoff to that big cabin should be coming up soon.

He had no doubt that he'd done the right thing, leaving that midwife behind on the roadside in that Jeep. That woman might identify him, help the police find him, endangering his plan to escape with the baby. She was just one more person out of the way. How amazing—how *lucky!*—that she'd hit that deer. It was all part of Simon's destiny, he was sure. But until he got the baby rescued, the fewer people he saw face to face, the better.

Ashleigh Logan was undoubtedly in labor. Why else would the midwife be driving on *this* road, in the dark, in *this* weather? But from what Simon had learned watching the *All About Babies* show, the birth could be imminent or it could take hours. He would have to be cautious, approaching the cabin. He would have to be wary.

The man he had seen at the door, her *boyfriend,*

no doubt, might pose a real problem. But now that it might just be the two of them in the cabin, Simon could wait until he was certain the baby was born, then create a distraction—a fire? a broken window?—and draw the boyfriend out of the cabin. Then he could break inside and take the baby from the mother—the *woman*. She was not a *mother*. She was a selfish harlot who had created a baby as if it were just one more possession to heap upon her sickening pile. Whatever he did, it would have to be soon after the birth while the *woman* was too weak to resist.

He parked at the bottom of the drive, in the shallow turnout where he had parked before. He killed the engine and headlights, got out and shivered. It was so cold out here! He would wrap the baby up good and tight. He could take care of a baby. He knew he could.

GREG TIMED THE CONTRACTIONS at three-minute intervals, told Ashleigh he had to go to the kitchen and that he'd be right back.

Away from the bedroom, where Ashleigh couldn't hear, he dialed Katherine's cell phone number but got a voice-mail message instead of a connection.

''Ms. Collins,'' he said, leaving his message rapidly, ''this is Greg Glazier. I'm trying to reach you to see if something's gone wrong. We seem to be getting closer to delivery here. I'm helping Ashleigh use the breathing techniques you taught us but—''

He heard a noise outside just as the motion sensor on that corner of the house switched on.

Greg raised the window over the sink and looked out into the snowy night. The bright light illuminated only silently falling snow, thick as down feathers from a burst pillow, and then darkness beyond. Greg stood stock-still and listened, heard only a soughing in the pines. He slammed the window down. Probably that old deer again.

''Greg!'' Ashleigh called out. He dashed into the bedroom.

She was raised up on her elbows, her expression pinched, her legs spread wide. ''I feel like I need to push.''

Holy God. *What should he do?*

''Not yet, sweetheart.'' *Not yet—the midwife's not here.*

''But I...I can't...I want to push.''

Raking his mind to remember everything he'd read and seen on the videos in the last few weeks, he said, ''Let me check you. We'll see if you're crowning.''

Just as he got her knees raised, a contraction hit her full force. He tried to stroke her forehead, meaning to wait until the pain was over, but Ashleigh, panting hard, tossed her head and said, ''No! Look now!''

He pushed her gown up and tilted the bedside

lamp and watched her perineum for any signs. Thing looked pretty swollen, but there was no sign of the baby's head.

Halfway through the contraction, Ashleigh thrashed, tossing her head side to side. If he didn't miss his guess, this was transition. They were close. He needed help.

He made his next call from the bedroom. He would not leave Ashleigh's side again.

"Trish? Greg Glazier. Ashleigh Logan is having her baby and Katherine Collins hasn't arrived yet. Yes. I'll hold."

Lydia Kane's voice came on the line next and Greg felt a rush of relief. Thank God those woman often worked late. "Mr. Glazier?"

"Yes."

"Can you see any sign of the baby at the vaginal opening?"

"Not really."

"Good. Then she's not crowning yet. Trish is trying to reach Katherine on another line right now. We have no idea what has happened to her. She left here over an hour ago. Trish will also try to locate a backup midwife who probably can get to you in thirty minutes. I have a patient about to deliver here, so I cannot come up there."

She let a beat of silence reverberate before her next question. "Have you ever delivered a baby, Mr. Glazier?"

"No."

"Attended a birth?"

"No." Greg pinched the bridge of his nose, wondering if pulling a foal counted.

There was a tense, thoughtful pause on the other end, then Lydia Kane said, "I think it would be wise for you to go ahead and bring Ms. Logan into the clinic."

"I agree."

"In the meantime, I am going to talk you through anything that happens. Stay calm and remember that birth is a natural event and that Ashleigh is very healthy. We expect a good outcome. All you have to do is follow my instructions."

"Okay."

"You have a four-wheel-drive vehicle, do you not?"

"Yes, ma'am."

"Good. With a first baby we probably have plenty of time, nevertheless, I want you to bundle Ashleigh up right now and bring her to the clinic. You're only twenty minutes away. We will deliver her here. Call me back on your cell phone as soon as you can get a signal."

Greg did not waste one millisecond. He snatched up the ziploc bag containing the gloves, sterile scissors, sterile clamp, cold pack and receiving blanket and jammed the thing into the pocket of his leather jacket as he jerked it on.

"Greg!" Ashleigh screamed. Greg turned to her and saw a wild-eyed woman, clawing backward on the bed as if she'd seen a ghost. Was this another bizarre reaction to transition?

"Oh, God!" she yelled again, pointing at the windows.

"What? What is it?" He ran to her, put his hands on her. She was trembling.

"There." She pointed a shaking arm to the black expanse of glass opposite the bed. "I saw someone. Out there. Running—" her voice squeaked with fear "—in the trees!"

Greg looked out the windows and at the black woods. Again, the motion sensor lights on that side of the house had come on.

"Are you sure it was a person? Not an animal?"

"I'm sure!" Ashleigh's voice was high-pitched and panicked.

Greg flipped off the bedside lamp, walked to the windows and peered out. Nothing. Even so, he went to the dresser, opened the lockbox, snapped a clip into his Glock, chambered a round, checked the safety and jammed the gun under his waistband at his back.

"Come on, sweetheart. We're getting out of here." By the reflected glow of the safety lights, he helped Ashleigh into her robe, hurriedly wriggled house slippers onto her feet, then wrapped her tightly in a blanket before scooping her up in his arms with the Navigator keys clutched in his left hand.

Greg carried Ashleigh to the front door, and he

gently manoevered her through. As soon as he kicked the door shut, there he was.

"She hasn't had the baby yet?" the large man said from the shadowy pines.

Ashleigh screamed, then buried her face in Greg's neck. "Ah," she cried immediately, grabbing her front. From the bowing of her back, Greg knew a contraction had started.

"I don't want *her*." The man stepped into the light. Several inches taller and considerably heavier than Greg, he was the reporter who'd tried to take Ashleigh's picture the night Greg met her. The same guy Manny had so accurately described. Wire-rimmed glasses. Burr haircut. Built like a tank. But tonight he wasn't a polite, smiling charmer. Tonight his lower lip drooped, glistening with a faint sheen of saliva, communicating his unstable state of mind, his evil intention. Grazing his thick tongue over that protruding lip, the man said, "I don't want to hurt anybody. I don't want anything but the baby." At that, Greg felt the blood halt in his veins.

CHAPTER TWENTY

WITH ASHLEIGH CLINGING to his neck, in the throes of a contraction, Greg thought his Glock might as well have been back up in the lockbox. His mind raced as he anticipated the weapon this crazed idiot thought he might employ to persuade Greg to hand over his only child. A knife? A gun?

"I have come to take the baby," the monster repeated.

"There's a problem," Greg lied, and tightened his grip on Ashleigh to communicate to her what he was about to do. "She's bleeding. I have to take her to the hospital."

"I have only come to take the baby," the creep insisted again and, reaching under his coat, started lumbering forward in the snow.

"Hold tight," Greg instructed in Ashleigh's ear. She clung to his shoulders and curled into a ball.

In one lightning motion Greg shifted her weight, securing his left arm in a vise around her hips. Simultaneously, with the right hand that had been under her knees, he whipped out his Glock, thumbed off the safety and slammed his arm back under her knees again. The gun barrel was pointed squarely at the guy's gut and the sight of it stopped Fischer in his tracks.

"Pull your weapon out—slowly—and toss it over there."

The creep withdrew a gun and flung it into a snowbank.

"Step over there, into the snow." Greg waved his Glock toward the deep drifts against the tree trunks where the lot sloped away from the drive.

The big man stumbled back, collapsing backward into a drift up to his hips.

Greg fumbled in his fist and hit the clicker to the Navigator, Ashleigh managed the door handle, and he swung her into the seat. He ran around, jumped in, reset the safety on the Glock, started the engine, rammed it in reverse, backed around and roared down the drive.

In his rearview mirror, he saw the man, with his long legs plowing through the snow, chasing them. Off to the right, he spotted what he assumed was the guy's wreck of a vehicle, parked off in the trees. Fischer would no doubt find his gun, get in that thing and chase them down this treacherous road.

Fortunately, Ashleigh didn't see the car. With trembling fingers she was busy trying to find a signal on the cell phone. "Nothing!" she cried in frustration as she slapped the phone shut. "Where in the *hell* are the cops when you need them! Greg…" She gripped his arm as a contraction hit her, almost causing him to lose control of the wheel. "Promise me,"

she ground out, "you won't let that son of a bitch...
anywhere...near...our baby."

"I won't," Greg vowed.

When the contraction ended Greg glanced in the
rearview mirror and saw headlights advancing.
"Buckle your seat belt," he ordered.

"I can't! I'm too busy having a bab—oooww!"
Ashleigh cried as another contraction hit her. She
arched on the seat, fighting the pain.

When this one was over, Greg said, "Sweetheart,
listen. I want you to try and calm down to conserve
your energy."

"I can't, dammit! I'm having a *baby* while we're
careening down a mountainside and some demented
maniac is try—ooww!"

The next contraction made her shut up and
breathe deep. When it subsided, she cried, "Omi-
god!" and looked down. "My water broke."

Greg cut a sideways glance—a dark stain of
amniotic fluid flooded over the seat of the Navigator—and then turned back to focus on the next hairpin turn.

In no time Ashleigh let out another pained moan,
spread her knees wide and grabbed her abdomen.
"The baby's coming!" she ground out through
clenched teeth.

"Try not to push," Greg yelled. "Blow!" He
knew they wouldn't make it to The Birth Place
in time.

With Ashleigh puffing like a fire bellows, the mile to Manny's place felt like a million.

The Navigator churned snow and mud as Greg spun into Manny's drive and roared up to the house while blasting the horn. He lurched to a stop near the front porch.

The porch light snapped on and Manny hurried down the steps as Greg was rounding the Navigator to Ashleigh's door. "She's having the baby *now*," Greg yelled.

Manny crossed himself as he ran to assist Greg.

"Can you pant through this next contraction while I carry you inside?" Greg asked Ashleigh as he put his arms around her.

Despite her pain, Ashleigh nodded.

Greg hoisted her out of the Navigator and Manny ran ahead. At the front door Greg looked back and saw headlights turning into Manny's drive.

Reading Greg's face, Manny looked up, too. "The midwife?"

"No. The creep."

"The one who came sniffing around here?" Manny followed Greg through the living room.

"There's a Glock on the seat of the Navigator," Greg told Manny as he laid Ashleigh on the bed. "Can you keep that guy out of here?"

"*Sí.*" Manny grabbed his rifle from a rack in the corner and started feeding shells into the magazine. "And I will call Miguel."

"Call Lydia Kane at The Birth Place, too. Tell her we're here."

"*Sí,*" Manny said, and dashed out of the room.

OUTSIDE, MANNY STOOD ON HIS porch, spread his legs wide and aimed the rifle at the massive man lumbering toward the house in the dark. Manny had known they had not seen the last of this character.

"Stop, amigo. You got no business here."

Fischer stopped, but then Manny saw the gun in his hand. Manny held the barrel of his rifle deadly still.

"Drop it. Or do you want to die?" Manny said. Fischer dropped the gun. "Put your hands up and lie facedown. Over there—" he flipped the rifle barrel toward a rocky spot in the drive "—on the ground."

But Fischer only lumbered forward. "I'm taking that baby," he muttered.

"Trust me, amigo, if you pull anything I *will* shoot you." Manny cocked the rifle, and Fischer halted again. "I've killed a lot of men in my time," Manny continued quietly while they stared each other down, "one more isn't going to matter much with God. Now, get your ass down on the ground."

"God *will* punish you," Fischer growled as he threw his huge frame to his knees.

"Probably so," Manny said as he hitched down the porch steps. He poked the rifle at the man's back, forcing him fully prone. "But not for this particular deed. Now, put your hands behind your back. I got to tie you up.'' Manny dug his trusty roll of duct tape from his baggy pocket.

MANNY ENTERED THE BEDROOM quietly. Greg's coat was off; his sleeves were rolled up. He was propping some pillows that he'd snatched off the boys' beds behind Ashleigh, who had started another contraction.

''That loco can't bother us now,'' Manny assured Ashleigh.

''I can help with the baby,'' he told Greg calmly. ''Me and my Rosa, we had one of ours at home. Everything turned out fine.''

''What's happening down there?'' Ashleigh wilted when the contraction was over. She seemed calmer and more in control now—Greg was relieved to see that the panic of transition had passed. He pushed her gown up above her hips, flexed her legs and gently rotated her knees outward.

''Looks like the baby's crowning,'' he pronounced.

Manny hurried off to wash his hands.

Greg's palms were sweating as he pulled on the latex gloves, then shook out the receiving blanket and opened the packages with the cord clamp and scissors.

Manny came in with a stack of threadbare but freshly laundered towels. Greg folded two into a pad and wedged the barrier under Ashleigh's hips between her skin and the wet gown. He laid another towel at the ready to dry the baby.

Manny was over in the corner, plugging in the new space heater Greg had given him only a few weeks ago.

"Okay, sweetheart." Greg sat on the bed and cupped one palm gently over Ashleigh's knee as he looked her in the eye. "Be ready to push, and keep pushing, on this next one."

The contraction hit with full force, but with Greg's encouragement, Ashleigh made good use of its power.

She wilted back against the pillows when it subsided. "I think I need a little courage here," she said.

"My sweetheart..." Greg kissed her forehead soundly. "You have enough courage for ten women."

The next push brought the top of a tiny blond head forth.

"Watch out for the cord." Ashleigh strained forward, trying to see. Her face was bright red, her eyes hyperalert; she was operating with total maternal empowerment now.

"I am." Greg looked down and never took his eyes off of his emerging child so that immediately he spotted it—a pale fleshy rope, tightly binding the baby's neck. Imitating the videos he'd watched dozens of times, Greg hooked a finger underneath and slid the cord up over the small, pinched face.

Next, he delivered the tiny shoulders smoothly. And then the baby's whole body slipped into his hands.

"Oh!" Ashleigh shouted, staring in awe. "Oh, my God! There he is!"

Greg swiped out his son's mouth with a finger, swabbed his tiny face with the corner of the receiving blanket, dried the slippery little body with Manny's towel. But the tense seconds ticked by while the baby remained colorless, limp and unresponsive.

"Rub him some more," Manny urged, pressing a fresh towel into Greg's hands. Greg rubbed the tiny body more vigorously, willing his son to grab hold of life.

"Breathe," he commanded.

The baby grimaced, gasped, sputtered, and then opened his cherubic little lips and started to howl.

When the baby started crying, Greg's eyes welled up. Which made Ashleigh cry, too. Even Manny swiped at sudden tears. For a few seconds everyone in the room was crying except for old Guapo, who had pushed the creaky door open with his nose and padded in. With mute canine curiosity he looked briefly in the direction of the squalling infant, then crept back out again to resume his usual post in the living room.

Miguel Eiden arrived, having stopped and retrieved Katherine at the roadside, trusting that Manny had done as thorough a job with the duct tape as he claimed.

Clutching her bag, Katherine leaped from the cruiser and dashed into the house.

While Miguel was in the process of cuffing Fischer, reading him his rights, and stuffing him into the back seat of the cruiser, he was gratified to hear the intermittent sounds of a wailing infant from inside the rickety old house.

INSIDE, KATHERINE SOOTHED them all with her gentle ways. "Oh, my, he looks fine," she said, examining the baby. "The cord looks good—good work, Greg. And he's a nice size. About seven pounds, I'd guess. Good color. Good reflexes." She inserted a freshly washed finger into the baby's mouth and he latched on. "We'll let him nurse in a minute. After that, Officer Eiden has called for a transport."

"But first, let me check the mommy."

Katherine massaged Ashleigh's fundus, checked her for excessive bleeding and made a concession to Greg, placing one of his fancy cold packs at the perineum to prevent swelling. They wrapped Ashleigh's shivering legs in one of Manny's warm flannel sheets.

When Ashleigh was covered, Manny came in with a glass of orange juice for her.

"Good idea." Katherine smiled at the old man, who then made his exit, quietly closing the door.

"Now," Katherine said as soon as Ashleigh had downed the juice. She folded her hands in front of her thin chest, like a fairy godmother about to grant a wish. "Are we ready to nurse?"

Ashleigh looked at Greg and Greg looked at Ashleigh. Without speaking he helped her ease her gown over her shoulder and exposed her breast. He sat by her on the bed and leaned his broad shoulders back on the pillows next to her. Then he settled his arm around her shoulders protectively. Katherine delivered the bundled infant into Ashleigh's outstretched arms. With only a stroke of the nipple to his rosy cheek, the baby latched on to his mother beautifully. His two parents watched the process in awe.

After a while the baby released the nipple, quieting into a newborn slumber.

"I was thinking about that name you suggested a while back," Ashleigh whispered as she and Greg huddled together on the bed, admiring their sleeping baby. "Gemariah," she said wistfully, tucking the blanket aside so she could see the baby's face better. It was a beautiful face, and his alone. She could see that already, although it was gratifying, so very gratifying, to also recognize hints of his father's strong, wide mouth and deep-set eyes.

"You'd really consider the name Gemariah?" Greg smiled at her profile. "You mean it?"

"Yes. I've thought about it and it's what I want. That was, after all, the name of this little boy's great-grandfather."

"Okay," Greg agreed softly, loving this woman with all his heart. "We could name him after

Gramps, but we wouldn't call him Gemariah. We'll call him what people used to call my grandfather."

"Oh? What did they call him?" Ashleigh never took her eyes off the baby.

"Jim. People always thought Great-grandma Sadie was saying *Jim* when she called him *Gem,* and after a couple of weeks his parents gave up and went with Jim."

"Jim Glazier," Ashleigh said, testing the name. "I like that. But back to Gemariah. What exactly does the name mean, by the way?"

"It means…" Greg bent his head, leaning close to Ashleigh and studying the tiny face of their baby alongside her. He touched a gentle finger to the little brow that was so clearly fashioned after Ashleigh's. He could see Ashleigh's good looks in the child already. And that little dusting of white hair, softer than dandelion fluff, would surely end up blond like hers. What a beautiful, perfect baby they had made together, in a roundabout, miraculous sort of way. "It means…" Greg's voice, thick with emotion, dropped to a whisper so as not to wake their sleeping child "—He Whom Jehovah Has Completed."

* * * * *

*Turn the page for an excerpt
from the second book in*
THE BIRTH PLACE *series.*

*Brenda Novak's
SANCTUARY*

*is a moving, exciting and completely
absorbing story, one you're guaranteed
not to forget!*

*SANCTUARY is available from
Harlequin Superromance books in
October, 2003.*

PROLOGUE

The Birth Place
Enchantment, New Mexico
February, 1993

LYDIA KANE had keen, shrewd eyes. Hope Tanner stared into them, drawing strength from the older woman as another pain racked her middle. The contractions were coming close together now—and hard, much harder than before. Her legs shook in reaction, whether from pain or fear, she didn't know. She didn't feel as though she knew much about anything. She was barely seventeen.

"That's it," Lydia said from the bottom of the bed. "You're getting there now. Just relax, honey, and breathe."

"I want to push," Hope panted. Though the baby wasn't overdue, Hope was more than anxious to be finished with the pregnancy. Lydia had put some sort of hormonal cream inside her—on what she called a cervix. The older woman said it would send her into labor. But the baby was proving stubborn. The pains had started, on and off, at sundown and only now, when it was nearly four o'clock in the morning, were they getting serious.

More of God's punishment, Hope decided. She'd run away from the Brethren, refused to do what her father said was "God's will," and this was the price she had to pay.

"Don't push yet," Lydia said firmly. "You're not fully dilated, and we don't want you to tear. Try to rest while I see what that last contraction did."

Hope stared at the ceiling as Lydia checked the baby's progress. She was tired of all the poking and prodding, but she would never say so. Lydia might think her ungrateful. After being alone for most of her pregnancy, wandering aimlessly from town to town, Hope wasn't about to do anything to anger the one person who'd taken her in. Lydia was so decisive, so strong. As much as Hope loved and admired her, she feared her a little, too. Lydia owned The Birth Place and had to be sixty years old. But she wasn't a soft, sweet grandmotherly type, certainly nothing like Hope's own patient mother. Tall and angular, with steel-gray eyes and hair, Lydia often spoke sharply, seemed to know everything in the world and had the ability to make other people—and apparently even events—bend to her will. She took command like Hope's father, which was an amazing concept. Hope hadn't known women could possess so much power.

"Is everything okay?" Hope asked, weak, shaky, exhausted.

"Everything's fine." As Lydia helped her to a few more ice chips, the pendant she always wore— a mother cradling an infant—swayed with her movements and caught Hope's attention. Hope had long admired that pendant. She craved the nurturing and love it symbolized. But she knew she'd never experience holding her own child so close. Not *this* child, anyway.

After mopping Hope's forehead, Lydia went back to massaging one of her feet. Lydia claimed that pressing on certain points in the foot could ease pain—she called it reflexology—but if reflexology was helping, Hope certainly couldn't tell. To her, its only value seemed to be in providing a slight distraction.

"It shouldn't be long now," Lydia assured her, but she kept glancing at the clock as though she was late for something and as eager for the baby to be born as Hope. "I'd transfer you to the hospital if I was the least bit worried," she continued in the same authoritative voice. "This is dragging on, I know. But the baby's heartbeat is strong and steady and you're progressing. First babies often take a while."

Lydia had once mentioned that she'd been a midwife for more than thirty years. Certainly after all that time she knew what she was talking about. But Hope was inclined to trust her regardless of her professional experience. It was men who always failed her—

Another contraction gripped her body. Biting
back a tormented moan, she clenched her fists and
gritted her teeth. She didn't know how much more
she could take. It felt as if someone had a knife and
was stabbing her repeatedly in the abdomen.

Except for the music playing quietly in the background, it was quiet. Parker Reynolds, the admin-
istrator, and the other midwives and clerical people
who worked at the center were long gone. They'd
left before Lydia had even induced her. She and
Lydia were the only ones at The Birth Place. With
its scented candles, soft lighting and soothing music,
the room was meant to be comfortable and welcom-
ing, like home. But this room, which had turquoise
and peach wallpaper, Spanish-tile floor and wooden
shutters at the window, was nothing like the home
Hope had known. She'd grown up sharing a bedroom with at least three other siblings, oftentimes
four. If there were candles it was because the elec-
tricity had been turned off for nonpayment. And the
only music she'd been allowed to listen to was clas-
sical or hymns.

"Good girl," Lydia said as Hope fought the im-
pulse to bear down.

At this point, Hope didn't care whether or not she
caused herself physical damage. She felt as if the
baby was ripping its way out of her, anyway. She
just didn't want to displease Lydia. The ultrasound
she'd had several weeks earlier indicated she was
having a girl, and Lydia had promised that her

daughter would go to a good home. Hope didn't want to give her any reason to break that promise. Mostly because Lydia had painted such an idyllic picture of her baby's future. Her baby would have a crib, and a matching comforter and bumper pads, and a mobile hanging above her head. She'd have doting parents who would give her dance lessons, help her do homework and send her to college. When the time was right, they'd pay for a lovely wedding. Her daughter would marry someone kind and strong, have a normal family and eventually become a grandmother. She'd wear store-bought clothes, listen to regular music and feel good about being a woman. Better than anything, she'd never know what she'd so narrowly escaped....

Hope wanted sanctuary for her child. She wanted it more than anything. After her daughter arrived and started her princesslike life, it wouldn't matter what happened to Hope.

She would already have given the only gift she could.

She would have saved her daughter from the Brethren.

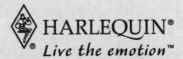